Returned

Alana, Thank you so much for the ♡!

KEELEY HOLMES

Keeley Holmes x

ALSO BY KEELEY HOLMES

PENDLE HILL SERIES

Returned

Other adult books

SERENDIPITY SERIES

Hope at Christmas

Dating Rules

Cupcakes & Chaos

Change of Plan

Published in 2018 by Keeley Holmes

Copyright © Keeley Holmes

The author or authors assert their moral right under the Copyright, Designs and Patents Act, 1988, to be identified as the author or authors of this work.

All Rights reserved. No part of this publication may be reproduced, copied, stored in a retrieval system, or transmitted, in any form or by any means, without the prior written consent of the copyright holder, nor be otherwise circulated in any form of binding or cover other than that in which it is published and without a similar condition being imposed on the subsequent purchaser.

A CIP catalogue record for this title is available from the British Library.

To the book club girlies - in no particular order –

Bethany "Mouth" Cunningham
Emma "Bert" Long
Ashleigh "Braids" Waring
Kerri "Cherry" Hughes
Jenna "Monster" Wright,
Kimberly "Maninizer" Durant
Samantha Wright

Thank you for five amazing years of fun, reading, gossip and parties. It was without a doubt the best book club, ever!

Preface

A thud of feet struck the hard ground behind me as the sharp crack of frozen branches echoed in the vast wooded area. I ran as each snap sent my heart into overdrive, that sound meaning they were gaining ground, but I couldn't run any quicker. I couldn't pull the much needed oxygen into my whimpering lungs.

My heart jackhammered, fighting its way out of its cage, trying to escape the overwhelming fear that coursed its way through my body. The thought of the many things that could happen tonight distressed me. Would my lungs give out? Would they catch me? Who I would meet when my legs, which were as strong as jelly, finally crumbled beneath me?

My biggest fear ripped the remaining breath from my body.

That fear…

Would it hurt when I died?

Cora

An urgent whisper embedded itself deep into my subconscious, but before I had a chance to push it away, it rushed through my foggy state of sleep, banging frantically on the door to get in. I groaned.

The voice was unfamiliar to me; the tone of it was almost musical, very soft and very feminine. It didn't sound like my mother. I pulled the cover over my face, shielding me against the bright sunlight that was shining directly in my face. The voice became fainter, but I caught some of the words which piqued my interest.

It wasn't them...

Not their fault...

You need to find...

I was no longer asleep, and the voice was fading. Seriously? Was this even a dream anymore? The woman's voice, a whisper, still held a bit of panic. It dawned on me that this wasn't a dream. How could it be? How often did someone realise that they could listen to a voice which was apparently a dream, but be consciously aware of being awake at the same time?

The woman's words were not getting through to me, there was an urgency and her voice erupted, the pitch becoming painful.

I opened my eyes and pushed the covers back, breathing in fresh air. That had to be a dream? Surely, it couldn't be anything else, could it?

No, it couldn't. I was just on edge about this whole move because I hated moving.

"Cora, sweetheart, are you awake?"

Jumping, I sat up in the bed and told myself to get a grip. Dreams were meant to be weird and unexplainable.

My mother gingerly edged the door open with a smile plastered on her face. "Cora?"

I eyed my mother suspiciously. That tone of voice usually meant one of two things: She had done something and felt bad about it, or, she was going to do something and felt bad about it.

"I need to go to work today," she edged cautiously.

I knew the look on my face could turn milk sour, but this whole move had been her stupid idea and now she was ditching me to go play teacher. I knew I was being childish, but I was so fed up with moving. Just within the last twelve months I'd lived in Carlisle, Manchester, York, Exeter and then finally London. I knew my mother's job as a cover teacher took us to different places, but did she have to cover the whole of the UK?

"I'm sorry," my mother sighed, "I have to go to a meeting about the new curriculum and my role within the school. It was a last-minute decision, but we can go explore the village this afternoon."

I'd caught a glimpse of things as we'd driven in yesterday. Hills had loomed high as they'd dominated in the distance; I'd seen tiny roads weave along between them. Houses had become sparser and more luxurious. As the sun had dipped lower among the hills, casting streaks of soft orange and warm reds that streamlined the early evening sky, I could admit that it was postcard perfect. I just didn't want to live here.

"That's fine, Mum." I shrugged nonchalantly, even though I struggled to hold back my disappointment.

Complaining and snide remarks got me nowhere fast. I accepted the orange juice from my mother. "I'll go for a walk and look around the village myself."

The deep worry lines that had hounded her hazel eyes, faded. The remaining lines were due to her radiant smile. I knew I was adding more stress for her, but this move also caused me problems. I wasn't homeless or starving, but my life was a mess and I was stuck in limbo.

"I will be back no later than 3 p.m., I promise." She flashed another brilliant smile as she left the room.

"Sure Mum, that's great," I mumbled, as I watched her shut the door.

As soon as the door clicked shut the fake smile slid from my face. I listened as my mother bopped down the stairs, each step emphasising how happy she was, and shut the front door behind her. A loud irritated groan sounded from our car as she drove away. Well, if I had to go and explore this village that excited my mother so much, I might as well get it over with.

The house we were currently renting was a standard two up, two down with a small garage which was hastily built on to the side of it. The drive was long and pebbly. It was imprisoned by trees, a tall, dominating wall which seemed to suck the light right out of the house and area. As first impressions went, I didn't like it.

The wind nipped, burning my exposed skin as it smashed up against me. It felt extremely cold for the late days of September. I couldn't understand how the leaves hadn't already died from hypothermia. One small walk around this village and I would be highly at risk.

I stopped next to a cluster of terraced houses. Up close, the doors and window shutters were tastefully decorated in different shades of pastel. The soft rainbow of colours lined the street to my left and directly ahead. This had to be the most colourful village I'd ever seen. Well, it was probably the first village I'd ever seen. I couldn't really remember, the moves had become a blur to me. It was something that bothered me, when I occasionally thought about it.

Wedged in between the houses were a few shops, a butcher, a newsagent, a small handmade card shop, a post office and another shop. I could see three figures occupying the space outside. There was nothing more than the few shops in front of me with a cobbled type road in the middle. Great, this was smaller than I first thought. What the hell was I meant to do here?

I approached the unnamed shop, a soft egg-white beautifully complemented the window shutters and the door which was painted a deep forest green. The building was stood quite crookedly, something I found odd considering the shop was stood at a wonky angle in the middle of two houses that stood square. The three figures that occupied the space outside the shop were witches, and they were dressed in what I considered to be the stereotypical long cloak and black pointed hat, each of them holding a broom at their sides. The weather had not been kind to them as paint peeled off their faces.

Pulling off my gloves, I lifted my hand and edged closer to the smaller, hunched figure of the three. I'd always had this uncontrollable urge to touch or lift things, which usually resulted in broken items. Most of my pocket money was lost due to it. The long grey hair held underneath the stiff, pointed black hat felt straw like in my hands. The crooked nose with the typical wart on the edge of it was chipped. Before I'd finished, a shadow fell over me and the witch.

"Watch out!"

Shocked by the yell, I jumped back right into the stranger. Before I could get my bearings, I was roughly pushed away.

"Hey! Watch where you're going, witch!"

Spinning around in shock, I faced him and immediately flinched under his intimidating stare.

His chocolate brown eyes, ablaze with fury, glared at me. He stood a little taller than me, my head just reached his shoulders. He was flanked by two boys, making them look like characters from a film; the ringleader followed by dumb and dumber. One boy was small with an oval shaped face and was currently smiling like a Cheshire cat, with a dopey look in his blue eyes. The other boy, tall and skinny, had a bowl haircut that flowed over his eyes, making them practically invisible. Only his stupid crooked grin could be seen under his mop of blonde hair.

Great. I'd obviously bumped into the village bully.

The leader's eyes looked over me, inspected every inch of

me, and as I followed the trail of his eyes I suddenly felt shy. Words weren't exchanged as he did this. I couldn't seem to get my words in order and my mouth was so dry, it felt like my tongue was glued to the palate. What the hell was happening? I'd been minding my own business.

"Sorry witch, I can't hear you." He lifted his hands to his ears, cupping them in an exaggerated manner.

Anger surged through me and pushed my nerves aside. For some bizarre reason, I felt the urge to punch him in the face. I'd never felt that urge in my life. What was it about him that angered me so much? I felt the pinch of my short nails in my palm. I didn't even know how to hit someone, but I sure as hell wasn't going to scratch him like a girl. I stood, letting my head and my anger play tug of war as ice cold wind surged around me. I sucked in a shocked breath as I realised the wind circled only me. This wasn't happening. It couldn't be. Wind didn't do that… On the undercurrents of the wind, I could hear a hint of laughter. I let out a breath as my head spun.

The boys in front of me weren't laughing, so where was the excited laughter coming from?

The leader's lopsided grin was still in place, the curve of his lips, Cupid's bow and all, made my heart stammer. Those lips, along with the chocolate brown eyes and the strong jawline, made him appear more man than boy. I stood straighter, and without thinking, crossed my arms over my chest hoping it looked defensive. My stomach was rolling around somewhere near the top of my chest. Confrontation was something I avoided, unless it was with my mother.

The wind lashed out at him, whipping his stomach with a sharp precision.

No.

That wasn't right. How could I even see it?

He stumbled back, a look of confusion in his eyes, but then they narrowed angrily as his gaze fell on me yet again. The wind swirled around me, as laughter seemed to dance right through me. He stepped closer, each step making my heart thud a little bit harder. His strategic move forced me closer to the figures outside the shop. I edged backwards, having no other option since he was standing in the way of my only exit. I felt the pointy finger of a witch poking me painfully in the back. Holding back a wince, I took a deep breath to tell him to back off.

"I think it would be very wise that you do not touch her."

The voice was soft, but it held the bite of anger. It had come from somewhere behind me, but I didn't look. I could already feel a bruise forming on my back. The leader threw back his head and laughed, but I noticed that he cautiously backed away. Shaking my head in frustration, I moved away from the witches on the pavement, but made sure to keep my focus on him.

Without saying a word, the three boys sauntered up the main street away from me. I wished I'd said something to him and now I had a really good retort. Typical. A polite cough interrupted my thoughts. Turning, I faced the stranger and my mouth dropped open.

The woman was gorgeous, I couldn't find any other word to describe her. Her long, coal black hair complimented her creamy complexion, as a soft raspberry blush on her cheeks gave her a healthy glow. The intense leaf green of her eyes stood out against her pale skin. I'd never seen eyes that colour before. I caught a flicker of something cross her face, just a slight twitch of her full rose-tinted lips, and then her face seemed to smooth out again.

I looked from the woman's intriguing face and followed the length of her hair. It hung in locks which were full and bouncy, not the kind of knotted mess I would normally have if I tried to curl my hair. The woman wore a long dress, though it appeared to be more like a robe. The robe was a deep, luxurious purple, with a green belt wrapped around her small waist.

"Now, I suppose you're very cold," the woman said, breaking the silence.

I'd been a little bit preoccupied with the crazy boy and the wind that somehow laughed and danced around me to give the cold much thought. The woman gestured for me to enter the weird shop. I shouldn't enter a shop with a stranger. Should I?

"Please come in for a warm drink, you must be very cold in this weather," the woman repeated.

I felt a hand being placed lightly on the bottom of my back which gently forced me towards the door. I took one last look at the three watchful witches keeping guard outside and entered the shop I later found out was called *The Broom Cupboard.*

Cora

The shop was small, but that hadn't deterred the woman from making the most of it. Cauldrons in every size imaginable, broomsticks and huge pillar candles were scattered on the waist high cabinet to my left.

A bay window housed several witchy items and two bookshelves were crowded with hundreds of tiny bottles containing colourful liquids, and beautiful ornaments.

I knew I should leave, but something was keeping me here. The woman had vanished somewhere, leaving me looking stupid and awkward, but nothing new about that. I crept towards the books, straining my eyes as I read the titles, *'The Book of the Wiccan'*, *'The New Book of Organic Spells'*, *'Love, Love, Love Potions'*. Smothering my laugh in my hand, I moved around the bookcase. People had to be brainwashed if they believed this stuff worked, take *Harry Potter*, for example; I liked Harry Potter, most people did, but he wasn't real. The spells weren't real.

I shuffled to the rear of the shop where a small, round table accompanied by two chairs was positioned next to a banister. Should I sit down or just stand here aimlessly? I peered over the banister and noticed that the stairs seemed to sink into the floor. I turned and looked at the bookcase that spanned the full wall, when a soft click from behind me made me quickly sit on the chair. The woman walked up the steps that sank into the floor and placed two steaming cups on the table. I turned to assess the door at the bottom of the stairs. The door didn't have a handle.

Turning and facing the woman, I tried to form appropriate questions in my head, but they all sounded stupid.

Can you walk through floors?

Are you an escaped asylum patient?

I hated the silence that hung heavily between us. Maybe I should go with the asylum patient icebreaker?

"Th-thank you for your help outside," I stuttered. My voice sounded distant and I knew the blood pounding in my ears was to blame. The woman lifted the steaming, blue cup to her smiling lips, but her eyes remained focused on me over the rim. I hated direct eye contact like this, especially contact that was so intimidating. I fidgeted in my chair. Having nothing better to do, I put down my gloves and lifted the red cup to my lips and took small sips. I tried to keep the surprise from showing on my face, but I was completely unsuccessful. It wasn't tea, I'd expected it to be tea, but instead it was a lovely thick hot chocolate.

"What were those boys doing to you outside?"

Keeping the cup in front of my face like some sort of shield, I took another sip. I enjoyed the chocolate which was laced with something sweet and delicious. I dared to look at the woman whose eyes hadn't strayed from my face.

Sighing, I gave in to the stare. "I arrived here yesterday with my mum...I came to look around the village. I was supposed to spend the day with her..." I trailed off feeling self-conscious.

The woman waited.

I continued. "The witches outside caught my attention and then that boy was pushing me." I shrugged, trying to brush off the horrible feeling he'd left imprinted on me. "It was right after that you came to the door."

I could feel the anger rise again and as soon as it did I heard the wind protest outside. I dared to look at the woman; did the wind always behave like that? I shivered as laughter danced around me.

What *was* that?

My anger, fuelled by nerves, spiked again. He'd put me in this situation and I was the one stuck here in this crazy shop with this woman, whilst he was out there gallivanting around without a care in the world.

"Welcome to Millsteeple, you must be Cora Hunt, and I have to say I've heard so much about you already."

Stunned and more than a little freaked out by this woman's revelation, I sat in silence. This woman knew me? How? I tried to ignore the awkward silence between us, but I could feel the woman's gaze on me.

"Well I must leave, Mum is expecting me," I choked on the lie as it lodged in my throat. "Thanks for the warm drink." I stood up too quickly and nearly fell over my own feet.

"Cora...I would like to offer you a job working here."

My eyes darted upright in shock. The carefree smile remained on her face. A job?

No.

No way.

I wasn't going to accept a job from a stranger.

"I understand you do not know me, but I know young people need extra money and I have a free opening here in the shop." She attempted a shrug. It looked like the woman had never used the gesture in her entire life.

Shuffling from foot to foot, I stared down at the faded wooden floorboards. I didn't know what to do. This was stupid, why couldn't my mouth say no?

The silence was becoming unbearable.

"Errrrmmmm... sure," I stuttered. Without giving the woman a chance to respond, I started walking towards the door.

As I pulled it open, a refreshing blast of cold air hit my face. Taking a step onto the pavement, I was stopped by a polite cough.

Keep moving, don't look back.

I turned to look at the woman and only just managed to contain a shriek. When had the woman moved?

"Cora, my name is Tabitha Preston. You can start Saturday, please be here at 9 a.m."

Without waiting for an answer, she smiled and walked back into the shop. I had a job? What the hell was happening? The cold wind nipped at my bare hands. I rummaged around in my pockets and mentally kicked myself. My warm gloves were on the table in that ominous shop. I walked briskly up the main street and tried to shake off my nerves. Why did I feel like there was something about Tabitha that was so familiar to me?

"Hey, witch! You haven't got your witch friend to save you this time!"

The already familiar male voice shocked me out of my mental turmoil. As his voice registered with me, I heard the laughter that seemed to glide along the waves of the cool wind, a wind that circled my body, again.

Cora

He stood, tall and intimidating, mere feet in front of me. His eyes seemed to sparkle with amusement whilst my stomach turned in nauseating circles, knotting itself into a tight mess. Dumb and dumber who stood behind him, cackled.

"Leave me alone," I whispered, the show of weakness annoyed me.

His lips were pulled into an arrogant smirk, it grew wider as I looked at him. Two deep dimples formed in both his cheeks as he continued to grin at me. And a second later, I gasped. That smile triggered a switch inside me.

Had I seen that smile before?

The wind picked up in speed as the laughter danced around me. Seriously, they couldn't hear this laughter? I clenched my hands into fists as pain stabbed my stomach.

"Oooooooo... harsh words witch." His eyes danced with glee.

He closed the gap between us in three strides. His hair was

cut short at the sides, as the longer jagged, wisps of mahogany brown moved erratically in the wind, a wind that seemed to pulse from within me.

Anger flashed in his eyes as I heaved in a breath. There was a build-up of pressure in my head, like a balloon that was ready to pop. The muscles in my throat forced the bile up into my mouth. Panicking, I over swallowed to compensate, but it wasn't working. Heaving in another cold breath, I felt something click. Almost like something literally snapped inside me.

It hurt like a bitch.

He pushed me, hard. I stumbled back, my arms snapping out to keep upright. The agony I felt only intensified at the sound of their laughter. Squaring my shoulders the best I could whilst whimpering in pain, I forced my legs to pick themselves up and move.

"Get out of my way!!" I spat.

I felt his breath brush hot against my skin as I ground my teeth together.

He stopped laughing, his eyes narrowing as he glared at me. "What will you do if I don't?"

I felt little flickers of spit land on my cheeks. My long brown hair was suddenly flicked back as the wind's cool hands pulled my bobble free. Stepping closer to him, I watched as he dragged his hand through his hair, styling it to sweep to one side. His eyes portrayed nothing but confidence. A muscle ticked under his eye as his jaw popped. Stood toe to toe, we continued to glare at one another as if we were about to go to battle to save the world.

What the hell was we doing?

Without warning, my hands were pushed up and locked

into position near the centre of his chest. My skin tingled, increasing in temperature until it burned. I bit down on my lip, tasting warm copper pennies. The pain grew, the intensity of it ripping the breath right out of my lungs, I groaned and then as suddenly as it had started, the wind stopped and the pain vanished.

My hand remained between us, it was the only thing not trembling. I could hear nothing but our breathing, my short gasps, his steady breaths. Caramel infused with chocolate looked at me, his smile, slow and so self-assured returned.

Something blasted from deep within me.

Screaming erupted.

Confusion blocked my senses as I focused on the scene in front of me. The boy who had been stood at my toes only seconds earlier now lay crumpled on the floor some distance away from me. My teeth smashed together as my whole body grew cold. Why was he over there?

"Jack, are you all right? Jack!" Mop hair boy screamed.

I shook my head, trying to clear away some of the cobwebs. Dazed but able to think about my own safety, I needed to move. God, what had I done? I choked on a sob as I ran, the wind gently wiping away the drops that were rolling down my cheeks. Had I seriously hurt that boy?

I stumbled into the house, my hands grasping at my throat. I couldn't breathe. My legs fell from underneath me, forcing a desperate cry out of my mouth as I hit the floor with a heavy thump. I dragged my dead body to the kitchen, wheezing along the way.

I made it to the fridge and leaned against it for support, any movement made my head somersault as new waves of dizziness hit me. Taking a deep breath, I stood. Pulling the door open required strength I didn't have but I managed it, only falling to the floor once the door was open. I grabbed the nearest thing to my outstretched hand and unscrewed the cap. Sighing as the bubbles popped in my mouth, I took a deep breath and shut the fridge.

As soon as my hands reached the solid wood of the table, I pulled myself up and immediately regretted it. Bending my head to try and stop the onslaught, I inhaled much-needed air, but air wasn't going to work. Moving as quickly as my body would allow, I pushed my head over the kitchen sink.

I was going to die.

I tasted acid a second before sick erupted uncontrollably out of my mouth, slamming me closer to the sink.

Then the dark shadows rushed in.

Cora

I was stood, and rather bizarrely, I was surrounded by white fog. The thick heavy mass drained any warmth I may have had as it clung to my body. I couldn't see, yet instinctively I knew someone was following me. Where the hell was I? I strained my eyes to see through the thick fog and then stumbled over my own feet as a figure darted towards me.

The fog suddenly vanished. I tried not think about how weird that was. As the figure approached me, I told my body not to shut down, not to be a coward and faint. Keeping my eyes open, I noticed that the thing was draped in robes, similar to the one Tabitha wore. The figure didn't touch the ground. It literally floated. I saw the beginnings of long, brown hair.

I started to step back, to force some distance between the thing and me. I blinked and in that second the figure was gone. A whisper of a voice reached me.

It's in your blood…

Ask Tabitha.

I jolted back, hitting my head.

Ouch. My head throbbed.

I assessed my body, keeping my eyes closed so it didn't hurt more. My hand felt like a dead weight at the end of my arm and my legs were heavy and cold. My entire body battled against pins and needles as I lay on the cold kitchen floor. At least I knew where I was now. I wasn't going to think about yet another strange dream.

Opening my eyes, I was sat in darkness. What time was it? Inch by excruciating inch, I turned my head to the side and gasped as an explosion gripped my head like a vice. Closing my eyes, I held my breath, waiting for the worst of it to abate. Once the pain had subsided, I attempted to move again and put all my weight onto my knees.

Leaning over the sink, I sucked in deep breaths, trying to ward off the fresh bout of sickness that was sloshing around high in my chest. I counted slowly to ten, concentrating on the function of my lungs moving in and out. Once the new wave of sickness had passed, I opened my eyes and looked at the time, 7:30 p.m.

As elegant as a newborn baby on roller blades, I moved to the living room and noted that everything remained untouched from this morning. The house groaned as torrential wind smashed against it. The silence confirmed that I was home alone. Where was my mother? I slumped down hard onto the sofa and instantly regretted it, I slowly moved back and nestled into the pillows as images of the day flashed through my mind.

The image of his body slumped on the ground.

The sound of the horrible scream of his friend.

Tabitha.

The weird shop.

The dream.

Exhaustion washed over me, suffocated by the need to sleep, I sank under.

Movement shimmered, light and dark flickered across my face, the light caressing me with warmth.

"Cora, darling, are you awake?"

I opened my eyes. The first thing I noticed was the distinct redness that surrounded her hazel eyes, and her soft nutmeg hair hung limply around her face. I focused on trying not to scream, I didn't want to frighten my mother. My mother had walked over to the window. Squinting against the light that burned, I attempted to look at my mother's face, but she'd strategically moved so I couldn't see her. Had she been crying?

"Mum, are you all right?" The effort to talk was exhausting.

"Oh, yes," she murmured.

I didn't believe her.

"Where have you been?" I swallowed the very little spit my mouth could make. I needed a cold drink to wash away the sand pit that had taken up residence in my mouth.

From where I was sat, I knew my mother's eyebrows were drawn together deep in thought, the straightness of her shoulders gave that away. Her lips would be forced into a thin line, the crossed arms signalled that. This was my mother's signature look. She'd been crying, did she know about what I'd done?

I didn't know how injured he was, now that my anger had

fizzled out I hoped he wasn't too badly injured. I would have to face the consequences, whatever they were. Looking back on the whole thing, it seemed ridiculous. What had come over me?

With a sigh, my mother turned and looked at me. The smile on her face was forced, never quite reaching her eyes. Her lips quivered before she could control it. I watched in stunned silence as my mother left the room. The last twenty four hours had been the worst of my life, or what I could remember of it because I seemed to have issues with memory. I'd nearly died, no, I wasn't being melodramatic, and my mother had gone AWOL. And now she'd left the room leaving me with more questions. What was going on?

Half an hour later, looking and feeling more like my usual self after a long, hot shower, I was sat at the table. I was pissed, really pissed. My mother wasn't home, which meant I had to do something, anything, to get to the bottom of things and find out what the hell was going on because no one was rushing forward with the information.

Snatching my coat from the back of the chair, I set off. He wasn't dead. He couldn't be. But why would my mother be crying? Surely the police would have come here for me? I felt the first stirrings of panic grab me. What if I'd killed someone?

I closed my eyes, there had to be a reasonable explanation. The feel of my feet pounding against the concrete helped me focus on not hyperventilating. Inhaling another fulfilling breath, I heard it.

His laugh.

Cora

My body jerked at the sound. He stood ahead of me, blocking my path. A plethora of feelings fought for pole position. Anger, the winner. Fear came in at a close second. Relief was also present.

He was alive.

And we were here, again.

My nails embedded themselves in my palm as my body responded before my brain had caught up. There had to be some explanation as to why I felt like this with him? I'd never disliked someone so intensely without knowing their name.

The jagged wisps of his hair flew in all directions as his eyes glared fiercely at me, his Cupid's bow mouth was set in a thin line. I walked closer to him, this wasn't easy with the unsteadiness of my legs. He remained glued to the spot. The closer I stepped towards him, the more defined his features became. I caught a slight flicker of something in his eyes, was that fear I saw?

"Look, Jack c-c-come on, she could cast a spell on you," one of the boys behind him stuttered.

"We really need to stop meeting like this," he sneered, the grin on his face was easy, carefree. "You think you can push me and get away with it?" Jack edged closer.

I smiled. He seriously thought I'd pushed him? That thought alone was absurd. I could barely lift my own weight, let alone push him that distance.

"Go on then, do it again if you dare, or is witchy witch scared?" he said, taunting me.

Before I was able to respond, his movements blurred. One minute he was stood sneering at me, the next he was doubled over. My lip stung. One of the chuckle brothers grabbed Jack, pulling him up. Jack leaned on his friend but still managed to look up at me with that idiotic smile in place. Sweat glistened on his face, giving it a sickly blue glisten.

"I had been warned about this but I'm stronger than you," he hissed.

Shock snatched away my ability to speak. Warned about what? The pain in my stomach shifted from bearable to extreme in seconds. My abs contracted, sinking inwards, ripping and pulling. The sky that had been clear blue on this crisp autumn morning was now overcome with bulbous, midnight black bruises. One hell of a storm was brewing, but Jack didn't acknowledge the darkening sky.

I felt the pain build as a crack of thunder protested, roaring across the dark sky. The ground shuddered beneath my feet. Neither of us outwardly acknowledged this change in the weather. He smiled, dimples deepened in his cheeks, and then something hit me, hard.

My feet flew from beneath me and the world rotated. The

ground smashed into my battered body as my hands flew out, scraping across the hard tarmac. I coughed, forcing my paralysed lungs to function. The skin hung limply on my hand, blood and road mingled together.

I stood up, shaking from the force that had just hit me. What had just hit me? His fist? Clenching my fists and ignoring the sharp cry from the fresh wound, I willed the pain to leave my body and I felt the punch of power blast out of me. I witnessed the way the iron fist smashed straight into Jack's chest. The impact slammed his clothes into his skin. He flew back and hit the floor with a sickening thud. The wind continued to howl and encase me as I gingerly stepped a little closer to his limp body. He didn't move. His brow was scrunched together. I bent beside him as the thunder continued to rumble in the distance. He was still breathing and the relief I felt from that was frightening. I rubbed at my eyes and took several deep breaths.

And then I looked back at him. My blood ran cold as goose pimples broke out over my skin. He was…I could barely believe it.

He was…but he couldn't be…

I scrambled back, feeling the nauseating slap of pain in my hands. In my only clear moment of the last twenty-four hours, I stood and took one last look at Jack before I ran.

*R*elief flooded through me when I caught sight of the three protective witches guarding *The Broom Cupboard*. I couldn't stop thinking about Jack. If Jack wasn't currently unconscious on the floor, when would the fight have stopped? How much damage would we have inflicted on each other until that damage was something we couldn't recover from? At this rate, the death of the leaves wouldn't be the only one to happen in this village.

I skidded to a stop outside the shop and saw my reflection in the window. My hair, dragged free from the bobble restraining it, was puffed out at odd angles. My face was ghostly white, the dark shade of my eyes made me look paler than I was. As my hand touched the handle, the fierce wind that had followed me since running from Jack suddenly died away, leaving a quiet eerie calm. I walked into the shop and then I was falling, the unwelcome darkness was creeping into my vision.

"Hello, Cora." Tabitha's words were fuzzy, like they were wrapped in cotton wool.

My legs crumbled beneath me, before my face hit the wooden steps, I felt a strong arm slide around my waist. Tabitha guided me to the only table in the shop. Grabbing the cup as soon as I sat, I took big gulps of the hot drink, trying to push away the huge lump that had lodged in my throat. The sting of scolding water made my mouth numb. I repositioned the cup in my hand which made it throb painfully.

"I think I killed Jack, the boy who was at the shop yesterday."

He couldn't be dead, the dead didn't... they didn't do what he was doing. The high pitched laugh startled me from my thoughts. I looked at Tabitha. Not one part of this was bloody funny. Nothing made sense to me, the wind and the laughter. Why did she think this was funny? Anger fuelled every cell in my already aching body. The wind howled outside, bashing up against the closed shop door.

"Enough of that!" Tabitha snapped. "You don't need to conjure the wind every time you get angry."

I gasped and stared at her.

"I suspect you want answers?"

Had Tabitha said that I was controlling the wind? But that wasn't possible. No one controlled the wind.

"Yesterday, your mother came to me, she was upset because we both knew as soon as the weather changed and the storm built that something had happened. I know, I have seen first-hand, that we can get four different seasons in one day but the storm you created was beyond that. Just one moment," Tabitha murmured as she stood and left the room, heading down the staircase.

My mother had come here? Tabitha drifted effortlessly up the stairs carrying a big blue book covered in a sheet of dust.

"Wh-what has happened to my mother?" I stammered.

Tabitha looked at me, confusion making her eyebrows collide. "As far as I know, nothing has happened."

"She's not home, she was, but then she left and didn't tell me where she was going."

"Perhaps she needed time alone. She will be at home when you get back, I'm sure."

"You don't know that. She could be anywhere. You don't know me or my mother."

"Cora, I know you better than you know yourself. I've spent the better part of my life protecting you."

Protecting me? What from? Tabitha held my gaze, but it was too intimidating, so I broke the contact and looked at the book that Tabitha had placed on the table. Gold looping letters were etched on the front of the leather-bound book, my fingers moved to touch but then I jerked away as the book flipped open and the pages starting flapping erratically. As suddenly as they had started, they stopped. I moved as close as I dared to the archaic book, the epitome of this shop, and peered at the exposed page. It was blank.

"That is your page, Cora. The page is blank because your path is yet to be written, this page will fill with important everyday events you experience. When you look through the book you will read about the members of your family. Your mother came up with this idea, she wanted you to be able to look back and read about your family. It had never been done at the time and it has never been done since because she was the most powerful person I knew."

"I'm sorry to sound so rude but you're talking rubbish. I

know who my mother is because I live with her. I don't need a book to tell me that, plus, the trick doesn't work with me, the book looks fake."

"I can assure you that was no trick. The book is real."

"Well, I know my family history... so you're lying." I couldn't think of a better reply.

"Yes, you know your family history as you believe it to be, but your bloodline is very important. It guides you to who you will become, who you are inside. Cora, you have returned. You can now take your place."

I was at a loss for words. Clearly, this woman was mental. Even as I thought that Tabitha was a liar, why were the creeping tendrils of doubt snaking its way up my spine?

"I don't understand." I shook my head. "This can't be true."

"In 1612, members of the Device family were tried and killed as witches," Tabitha began, focusing her eyes on me, the gleam from the light making them shine like emeralds.

"Cora, you are a descendant of this family. Their blood flows through you. This means you're a witch."

"No. No, I'm not." I shook my head adamant that this woman was lying to me. Witches didn't exist.

"You have powers and you've had them since you were born. You are the most powerful witch of your kind because your mother was. After the witch trials, I cast a spell which diminished your power. There have been some cases where the trigger switch doesn't flick back on which meant you would have been a commoner forever."

Commoner?

"I held back your powers because it made things easier for your adopted family. Now your powers have developed, and I can't tell you how much of a relief that is, I must admit I was swimming in guilt over the lack of your abilities. We were sure you would have them by now."

"And I'm not a witch," I snapped.

"How do you explain the wind?"

I opened my mouth to answer but no words followed.

Tabitha shot me a knowing smirk. "Alizon Device was a powerful witch, the most powerful witch I've had the pleasure of knowing. She was someone who had a great deal of spirit and determination, she was also one of the kindest people I knew. She had such a stubborn streak in her," she smiled. "I can already see you're very much like your mother."

The wind pulsed around me, an obvious sign that something was amiss.

"Of course, your mother, for all intents and purposes, was to tell you about your family history when the time felt right, I'm afraid this has taken us both by surprise. I suspect you want me to tell you about your family now?"

I was semi aware of my head bobbing up and down in answer to Tabitha's question.

"During the reign of King James I, people, and the King, believed that witches had made some sort of pact with the Devil-"

"Did you?" I interjected.

"No. I cannot abide by witches who use their craft for evil. England was unaffected for a short while, but it was only a matter of time… He became King of England sometime later and so the witch trials spread like wildfire.

"We were trying to remain under the radar but the Chattox family, our friends, or so we thought, turned us into the law. We could not defend ourselves because to show magic was disastrous for our kind. You must know that people with our abilities cannot show themselves. There are rules against Commoners knowing about what witches can do-"

"Commoners?"

"It is a name we give to people that are not witches. We didn't like using the terms humans because we are also human."

"But common makes them sound…well…common…"

"Yes, well, we couldn't think of another term. People in this very village were baying for the blood of a witch, any punishment would do but they favoured hanging and burning at the stake. We can never show ourselves. People don't understand. Cora, I can understand this is difficult for you to comprehend, but you must come to terms with it."

"No." I shook my head.

"You're a witch."

"Please stop saying it."

"It wouldn't change anything," Tabitha said, trying to contain a smile.

It couldn't be true. If any of this was true then I'd just been told that my mother wasn't actually my mother, that my birth mother had been murdered because I was a witch. And I couldn't remember any of this.

But that creeping doubt still played a deadly tune along my spine. What if it was real? What if I was a witch? It did explain the wind and the laughter. The pain that I'd had that was now gone too…

Well, hell.

Cora

Shaking my head in denial, I looked at Tabitha.

"I know what you're doing. You're playing with my insecurities, you somehow know that I never felt like I belonged in this life, but that's because my mother pushed me from home to home."

"Yes, we had to move you."

"Yeah, yeah. I have moved around because I'm a witch," I replied sarcastically.

"I believe I'm responsible for this and I deeply apologise. You don't know me... but you should. I have visited you every year for... let's say a lot of years. I cleanse your memory which makes it easier for Laura to keep up with the act of being your sister, aunt, or mother."

"What do you mean by cleanse?"

"We had to keep your true identity from you or you would see yourself every day and question it."

Question what? "This whole conversation is absurd, seriously have you sought medical help?"

Tabitha laughed. "I can see why I'd appear insane to you, but I can assure you, I'm perfectly normal. Well, as normal as a witch can be."

If Tabitha was telling me the truth, then I'd spent all those years moving around because of her. I should hate her...but I found myself fascinated by her.

"Why is it happening now?"

"Jack," Tabitha replied bluntly.

Startled, I dropped my cup on the table and watched the contents fly in all directions. I dragged my coat off my shoulders to wipe up the spill.

"What are you doing? Here, you'll ruin your coat, step aside."

I stumbled aside as Tabitha spread her hands over the table. Heat instantly fired up around me and I could feel it dance happily alongside the wind. The chocolate evaporated. The heat vanished. And my mouth dropped open in shock.

"My gift is not unusual, please don't look so terrified," she chuckled. "I have the gift of fire, it is quite clearly a very useful gift. Elements are very useful when they are controlled properly."

I bent and quickly looked under the table to see if there was a hole that let the liquid disappear.

"Does your...power speak to you?" I blurted.

Tabitha's eyebrow shot up. "No, does yours?"

"Yes. No. I don't know," I sighed.

"What does it do?"

"It laughs," I mumbled meekly.

Tabitha laughed. "Great, well obviously one part of you is happy."

How was any of this great?

Tabitha coughed. "Rather regretfully, Cora, you haven't controlled your element and we have a bit of a problem on our hands."

This wasn't just a problem, it was a train wreck. "Well, if I'd known about this before I'd been attacked then maybe you wouldn't have this dilemma to deal with. You're to blame for that, not me. Jack said he knew, he said he'd been warned about this. Where was my warning?"

"I was afraid Jack would already know. I didn't tell you, and that decision was made by Laura and I. We didn't think you needed forewarning. Your element may never have developed, and what then? You would know you were a witch without having an element, are you to convince me that you wouldn't have felt inferior? Or in fact that you would have believed what we told you without proof?"

"Still, you had no right to hold this from me. You could have warned me yesterday when I was here. You witnessed first-hand Jack's temper, right here at the shop, yet you did nothing," I snapped. "I thought I was dying." My voice broke.

"Oh, Cora, I'm sorry that you went through that alone. Yes, I could have told you this yesterday, but you wouldn't have believed me."

"I would have..." my reply trailed off. "Okay, fine. You mentioned that Jack was the reason my powers have surfaced?" Rubbing my fingers over my eyes I tried to shake the first stirrings of a massive headache and focused on one thing at a time.

"What did you do to your hand?"

I stupidly looked at the loose skin. "I fell, well, that's not entirely true. I was pushed. Who knew concrete could do that?"

"Wait a moment." Tabitha stood and made her way to the door behind the counter. She came back holding something in her hands. "Here."

"What is it?"

"It will help."

I allowed Tabitha to wrap the warm towel around my hand and immediately smelt summer heat and flowers. "Jack?" I prompted Tabitha.

"Oh yes, he is the only direct living descendant of the Chattox family, that makes him-"

"Not a very nice person," I interjected.

"Well, yes. I believe the anger you have for each other is the important key as to why this change has started. I can only assume this is the reason why your powers have emerged so quickly. I believe when faced with someone who is a threat to you, your power came into being, how else were you supposed to protect yourself?"

"My fists?"

Tabitha shook her head as a smile tugged at her perfect lips.

"Oh, that wasn't a question?"

"No," she laughed. "However, now that this has happened and now you can protect yourself, there is only one thing that will solve this, and it will sound rather brutal… Cora, I'm afraid you have to eliminate him."

I jolted in the chair. "When you say eliminate..."

"I mean exactly that."

Tabitha's face remained expressionless.

No.

No way. You didn't go around killing people. It wasn't right.

"You have to," Tabitha said almost like she sensed my reluctance. "I know that this revelation is difficult to grasp, especially as you've just found out you're a witch, but it has to be done. It's not something I condone, I hate violence, but I'm afraid it comes down to that. You die, or he dies. You have no option... unless you want to die?"

"No," I said in the same instant my mind said maybe. Would I rather die than kill another human being? Why did I have to kill anyone?

Tabitha stood, her dress today was snow white, the slim green belt wrapped snugly around her waist.

"If you don't want to die then you have to kill Jack," Tabitha insisted. "This is the only way to ensure peace. To ensure you don't die, and you will not die on my watch because I've spent too long protecting you."

This wasn't happening. I didn't know which revelation was the worse... that I was a witch or that I would have to kill someone.

"We must learn from the mistakes of the past, which means neither Device nor Chattox can live peacefully within the same village."

"Wait a minute, shouldn't we learn that fighting gets you nowhere other than very dead?" I argued.

"Yes, inevitably fighting leads to death, but what happened between your mother and the Chattox family was about power. I knew the Chattox family and they wouldn't want to lose. Dominance battles are a very tricky business, no one is ever going to admit defeat."

"Okay, then should we not show them, and this Jack, that we don't want a power fight?"

Why didn't Tabitha get it? We didn't have to fight, why couldn't we talk instead?

"Cora, he doesn't want peace, haven't you already witnessed his need to dominate you? To intimidate you? Look at what's occurred since you two have met. You may not want to admit it, but I can imagine when you were stood in front of him you wanted to win." She raised her perfectly shaped brow in an invitation to argue.

She was right, I had wanted to win, but I wasn't going to admit that.

"But times have changed, and people don't go around burning each other anymore. We can see who wins in a fight and then leave it. We haven't been caught so far."

"Yes, and for that you are very lucky. We can't just allow you to do this. Let me ask you this, if you lost, would you be satisfied and leave it be?"

"Yes." Of course, I wouldn't leave it.

"What would happen if one day you were walking on this very street and he was there too, would you just walk past each other without a challenge?"

I couldn't answer.

Tabitha nodded and continued. "People may believe that witches are real but to see and be part of a witch war is entirely different, they won't stand for it."

What was I meant to say? It was clear Jack didn't like me and I wasn't exactly rushing to be his best friend. "Can't I just move again?" I whined.

"You could, but now you know about your true self would you want to be anywhere other than here?"

I didn't have an answer.

"I find it really ironic that you were brought back here," Tabitha commented, breaking the awkward silence.

"Why?"

"Your mother, Laura that is, didn't tell me that you had moved here. I found out the day I saw you in front of my shop. Before the trials, your mother's house would have been where the woods are now, so you live close to where it all began."

"Can't I have my memories back?" I wanted to remember this past life.

Tabitha was already shaking her head. "I wish I could but once the spell has been cast it is up to the individual mind whether it repairs itself."

"You're saying that I might never remember my life?"

"I'm sorry, this was the only way to keep you from knowing who you are and asking questions about your appearance."

"My appearance?"

"Yes, you never change in appearance."

That didn't make sense, I grew older every year. "Why didn't you just go with the easy option and just tell me? Why not let me decide how I wanted to live my life. Why did you have to take my memories?"

"It was the only option at the time, things were too dangerous and by the time things settled down you were already living your life and your memories were gone. We had to give you time to find your power, we just never imagined it would take this long. I want to assure you that you've had a good life."

"Well, you would know," I replied smartly. "I don't want my memories taken from me. From now on I want to remember everything."

"Yes, of course."

"How am I meant to deal with this? How can I?"

"Cora, his family are the reason you don't have one."

Anger tightened my chest. "I'm just one person, how I am meant to do this?" I couldn't actually believe I was even contemplating it.

"You're not alone, you have an entire coven to help you."

"I have a what?"

Tabitha smiled and then stood aside. A coven? Hundreds of people?

Tabitha motioned for me to stand, which I did. Tabitha placed her hand on my back and guided me towards the staircase. I had a funny feeling that after tonight my life would never be the same.

Cora

As we stood on the last step facing the wall, Tabitha whispered something foreign. The wall moved, revealing more steps into the darkness. Darkness engulfed me, taking away my sense of direction. I picked up the faint smell of... mud. Wet mud. I felt the reassuring warm arm around my waist, it was the only thing restricting me from running back up the fake stairway.

We continued walking in silence with only the sound of Tabitha's robe as our companion in the silence. After several turns, Tabitha eventually stopped. The arm left my waist, the air stalled in my lungs. I caught the sound of a crackle of energy before it snapped, and light filled the area.

I was stood in a cove which was large and circular in shape. Tabitha seemed to like dusty books as every wall was lined with them. In the middle of this room, taking pride of place, was an oak table surrounded by four tall high-backed chairs. A symbol engraved in the middle of the table caught my eye. I knew I was looking at was the Wiccan symbol. My fingers brushed against the engraved letters.

"Those are the names of the members of your coven, they are engraved in old English. That one is Preston," Tabitha said as she pointed to her own name. "Then there is Smith, Quinn, and of course, Device."

There were three members of my coven. That wasn't as bad as I'd first thought. I noticed that Tabitha held something in her hand. I looked at it as she passed it to me.

It was a photograph of a woman who was laughing. She had long brown hair which hung loosely, just hitting the small curves of her hips. Her jade green eyes danced mischievously. My pulse quickened. There was no denying it, the shape of those green eyes were the same shape as mine, our lips identical.

It was the woman from my dream.

"This is Alizon Device, your mother."

A thick black haze started to fill my vision and then everything went fuzzy. For what seemed like the hundredth time in my life, I fainted.

Taking a deep breath, I opened my eyes and moved into a sitting position whilst holding my head in my hands. The spinning room was making my stomach lurch, the result of which wasn't going to be pretty.

"Cora, are you okay?"

I looked at a wavy Tabitha. No, I wasn't okay. Shuffling off the table, I sat in a chair. "I'm sorry."

"Please, don't apologise. This is rather big news."

"Yeah, you could say that. On the one hand, everything you've told me makes sense, it all just slips into place and then, on the other hand, I just don't want it to."

Tabitha noisily scraped a chair back and sat next to me. "Cora, I don't know how much more you are ready to handle tonight, this has been enough already." She held her hands on her lap and studied me.

"I want to know everything," I insisted. If I didn't hear it tonight, I was afraid that my mind would make up an excuse, any excuse, to tell me this entire thing wasn't real.

Silence followed as Tabitha held my gaze. Sighing, Tabitha held up the photograph for me to see. "This is your mother. I took this picture in 1602, she was nineteen years old…"

Laughter interrupted Tabitha, and I was startled to find that it was coming from me. "Well, if all that is true…you couldn't take pictures in 1602, the camera wasn't even invented!" I smiled, quite pleased with the flaw.

"You forget that I am a witch," Tabitha's smile remained in place, but I felt the whiplash from her words. "I do not need such technology to take pictures."

"Okay, so, if you did take this picture of…" I couldn't quite bring myself to say it. "Then, how is it that I am still living? If this is… then I would be old… like…" I stumbled on the maths. It wasn't my best subject.

Something Tabitha had said earlier came screaming back, my appearance. Tabitha said we'd moved because of my appearance.

"Cora, you are four hundred and seventeen years old."

I nearly fell off the chair. My God! But I was seventeen, I'd recently had a birthday. I *looked* seventeen.

13

"Your mother never did tell me who your father was," Tabitha said, continuing even though I struggled over the age issue. "The law, our own Wiccan law states that a witch can be with a commoner, but she can never tell him what she is. The same goes for you. If you meet and fall in love with a commoner, you cannot let him know who you truly are. Take my advice, relationships always work better with another witch."

"I don't think I have the time for a boyfriend right now." I was trying to sound sarcastic but it just came out as one big sigh.

"Good," Tabitha smiled, taking my comment literally.

Tabitha's smile soon faded as she continued. "Your mother, my best friend was murdered in 1612, you were seventeen years old. A powerful witch goes through a change and this change is more commonly triggered by an emotional or physical experience. Once a witch goes through the change they will never age in appearance, their age will not change.

"Death will also come from the same things that can kill commoners, guns, knives and such things. Disease, cancer or infections do us no harm. The less powerful become old and die," she smiled before saying, "that is how they become the three decrepit witches outside my shop. It was believed many years ago that this was how the Devil rid the world of the weak. He only wanted the strong representing him here on earth. Of course, it isn't true. You remain seventeen years old because the death of your mother was the turning point for you."

"So, you're saying I will look seventeen all my life?"

"Yes."

No!

That wasn't right. "But I just had a birthday. I'm seventeen and next year I'm eighteen. I *will* be eighteen."

"You are seventeen, but every time we go through the process of taking those memories we make you believe you are nearly sixteen. I'm afraid you will never be eighteen."

That was depressing. What did you live for if you didn't die? What made you strive to do things in life? I looked at Tabitha, her coal black hair was pulled to one side, her eyes were focused on me.

"Wait, how long have you been running the shop?"

"A number of years." Tabitha skilfully evaded the intended meaning behind the question.

I wasn't going to let her off the hook just yet. "But won't people start asking questions? You look the same, Tabitha, years later you will still look the same, people may just notice this."

"Well, I have weaved a complicated spell that no one questions. They don't notice how I look."

"Isn't there a law against that?" I asked.

"I imagine there is, but I have a life here, one that I'm unwilling to give up."

Well, who was I to argue? I didn't want to move now either.

"Does the spell apply to me?" I asked, feeling uncertain.

"If you would like it to?"

It helped that Tabitha would extend the spell, that it would allow me to make a home here. If I wanted it. "I need more time to figure this whole thing out."

"I understand this must be hard for you, Cora, and we have discussed a lot tonight. I will suspend your first coven meeting for the time being."

The cove blacked out, signalling the end of the conversation. I stood up and felt Tabitha's warm arm slide around my waist. The life I'd lived and hated felt like it was over. I could start again, how often were people given the opportunity to do such a thing?

Jack

The motion of going up and down was quite soothing, like the soft rise and fall you got when you fell asleep on a boat… I'd never been on a boat, so I could only imagine. So why did this feel like what I imagined it to be?

My brows collided in the middle of my head in concentration. I opened my eyes and tried to look around the black spots that were floating in my vision. To my left was the farm owned by Andrew Bruton and to my right were the woods that branched off in the direction of Lemon Tree village, a village smaller than this, if that was at all possible. I knew where I was. The memory of what had happened came screaming painfully back at me.

I wheezed and rubbed my chest. Again, why did I still feel like I was on a boat?

I glanced casually to my left.

Oh Jesus Christ!

I wasn't on the floor!

My body quickly hit the concrete, grazing my elbow as it made contact with the hard tarmac. Rolling over, I shifted my weight onto my knees and felt the ground ripple beneath me. Gritting my teeth, I pushed the onslaught of sick back down, I would not throw up. I slowly pushed myself into a standing position as every muscle from head to foot whimpered. I needed to speak with Eli. Eli had warned me, but I hadn't listened. I smacked myself on the head with the flat part of my palm which made it spin. I took a deep breath and limped back home.

Eli was sprawled on the sofa watching TV when I crashed through the door. Eli's bored gaze moved from the TV to my face and I saw the confusion cloud his eyes, the green and blue dancing together, becoming turquoise as he tried to figure out what had happened.

He gingerly picked up the remote and switched the TV off. That was my cue to start explaining, but I couldn't form the words.

"So, judging by your entrance and by the look of you, which, by the way, you look like hell, I guess you finally want to talk."

I urged my legs to move and made it to the end of the sofa where they gave way. I rubbed my eyes with the back of my hands and took a deep breath. "I think it's happened."

"Good, I've been trying to explain things to you-"

"No, Eli, something happened, I can't explain it, she deserved it, it was-"

Eli abruptly stood, cutting me off. "What do you mean?" He towered over me, his hands fisted at his hips and a look of horror on his face.

Oh, Jesus, I'd gone and done it. Eli's expressions usually consisted of two things. Concern, for example, when I'd broken my leg. Or concentration, when he was developing a new gadget to sell. This look, where his eyes narrowed, his mouth pulled into an angry scowl and his jaw pulsed as he ground his teeth together, wasn't a great one. Last time I'd witnessed such a look, I'd had verbal whiplash for months. I'd made the grave mistake of setting Eli up on a date. It hadn't gone down well.

"Well... remember when you told me I would have some sort of power?"

"It's not something I'm going to forget, Jack, and I recall you laughed at me and continued to watch the garbage on TV." His jaw pulsed some more.

Christ, it was getting worse. "Well, I think I've got my powers today. No big deal though." I shrugged and held back the wince that one small action caused. I stood up and made my way into the kitchen.

The kitchen was as long as the cottage, it was situated at the back overlooking a shield of trees. It was light and airy and creamy yellow in colour, with light wood cupboards. Walking the short distance, in my condition it was a marathon, to the fridge, I opened it and reached for a can. My mouth and throat wept with gratitude as the cold liquid exploded in my mouth and rushed down my throat. I heard Eli's heavy footsteps behind me. Three, two, one-

"Jack, you need to do some explaining! What the hell happened? What do you mean you just have powers now? That she deserved it? If I know the person you said deserves it. Christ, we're in serious trouble."

I turned and watched Eli have some sort of middle age

breakdown as he pushed his hand through his short conker red hair. I warily approached him, past experience had taught me to be careful when someone was angry. I cautiously placed my hands on his shoulders and looked deep into his eyes. Why was Eli worried? I could handle a little girl. "Listen, I can handle the situation."

Eli laughed loudly. "You cannot handle that witch, Jack. She is very powerful, as you've probably already found out." Eli looked me up and down before focusing on my face. "I can see you already had some sort of fight. What happened?"

"Okay, I was with Lee and Adam," I began as Eli paced. "We spotted this new girl outside the witch shop-"

"When?" Eli interrupted.

"Errrmmm, Thursday I think."

"Jesus, why didn't you tell me sooner?" Eli scolded as he pushed his hand through his hair in exasperation.

"Because nothing happened...well, nothing much," I mumbled. Before Eli could shout again, I continued. "Anyway, I thought I would have a laugh with her, yer know... So I had a go at this girl and then that woman who owns the shop, the weird one, she came out to rescue her. Then we left. That was all that happened...the first time."

Eli had stopped pacing and he was now fixing me with a lethal stare.

"The next time I saw her we were messing around in the field. Something happened to me, Eli. She was so deep in thought I managed to creep up on her, her face was a picture. She was scared, and I seemed to feed off it. I don't know what it is about that girl but whenever she is near I just feel so overwhelmed with emotions. I felt it, something in here." I smacked my gut, ignoring the instant rise of bile. I shouldn't have done that. "The power I felt was immense, God, I can't tell you how much it hurt-"

"I know how much it hurts," Eli interrupted.

Right, Eli was a witch too.

"Anyway, I remember something pummelled headlong into my chest and then I was flying through the air. I remember feeling the ground smash into my back and then complete blackness. And then I woke up, but I wasn't on the floor."

Eli's brows shot up into his hairline. "What do you mean?"

"I was flying like bloody Superman. Once I realised what I was doing, I fell and hit my head, whacked it good and scratched my elbow to bits."

There was silence as Eli digested the information he'd received. "You can levitate, that has always been your gift. Come and sit down, Jack." Eli placed his hand on my shoulder, making me wince as pain shot across my shoulder blades.

Eli dropped the hand and made his way to the sofa. "It's time you were told everything about your family."

Jack

"Pay attention to what I tell you because you didn't listen last time I mentioned this to you and now look at what's happened. This situation could've been avoided, now that it's here, we will have to deal with it because your life depends on you listening to me."

Talk about being melodramatic. Eli narrowed his eyes just as I was about to roll my eyes.

"In 1612, thirteen witches were hung for witchcraft. They are known better nowadays as the Pendle Hill witches. The majority of the witches resided here and according to the commoners living here, the witches had shown themselves to the public, but I don't believe it for one second. We didn't do such things and I did warn you last time I discussed this with you that demonstrating your magic in front of people is forbidden within our community. The law needs to be upheld at all times."

"All right! No need to poke your finger in my face." I playfully slapped Eli's finger away.

Eli ignored me. "Villagers were hunting anyone they believed to be a witch, they became so obsessed with finding us that they killed innocents. If you took a breath and they thought that you did it wrong, they would declare you a witch. It was that simple, and you didn't have a hope of being found innocent."

Eli faltered, his head was in another time and place.

I shrugged my shoulders. "Thanks for the history lesson," I said, and flashed a smile. "But I really don't understand why I should pay attention to this?"

"Jack, that is your history. There were two main families who lived in this village, one family is your own. Your mother is Anne Whittle and she died in 1612 leaving a seventeen-year-old boy-"

"What?" I interrupted. Why was Eli only revealing this now?

"She left you because she didn't have any other option."

"It isn't true." It couldn't be.

"It is, I'm sorry."

I'd hurriedly accepted that I had powers, who wouldn't? It was a cool Superman moment, but I'd refused to acknowledge the link. Power didn't just come into being, it was passed down.

"You're a witch, it's as simple as that. I've told you this before but now you will have to believe me."

Eli had informed me a little less than a year ago that I was a witch and that one day I'd have powers that he would later explain. I'd ignored him. I'd believed he was a little crazy, but living with him was better than living with the people before…

"Powerful witches go through a change and when you witnessed the death of your mother you went through your change. The country wasn't safe at that time as witches were being tortured, I knew you would seek revenge; I couldn't let you, so I agreed it was for the best that your power was suppressed, and your memories were taken from you. It was best that you didn't remember your past. I wanted to give you a shot at a normal life."

I inhaled deeply and then held the air in my lungs. I'd watched my mother die? Exhaling, I took deeper breaths, trying to clear my head. I didn't know what to say.

"I was there too," Eli spoke. "I was hiding in the shadows to make sure they didn't take you; that was my job. I hope that one day your memories come back to you so you can see what happened that day."

"Why don't I remember anything? Who did this to me?"

"Tabitha, the witch at the shop-"

"I knew it!" I shouted, "She looks like the type to go meddling in people's business!"

"As I was saying, Tabitha was also involved in the witch trials. Her best friend was Alizon Device who has a daughter." Eli held his finger, signalling that I should remain quiet.

I knew who it was. The picces of the puzzles were falling into place.

"You and Alizon's daughter were at high risk at the time of these trials. Sons and daughters of witches were often taken and killed, they believed the Devil would jump from the mothers to their children. It was a miracle you were both able to escape. Once you'd witnessed the..." He shook his head and sighed. "You were both adamant that you wanted to be there at the end and we couldn't deny you the chance to say goodbye. Once it was over, Tabitha took you both into hiding.

"Since that day you were placed in a family in which the relatives over the centuries have watched over you. Tabitha continued to do a spell on both of you every year or so to keep your past hidden from yourselves and from others. I'm not sure if, or when, your powers would have shown themselves. I was pre-warned by Tabitha that your power may never develop because we'd manipulated it and stalled your body doing what it should naturally.

"Until this moment Tabitha has remained neutral for the safety of you both. No one knew about this arrangement other than the two families. It was just the Thomas family for you, Jack, and the Hunt family for Cora, Tabitha, the coven members and I."

That girl was the reason behind my family's demise. "So, what you're saying is that my powers somehow barged past Tabitha's spell because I met Cora?"

"I believe so."

The room was silent.

"And there is no possibility of my memories coming back with another type of spell?"

"That process is too difficult, the result could be disastrous. We didn't want to risk it."

"Right."

"We need to prepare you and your powers so we can face whatever is thrown our way," Eli urged.

"My powers are just fine," I sang.

To prove it, I jumped off the sofa and ignored the way my head throbbed. My element responded instantly and I found myself levitating a few feet off the floor. But I couldn't hold it. My concentration lapsed and my legs collapsed beneath me. I hissed as the pain intensified.

"I need to work on the landing," I smirked. "What do I

need to know? How do I deal with Cora?" How else was this going to be resolved?

Eli shot me a stern look as he left the room only for him to return moments later holding some sort of book which was the size of his chest. Christ. I hated reading.

"This is your family book, but what I do know without looking in this book is how to handle her."

"How?"

Eli placed the book on the coffee table and looked at me. "You need to meet with her and sort the problem out."

Something in Eli's tone didn't suggest sitting down with Cora and having tea and biscuits. "When you say sort the problem, do you mean like fighting?"

"Yes."

"Right, I don't know if that will work because we've had some sort of thing that has happened between us and that hasn't worked. It always ends with one of us running off or blacking out."

"Well, we will control the fight. One way or the other, it will end."

That could only mean one thing and that wasn't something I'd considered, ever. Yes, the girl irritated me, there was some emotion that seemed to surge through my body whenever I was in her presence. I couldn't understand it during clear moments like this, but to actually kill her? Could I kill another human being?

Her family had sent mine to be murdered. They had died, and I'd lost a mother because of her. Within the space of days we'd fought and both times I'd walked away with injuries. I couldn't believe I was thinking about this, but in the great scheme of things I had only two choices, kill or be killed.

"I can't believe we're talking about killing people…it's not in my nature to hurt people, that would turn me into something like him, and he made my life miserable. But when I see her or think of her, I get such a rush of emotion too difficult to control or understand. I can't live in this village, walk around this village whilst she does."

"We could move?" Eli suggested.

"Why should we? I lived here first, she should move. No, you're right," I sighed. "We have only one option."

"Right, then you will need the help of your coven."

Eli grabbed the phone on his way out of the room. Several tidal waves of regret, worry and concern washed over me. I'd either agreed to do something that would save my life, or it would kill another human being. It wasn't a decision I liked but this was far beyond anything I could control.

Jack

Blocking out Eli's muffled voice from the kitchen, I sat and brushed off the layer of dust on the book to reveal the name, Chattox. The letters had a flowing, calligraphy feel to them. I opened the book and found the beginnings of a family tree. Names I didn't know curved in several directions, creating branches. Turning the page, I found my name, a short branch born from another slightly bigger branch. I followed the sweeping name. My mother's name. I felt my heart painfully tighten for someone I would never know.

Opposite my mother's name was another large branch that was also connected to mine. The name was illegible as I followed the curves and sweeps. I gasped. The letters read, Anne Redfern. Our names were connected by one single flowing branch.

"Eli!" I shouted, "Eli, get in here!"

Eli walked into the room with the phone placed on his chest. "What's wrong?" he hissed.

"I have a sister!?" I waited for Eli to tell me that I was wrong, but it didn't come.

Eli mumbled something into the phone and sat on the sofa. "This is a very difficult thing to talk about," he sighed, "but I will try to tell you everything, please bear with me."

"You should have already told me everything."

"I know..." Eli took some deep breaths. "Your sister, Anne, was a funny, caring woman who loved with her whole heart. She had the same deep rich brown hair as you, the same eyes, you both inherited those eyes from your mother. The witch trials were a mass of confusion and Anne and your mother were taken. Anne came back, I believe they'd found new evidence condemning someone else, so she was released. She believed that she was acquitted but they came for her again, and this time they declared her guilty of witchcraft."

I pushed aside the sting of tears. "I don't understand why you didn't tell me?"

"I didn't tell you because... it was such a painful time for everyone..." Eli stumbled over his words.

"What aren't you telling me?"

Eli had placed his head in his hands. The hairs on my neck stood to attention, preparing me for something more. The seconds slowed as I waited for an answer. Eli's eyes finally found mine and to my horror, I noticed the tears.

"Jack, I was married to Anne, she's the love of my life." Eli wiped his face. "I've never felt pain like that. In that one second, I lost the one person who completed me, the one person who understood me. I went that day to see her, but I couldn't show myself for fear that they would take me. They presumed marital spouses were also witches, and their presumptions were right. She had this iron brace around her neck. Oh God, the blood." He looked down at his hands like he could see the blood there.

"I would have done anything to take her place that day, to die instead of her. It wasn't her time, I stood and watched her, murdered in front of my eyes. It was agreed that I was to look after you and if I'd saved her then you would have been left alone."

A wave of pity and guilt crashed over me.

"The crowds spat and shouted at them as they stood, waiting for death. It took every ounce of strength I had not to retaliate. I looked at Alizon Device who stood on the same platform as my wife. The moment I felt at my weakest with my hands fisted ready to pummel someone, was the moment Anne's eyes found me. She smiled at me and she'd never looked more beautiful. From the first moment I'd met her, her bright smile hooked me, and it's never let go. In the final seconds her lips moved and uttered three words that broke my heart. Then she closed her eyes." Eli took another deep, shuddering breath wiping the rest of his face and then he looked at me.

"Jack, I'm your brother in law."

My heart had stopped beating. Swallowing, I pushed my feelings down. "So, you went through the change? How old are you?"

"I am twenty-seven years old. I've been twenty-seven since 1612. I'm not an extremely powerful witch because my mother married a commoner, she fell in love and she loved breaking the law," he smiled.

"My dad, who was he?"

"I don't know, I'm sorry."

Was it bad that I felt happy about not knowing the name of another loved one? Two names already weighed heavily on my heart.

We sat in silence as the sun lowered in the sky, a soft pink hue danced across the wall and was quickly followed by the harsh cold blue of the approaching night. Neither of us stood to turn on a light. A soft tapping at the door forced Eli to stand.

"Jack, we're going to have our first coven meeting."

I turned around as the light came on; Eli stepped aside to reveal two people.

"This is Clay Barnes and Clio Merle, they are members of your coven."

Clay stepped forward and bowed to me. I smoothed out the slightly shocked expression that had jumped onto my face.

"Merry meet."

"Errrrmmmm… yeah, right back at ya."

Bowing and a different language? This night was about to become a whole lot stranger. Clay stood with his hands in the pockets of his dark ripped jeans, a royal blue shirt covered his large, muscular frame. His dirty blonde hair hung loose, strands of it just hitting his shoulders. His green eyes studied me. I could sense them on me as my gaze moved towards Clio.

Clio bowed as Clay had done. She was dressed from head to toe in a ruby red robe. Her brown hair, infused with several highlights of honey, was pulled back into a messy bun; her straight cut fringe shaped her face, highlighting her high cheekbones and exotic amber eyes.

"Merry meet, Jack," she said.

"Merry meet." The words felt rather strange, but I made an effort regardless.

"Do we hold meetings regularly?"

Please say no. Please say no.

"No, we generally meet once a year, but we have to meet when a new leader comes into a coven."

I let out a relieved sigh and followed the three of them as we made our way to the back garden. Eli stopped in front of the group and opened the shed door. I couldn't believe that a meeting took place here. What was wrong with the kitchen table?

As Clay and Clio followed Eli into the shed, I stepped forward and my mouth dropped open in shock. The lawn mower still stood dormant in the cobwebbed corner, the mud-caked tools hung precariously on the rusted nails, but a huge gaping hole occupied the floor that I swore was unfamiliar. A staircase sunk into complete darkness. I followed them with a huge grin on my face.

Jack

*D*arkness washed over me as I followed the sound of footsteps. Amongst the sound of our feet, I caught the sound of water. I had several fears, I'd listed them in my mind in accordance to which was the worst.

1. Darkness
2. Drowning.
3. Fire.
4. Shooting.

I started gasping for breath before I could control it. If the water rose, I could suspend myself in the air but for how long? The inevitable would happen, this cave would fill up. Before I could ask where we were, the group came to a stop and then a light snapped on, giving me my first look.

A large room, square in shape, housed a table, chairs and several cabinets. Thousands of little square shelves were scattered over every inch of the wall space. On each shelf sat many small bottles. I stepped to the nearest display, fascinated by the mix of colours in one small glass vial. Pinks and yellows meshed together as they curved along a delicate petal.

Light built into the shelf illuminated the bottle which threw out a mix of pastel colours into the room.

"Jack, we're ready."

I turned and realised they were waiting for me. Making my way to the last chair available, I got my first real look at the table. Engraved in the middle was a symbol, a circle with the odd star shape thing. A witch symbol… I slumped into a chair and saw the three of them looking expectantly back at me. What did they expect me to do? Balance on my head and juggle? My index finger brushed against something as I shifted in my seat, looking down, I saw symbols that were engraved in the old wood.

"Jack, that lettering is your family name in Old English. It has been engraved in this table since 1612 waiting for you to take your place."

"And what exactly is my place?" I looked at Clay as he was the one who'd spoken to me.

"You are the High Priest of your coven," Eli answered.

My head whipped towards Eli in shock. "What?"

"Your mother was High Priestess. Anne was placed second and you were to follow. You take the role because you are the last member of your family."

That was poor reasoning. What if I couldn't take on the role? "Eli, you were married to Anne. You can do it."

Their laughter filled the room, but I didn't laugh. Instead, I felt the first stirrings of anger move around in my gut. Gripping the table, I closed my eyes.

"Jack, can you stop doing that?"

My head shot up and I realised the laughter had died and I saw why. The entire table was levitating.

"You have a very powerful gift, Jack." Clio's voice was soft, appraising.

I smiled in her direction, but my eyes were focused on Eli's face. I felt the relief, a heavyweight I didn't know I'd harboured; leave my body when I caught the twitch in Eli's lips and the smile in his eyes. I felt the tug and pull as my power weaved in and around the people and the table trying to bring us down safely. The table landed with a thump as we touched down on the floor awkwardly.

"Need to work on the landing," I chuckled.

"Yes, you still need to work on your gift," Eli remarked. "But you also need to stop letting your anger rule you. It gets you into trouble, just look where your temper has got you so far." Eli gave me the look.

I knew such a look from my past. The look usually came just before gut wrenching pain from a fist.

"Are you ready for your induction, High Priest?"

I coughed to clear my throat which suddenly felt very tight. "Yes."

"Clay, if you will." Eli gestured with his hand.

Clay bent to the floor and then stood. Moving around the table in a clockwise direction, he placed a candle on each corner of the star inside the circle. Clay then moved around the table, now anti-clockwise, and lit each. Tiny flames sparked, burning a brilliant deep red. The flames from the candles danced higher, the tips licking hungrily at the ceiling. Clay placed two gold candles in front of me and then walked back to his chair and placed a tarnished dish on the table. Holding his hands palm up and resting them on the table.

"O God within, I am created from your essence, I thank you for the gift I hold dear within me. I offer you my gift on this night in welcome of our High Priest who has joined us at long last. Blessed Be."

Clay moved his left hand over the bowl once and laid it back on the table. I sat bolt upright to look in the bowl which was now brimming with water, but I held back the rush of questions. Movement from Clio caught my attention.

Reluctantly tearing my gaze away from the dish, I watched as Clio placed her hands in her robes. Would she produce a sword and go all samurai on us? She looked like the sort. She was lean, dangerous and sexy. She pulled out her hand and dusted her side of the table with small red crystals.

"O God within, I am created from your essence, nourish me with your love as I hold your earth's power in my heart. I offer this gift in welcome of our new Priest. Blessed Be."

I felt the earth respond to her. Little tremors vibrated, becoming greater in strength. Was that an earthquake? My hands grasped the table for support as my heart leaped into my throat. I had a feeling if this continued the room was going to cave in. A new terrifying fear rushed to the forefront of my mind.

Death by earthquake.

Her gift was amazing, despite my fear.

"O God within, I am created from your essence, I offer you my gift as a celebration of this night. We welcome our new Priest, my brother." Eli stopped speaking and looked at me.

A lump the size of London dropped heavily in my chest. I had a brother, a family.

Eli continued. "My gift to you is the athame. May you accept this gift with my love and protection. Blessed Be."

Something flew across the room and came to an abrupt halt in the middle of the table. I barely managed to stop myself from jumping out of my seat. It was a knife, and not any old knife. The long handle was death black and encrusted with jagged glittering red crystals. The blade, at least ten inches long, flashed dangerously in the red candlelight, the blood red dripping within the mirror of the blade. The knife floated silently down to the table. Eli never touched it. They turned their attention away from their own gifts to look at me.

"Errmmm… O God within, I am created from your essence." I faltered, maybe I could quote a song? I tried to think of a song… "Thank you for the gift you gave to me, I hope I can be successful as your High Priest. Blessed Be."

As speeches went, mine wasn't the greatest. I lifted my hands and pushed myself and the candles into the air. I grabbed my power and forced the candles to fly faster. I knew that speed would make sure my idea worked. With one great push, they rushed into the middle of the table and collided. Wax shattered, cascading like glitter to the table. Flames took hold of the tiny pieces and as they landed on the table I was satisfied to see the symbol set on fire. The larger candles sparked to life, the flames shooting higher and higher.

I descended and once I landed Eli held my hand as we chanted, "So may it be."

The flames died and then the lights blinked back on. I had to sit, not trusting my legs. I lowered my head, taking deep breaths. Now that I was focused on my breathing it was becoming more erratic. I wheezed a little but tried to do it silently, I didn't want the others thinking I couldn't handle the situation. I couldn't handle it, I was hyperventilating, but I still didn't want them to know.

"Jack?" Eli approached me. "Are you okay?"

I nodded and gave a very limp smile.

"We're finished here and I'm sure you're shattered, it's past your bedtime, little brother," Eli teased me, whilst he put an arm around my shoulders.

"Less of this little brother business," I smiled and stood on shaky legs.

Clay and Clio moved in unison in front of me, ready to bow or do whatever it was that they did. "Whoa… okay look, stop with the bowing business, it's the 21st century and I'm not the king, so just please stop."

Clay laughed whilst Clio smiled and still bowed. As I battled a jaw-cracking yawn, I listened to the three of them excitedly discuss spells.

I was a witch.

I was the son of a powerful witch.

It took less than a second for me to decide that I would rather be the son of a witch than the son of that low life who'd apparently been my father. And because I accepted this change, my next port of call was to seek revenge for their unnecessary murders.

Cora

I reluctantly climbed from the warmth of my bed and fished around in my wardrobe, which was otherwise known as the not so neat pile of clothes on the computer desk. I settled on soft grey trousers, a white shirt and a long beige cardigan. I headed to the small bathroom and washed my face and then blew out a nervous breath knowing I couldn't put it off any longer. I had to speak to my mother.

I crept quietly towards the muffled sounds in the kitchen wondering how the hell I was going to handle this mess? I'd barely got a grasp on it myself. I pushed the door open to see her stood over the hob, the smell of scrambled eggs drifted across the room.

"Morning," I murmured, my head down and my steps quick so I could reach the fridge without looking at her.

I poured orange juice for the two of us and sat at the table as she served up the breakfast. Blue bruises hung like sunken bags under her eyes. She looked sad. I hated seeing it. Taking a deep breath, I addressed the elephant in the room. "Mum, are you okay?"

She shrugged. "You're a witch, I've known it most of my life. My grandmother told me you were precious when I was a little girl, at that age I believed she called everyone precious." My mother stopped talking and started playing with her scrambled eggs.

"I used to play with you," she smiled at my shocked expression.

"We used to run around the garden playing hide and seek. It's unbelievable to think that I am now the adult."

My mother pushed her plate aside as I nibbled on my nails, nervously waiting for her to continue.

"Tabitha had researched many families after the witch trial that killed your mother, she met with my ancestors and Tabitha believed we were the best family to place you with. She wanted you to live a normal life. I was eighteen when I was told about you and I remember that day clearly, it was a warm Saturday afternoon in late July.

"My mother sat me down and explained everything. She started with your history, your mother, what you'd survived. I remember sitting there and letting the whole conversation wash over me, waiting for the hysterical laughter, but it wasn't a joke. Somehow, I always knew you were different. You were our family treasure and I felt honoured that I was the next to look after you. It was the day I met Tabitha for the first time."

"Thank you for taking on the role of my mum."

"You are most welcome. I do not regret it for one single minute. I'm sorry that I moved you around all the time."

Knowing what I knew now, how could I blame her? She'd done everything to protect me. "I'm so sorry about the way

I've treated you about this move and the other moves in the year. I now know why you did it. I'm sorry that you had to give up your life for me."

"Cora, I have had the best life so far and that is down to you. I don't need you to apologise, darling. I love you, you are my daughter, and as far as I'm concerned you always will be. I have been your friend, your aunt, and now your mother, who can say they have been through as many stages with their daughter?"

"I'm still so very sorry," I apologised.

She pushed some of the hair behind my ears. "No, you listen to me, don't be sorry, I'm not. My life with you has been one hundred percent worth it. I look at you and I see this strong, young woman who survived what you did."

I took a deep breath, blowing the stored up air out of my lungs. "You've still moved around your entire life, you've never lived in one place long enough to call it home."

"It was hard. The loss of your memories helped with every move. You would become so disconcerted after your sessions with Tabitha that I could control what we were to each other, but you will not apologise for who you are, I won't allow it. I've lived in and seen more beautiful places than other people dream about, for that I'm thankful."

"How did we afford to live in all these places?" We weren't poor by any means, but we'd never been swimming in money.

"Your inheritance."

"Eh?"

"Your mother's family were rather wealthy but at that time they chose to live a rather simple life. They didn't want the attention that came with wealth. Tabitha had full ownership of it until now. Now, it goes to you. We decided as your guardians that moving you around the world using your money wasn't such a bad thing. I'm sorry if you think so."

"You did the right thing." I nodded. "I'll be honest, I don't know what to do with everything I've learnt, you're my mother and I couldn't even put into words how much you mean to me. How selfless you are for doing what you've done. I don't remember my real mother and I don't remember my past life, but I would like to, and I hope that doesn't hurt you?"

She smiled a real smile for the first time. "You're curious, why wouldn't you be? I want you to remember your life too, I know that Tabitha said it may never happen, but I sincerely hope it does. You do have one memory that I know of, Tabitha was never able to take it away."

"My baby memory?" I whispered.

It was my only memory. I could remember the sound of the waves roaring, the loud crash and sigh as water caressed sand. I could remember the sun beating down on me, the itch of sand between my toes.

"You've told me the memory before and I said we'd been there. I'm sorry I lied to you but I couldn't tell you the truth for obvious reasons. You spent that day with your mother and Tabitha. Tabitha told me that you put sand in a bag and you brought it back with you. You fed it to the pigs, your mother laughed until she cried."

I should feel happy knowing my memory was one with my mother, but the pain in my chest made it difficult to breathe.

"Cora, I was wondering if you would show me what you can do. I've always known what your gift was, but I've always wanted to see."

"Well I was able to push Jack very far, there was also thunder." I smiled sheepishly.

I thought of my two meetings with Jack, he wasn't weak, and I had a funny feeling that he would force an opportunity to attack me. I would do the same if I had the confidence.

"He can levitate and he is very strong. I don't know how to handle the intense hatred I feel when I'm near him. It scares me."

"Cora, love, you're not a violent person and there is something deeper happening here. It doesn't matter what power he has, it sounds like you can control something very big."

"Yeah " My gift was growing stronger by the hour, I could feel it.

"Plus, we have our first home, we don't have to move," my mother sighed happily.

I grinned, I was even more determined that Jack would not take that away from me. "So you want to see what I can do, if I can do it again?"

She nodded enthusiastically, her eyes lit up which made her entire face glow.

I picked at the small knot of power and played with it and then held up my right hand. Laughter echoed around me and that was when I knew that I was ready. A gust of wind exploded around me as the pan launched itself towards the window spraying scrambled eggs as it flew. Landing with a thump it rattled on the floor. I looked at the mess and knew my mother was going to kill me. Debris littered the kitchen window, the counters and the floor. Floppy pieces of egg clung precariously to the ceiling, I watched as one sticky piece of egg let go and plopped loudly on the floor. The look on my mother's face was thunderous.

Oh, Lord.

I took a breath ready to blame her for asking, when she abruptly burst into laughter. "That was fantastic, Cora." Clapping her hands together, she grinned at me. "You have such a fantastic gift! Now, off you go, you don't want to be late on your first day."

My mother stood, brushing her hands on her jeans and then she started pushing me towards the front door.

"Wait, how did you know that...?" Sighing, I gave in.

My mother knew most things. For any normal teenager that was a curse, in my case, it was a blessing.

The bell tinkled above my head as warm cinnamon engulfed me. Tabitha was stood at the till ripping open packets of money and emptying them into the chunky slots of the till. I shook my head, she was wearing robes again. The dress was lovely, despite its lack of normalcy; the colour a rich burgundy with the slim green belt placed around her hips.

"Morning, you can find an apron in the room behind me."

"Morning," I mumbled and made my way to the door.

The room I entered was small. A lone window let little light in, but Tabitha had placed several lamps around the room. Finding the green apron, I tried to tie it around my waist, the slight shake in my hands a sign that I was nervous. I left my coat and bag on the floor and stepped back into the shop.

"You won't need to use the till today," Tabitha smiled as her hands continued moving money around. "I will show you how to use it another day, but for now you can tidy the books and the displays as you go along, trust me, the customers will take up your time. This right here," Tabitha turned away from the till and motioned for me to move with her, "is the stock room. Everything is labelled and ready to go. On the back of the door is a stock list, if we run low on anything you need to write it down. I'm no mind reader, that's one element I don't have, so please remember to write it down. Here you go." Tabitha gave me a duster and left me stood in the doorway.

"Just one thing," I whispered, making Tabitha turn. "I would like for you to do the spell, the one that means I can remain here and the locals don't notice."

Tabitha's face lit up. "Wonderful. Of course, I will do that for you."

I nodded, swallowing the lump in my throat. A customer walked in and Tabitha nodded at me. The woman stood, looking around the shop, her small hand absently rubbed her swelling stomach. Smiling, I walked towards the customer, I had a feeling this was going to be a long day.

The last customer left the shop precisely 30 seconds before closing, I'd been right; my day had indeed been long.

"For such a small shop you have a lot of customers," I sighed as I sat down at the table holding a cup of Tabitha's hot chocolate.

Tabitha blew the hot chocolate before taking a sip. "People are curious about witches, it brings customers. Of course, everyone knows I am one, to a certain extent, and they visit the shop to see if I am sat over a cauldron casting spells," Tabitha laughed.

If people were curious about Tabitha that could only mean

they would be curious about me. I wasn't sure how I felt about that. I was a witch, I would come to terms with that, eventually, but having people look at me in that way made me feel like I was some walking freak show.

"Have you enjoyed your first day here?" Tabitha asked, breaking the silence.

"Yeah, I have, but I wanted to ask you something, the first customer, was that the woman, you know?"

Tabitha took her time taking sips from her cup and watching me. Her leaf green eyes were so intense sometimes. "The first customer was Annabelle and she is the wife of Mark, the butcher's son, so yes, you obviously know about the village scandal with him running off with another woman."

"She seemed really nice. I don't know how he could have..."

"Some men are not worth the air they breathe."

From that statement alone, I assumed Tabitha didn't hold a candle for the opposite sex. "Are you married?"

"No. I have, of course, found certain men interesting and they have over the years filled up my time quite nicely, but I would never take it further."

"Why?"

"Well, I do not feel like I need a man to define who I am as a woman and I'm more than happy with my little shop and my life. Do you want to marry?"

I spluttered, sending my hot chocolate firing in every direction. "I'm seventeen!"

"Actually, you're not," Tabitha said with a sly smile and lifted her hand, guiding the heat to mop up the spill. "But I just wondered if you had ever thought about it?"

"I don't know." I shrugged. "She was looking at some interesting spells though."

Tabitha nodded. "Yes, she's been in quite a few times looking at those kinds of spells, but he wouldn't get anything more than acne or warts. Nothing that would be life-threatening."

"Tabitha! That's terrible!"

"That man left her with child, one that is ready to come any day now, acne won't hurt him. Anyway, I would intervene if she decided on something a little stronger."

"Would you?" I asked. I wasn't entirely sure Tabitha would.

Tabitha smiled. I noted the lack of an answer. "You seem to be handling the whole situation better. Have you spoken with your mother?"

"We talked this morning. I feel so much better, she's been amazing."

"Yes, Laura is quite unique, you are very lucky."

"I am. She wanted a demonstration this morning, but it didn't go well. I can't control my power much."

"That will all come with time and practise. It's been dormant for so long, you have to give it time. I didn't master my gift until later in my life."

"How old are you?" I'd wanted to ask the question all day.

Tabitha laughed loudly. "I'm not going to tell you that."

"Are you over a thousand years old?"

Tabitha continued laughing. "I'm not telling you."

"Fine, so, I could become more powerful?"

"Yes. In time you will be the most powerful witch in your coven."

"I couldn't become more powerful than you." I refused to believe it.

"Hmmm..." Tabitha looked at me. "You will."

"One more question, when Jack and I, you know, the wind flew around me which I know I was controlling but there was thunder, no rain, just thunder. What does that mean?"

Several expressions crossed Tabitha's face. "This is very unusual, usually a witch's power takes on one form, for example, I can only deal with fire. I need you to be clear when you tell me this, the thunder that came, when did it happen?"

"It happened when the anger became unmanageable, when I knew how to accept my power and kind of pulled it towards me so I could use it."

"It would seem your gift is more powerful than even I had expected. Your mother was a very strong witch, her gift wasn't entirely different from yours. She had the powerful ability to manipulate air. Everything slowed down, birds, animals, cars, people. I will have to look into your dual power."

I sat and mulled this over as Tabitha stood.

"Well, I understand you may be tired, but we have a very busy night ahead of us."

"What busy night? I need a hot bath and my bed." I tried to bite back the sound of a whine, but I was unsuccessful.

"You will go to bed at a reasonable hour so there's no need for any whining, but first you must meet your coven."

I repressed a sigh and followed Tabitha down the staircase into the darkness.

Cora

The door clicked behind me, taking away the only light source. "Wait, I have an idea." My words echoed.

"What is it?"

We had both come to a stop in the darkness.

"Well, you have the affinity for fire, so does that mean you can make things light up, like a fire?"

"Yes, I can make things light up, why do you ask?" I could almost hear the smile on Tabitha's face.

"I want to try something, do you trust me?"

This time Tabitha did laugh, the tunnel intensified the sound. "I trust you."

Tabitha raised her hand and summoned a small flame. My stomach knotted with concern, it didn't sit right to see a person's hand on fire. My gift reacted quickly to hers. How was I meant to control it so it focused on just one area? That was my next problem.

Holding my breath, I lifted my hands to meet Tabitha's

small flame and very gently forced my element out. The flame on Tabitha's hand disappeared. Darkness surged forward. My heart sank. I was about to tell Tabitha we should continue walking when I heard the laughter. There was a sharp hissing sound before the tunnel was alight with a soft glow. Yes. I'd done it. Tabitha smiled and nodded. We walked in silence until we entered a room.

"Cora, I would like to introduce you to Ember Smith and Ayden Quinn, they are members of your coven."

The woman introduced as Ember stepped forward with her hand extended. "Merry meet, Cora," she said, flashing perfect white teeth.

I felt a little dumbstruck. I'd never seen someone who was so flawlessly beautiful before. I'd believed Tabitha to be beautiful, but this woman blew her out of the water. An oval face was surrounded by long silver hair that was parted to one side, stray strands curved delicately around the contours of her face. Little yellow flecks flashed within the light grey of her eyes as she smiled.

Ayden moved towards me, his large muscular frame made me feel a little intimidated, although the twinkle in his blue eyes tugged at a smirk on my lips. He picked up my hand, gently brushing his lips over my knuckles.

"Merry meet, High Priestess," Ayden winked as he stood back.

He had a very nice smile, the kind of smile that was sexy on an older man. His blonde hair was cut close to his head.

"Right," Tabitha spoke, "introductions are done so we can get down to business. Cora, it is very rare that we actually sit down and give thanks to the Goddess, however, this is a special occasion so to welcome you into your rightful place we shall begin our first ceremony with you here."

I didn't ask which Goddess because I didn't want to appear dumb. Tabitha walked to a chair as the others began to take their place. This left one chair for me at what seemed like the head of the table. I sat down as butterflies exploded in my stomach.

"We are ready to begin."

The cove went black as I felt my element snap back. I panted I really didn't like the dark.

"I pledge allegiance to the Blessed Goddess, here we are, gathered on this night to offer you our gifts in celebration of our High Priestess joining us at long last."

Fire ignited in the darkness. Tabitha hands were in the air, the fire dancing between the two. The blends of oranges and reds shimmered over her beautiful features. Tabitha threw her arms and hands wider, fire flew towards me which made me scramble back. Candles glowed to life around the room.

"Blessed Be," Tabitha whispered.

How had Tabitha controlled her fire like that? Ayden stood up and walked to a smaller table, picking up two tall white candles. He flashed a mischievous grin as he placed them in front of me.

"I pledge my allegiance to the Blessed Goddess, you bring eternal peace into this world and I am honoured that I do your work here on earth. Accept these wands which represent the ability to acquire knowledge. Blessed Be."

I gaped at Ayden. Five Ayden's were now stood in the room. Their appearance was identical; they all wore the causal jeans and blue shirt, faces held the same wolfish expression. I shook my head as words failed to form. Ayden looked directly at me and with a sucking *pop,* he was one again.

Bloody hell.

I sat a little straighter in my chair and watched as Ember took a deep breath.

"I pledge my allegiance to the Blessed Goddess, I give you the chalice filled with ritual wine." She stopped to take a sip before passing it to Tabitha. "I commit myself to you. Blessed Be." Ember's chin fell down to her chest and then her body stilled.

I could see from the corner of my eye that Ayden was trying to pass me the wine goblet, but I couldn't take it. I concentrated on Ember, willing her to move or do something. Had her spell gone wrong? Shoving my chair back, I reached across to Ember.

"High Priestess, I'm fine."

A hand touched my shoulder, making me squeak. Ember took the wine goblet from Ayden and raised the goblet to my lips. My eyes must have looked like two saucers because Ember laughed.

"High Priestess, please do not look so distressed, I can astral project which means leaving my body, as you can see." Her hand pointed towards the sleeping Ember.

It looked like she was dead and that was very disturbing.

Ember placed the goblet on the table and sort of shimmered back into her own body. With a sigh, Ember's eyes opened and she looked up with a smile on her face.

It was my turn and I hated public speaking. I didn't care if it was only three people. "I pledge my allegiance to the Blessed Goddess, I have no gifts but my own gift to give you.

I want to thank you for my gift because it makes me feel like I belong in this world for the first time in my life. Blessed Be."

My ponytail whipped erratically as the wind built around me, stray hairs broke free of my bobble, caressing my face. The candles flickered then sizzled out. Darkness surrounded us. Gathering the wind, I knew what I had to do.

"Tab?"

I sensed Tabitha lift her hand, heat danced happily within the wind.

"Light."

The candles ignited and then I playfully flicked my index finger towards the two remaining candles. They lit, burning a brilliant emerald green. Feeling quite pleased, I smiled and then noticed Tabitha's expression. Her eyes shimmered until she blinked, allowing tears to escape and leave trails down her cheeks.

"Cora, you need to name this coven as your own," Ember instructed me.

"How do I do that?"

"Every High Priestess has given a name to their coven, it is something that is written deep inside your heart. All you need to do is concentrate and look deep within yourself."

I wasn't entirely sure how I could be the High Priestess. I was seventeen years old with no life experience, with no memories of my life, this or the previous one. Tabitha should be the one here in this place.

I closed my eyes and thought about a name, the coven, my family, Tabitha. The answer didn't scream out at me, but I knew it. I opened my eyes and focused on Tabitha.

"This coven will be called Gréne Coven."

Gasps from Ayden and Ember made my stomach drop, I focused on Tabitha, on her reaction. "Tabitha, what's wrong?"

"Everything is fine." Tabitha held her arms tightly across her chest.

"Tabitha, if I may?" Ember looked at Tabitha and received a small nod. "Cora, where did you get the idea for your coven name?"

"I don't know. It just came to me. Can you please tell me what's happened?"

Ember placed a hand on my shoulder. "You did nothing wrong, please do not worry."

All three of them looked like they were struggling to swallow a rock. I was going to worry.

"It was her chosen name."

I looked at Tabitha.

"It was your mother's chosen name for her coven. Gréne is the old term for the colour green, this is my colour. As you have probably already noticed, I wear green belts," she whispered. "Every family was represented by a colour. At one time that family would be the sole members of the coven. As time progressed and the witch population decreased covens made the decision to join as one. When your mother became the High Priestess of the coven, she named the coven after my family colour. It was her way of showing her love and respect for me."

"What was my family colour?"

"Pink."

I snorted. I hated pink. "Well, that will be our coven name," I informed them, certain this was the right thing to do.

Tabitha stood and walked to me. "Thank you." She hugged me. The action felt familiar, comforting.

"It makes more sense, you're the one who will guide me, the one who will help me."

"I can imagine my reaction startled you, I'm sorry I was a little taken aback because you called me Tab."

"Huh?"

"When you asked for my help lighting the candles you called me Tab. Your mother called me Tab, you remind me so much of her. I see her in your eyes and hear her in your sarcastic comments. I miss her, but I'm so happy that you are back in my life, that we can continue as we were before the trials."

Cora

I lost myself in the task and jumped when the shop bell sounded. Placing the last potion on the shelf, I turned and found that Tabitha wasn't in the shop. Glancing at the cat shaped clock I realised it was nearly five which would mean Tabitha was making her special hot chocolate for our after-work chat.

The customer stood looking at sachets of brilliant white viburnum petals. "Can I help you," I asked as I approached the customer.

He turned, holding the sachet in his hand and that was when I lost the use of my tongue. Holy Christ. His shoulder length, dirty blonde hair was pushed behind his ears whilst his faded brown leather jacket was open, the shirt he wore underneath revealed the beginnings of a toned chest. There was something about him, something rough, all man, that had my heart racing. My eyes continued to travel upwards and then green eyes hooked mine, he smiled, the green flirted with tiny specks of yellow. I looked down at the floor.

"I was thinking of buying this sachet, I'm in need of some strength."

I looked back up in time to catch his easy smile and watched him glide his hand through his hair. "Yes, that is very good for strength." I fought for concentration. "But you could also try dandelion leaves or perhaps wolf's hair?"

I silently thanked Tabitha who'd taught me the importance of spell ingredients during quiet moments in the shop.

"What exactly does wolf hair do?"

"Errmmm… well you mentioned that you are in need of strength, dandelion leaves and wolf's hair give strength. Wolves hair is particularly good for strength and protection."

I did an internal high five.

"Have you got any of those items in the shop?"

"Sure." I moved around him, leading the way to the small cabinet that was stood nearest the fake staircase. "Here they are."

I stood back behind the till, and unashamedly watched him.

"I'll take these." He handed me the items.

"Sure." I worried my lip, how hard could it be to use the till?

Famous last words.

I glared at the brass buttons, silently telling them to behave as I pushed the numbers. Why did Tabitha use such an old thing? The majority of the buttons were numbered but the important ones weren't, shiny brass buttons reflected my terrified face back at me. Which one opened the coin slot?

Holding my breath, I hovered over a button for an uncertain second, and then took the bull by the horns and pushed it down. The till made the satisfactory ping, and popped open. "That will be £5.79."

He gave me a note and I pulled the change for him. "Thank you for shopping at *The Broom Cupboard*."

"Oh, the pleasure was mine," he smiled, taking the bag from my outstretched hand. "I haven't seen you around, are you new?"

"Yes, I moved here last week." And in that time it already felt like home.

He nodded. "Well, hopefully I'll see you around, what's your name?"

"Cora".

He made his way over to the door and opened it. He turned. "By the way, my name is Clay." The door closed behind him.

I let out the breath I'd been holding.

"What are you smiling at?"

Jumping, I turned and found Tabitha stood at the top of the fake stairs. "The last customer made me smile."

"Good, you seem to be settling in."

"Yeah, rather shockingly I love working here."

I parked myself on the chair next to Tabitha. "I feel like I've finally found where I should be."

Tabitha smiled. "Good."

The bell tinkled above the shop door.

"Well, well, well, if it isn't my two favourite ladies," Ayden proclaimed extravagantly as he sauntered up the steps into the shop.

"What about Ember?" I teased.

"She's not here, so she doesn't need to know." His eyes twinkled as he bowed.

"High Priestess, Tabitha, what have you been doing today then?"

Ayden stole Tabitha's cup and was gulping down the hot chocolate like it was cold.

"Serving customers, cleaning, serving customers, cleaning," I said, and then I scrunched up my nose when I remembered the elderly lady. "One customer may be receiving too much... well...that...I feel sorry for her poor husband."

Tabitha laughed and with great skill she snatched back her drink without spilling a drop.

"Well, I believe you can never be too old for shaking the bed."

"Ayden!" I spluttered, choking on my drink. I never wanted to think about it.

He laughed. "According to *my* sources, the weather is going to be glorious this weekend, how about when you get off work on Saturday we all go for a picnic in Andrew Bruton's field?"

"Yes! That would be great, I would love that. Does that mean I can practise using my power?"

Ayden looked at Tabitha. His brows knitted together, becoming one thick line. "She hasn't been using her powers?"

Tabitha shook her head.

Oh dear. I should control my excitement better. But it was hard when I knew I had a power that I'd barely used.

"But she must!" He turned to me, ignoring Tabitha's thunderous expression.

Not a wise move.

"Cora, I can promise you we will have some fun with your powers on Saturday," he assured me.

I grinned, avoiding Tabitha's glare.

"Oh, and you must bring your mother to the picnic because I want to see if she looks like her great, great, great grandmother. She was one foxy lady!" He whistled.

The hot chocolate I just sipped sprayed all over the table. Tabitha stood up and clucked her tongue at the mess.

"Sorry Tab, it was his fault," I choked out the words, wiping my mouth.

"It is not you it was aimed at, Ayden, you know better."

Tabitha turned away, but not before I caught the glimpse of a small smile on her lips.

"Right, I will be off, things to do, people to see. I'll see you both on Saturday." With a final wink, he left the shop with a bounce in his step.

I like him," I announced as we watched him leave.

Cora

"I'm going to head out for some more supplies; do you think you can lock up?"

"Sure, will you be back for when Ayden arrives?"

Nodding her answer as she placed her purse and keys into a hidden pocket of her robes, she smiled as she walked out.

The bell sounded just as I was aligning the sand filled glass vials on the bookcase, I stepped off the box and right into the path of the customer.

"Oh, hi," I smiled as butterflies scattered in my belly.

"Hi, I need some more dandelion leaves."

"Sure."

Heading to the till, I used this opportunity to observe him. Today he wore a loose-fitting sky blue shirt which highlighted his warm brown tan, that shirt coupled with maroon chinos made him very easy on the eye.

"I'll take these." He pushed several bottles my way.

"Sure." Did I have any other words in my vocabulary? Why couldn't I focus near him?

"I noticed the sign on the door, the shop is shutting early?"

Momentarily forgetting my embarrassment, I smiled. "I'm going for a picnic with my friends and my mum this afternoon, we're taking advantage of the weather."

"It's lovely out there, where will you have your picnic?" he asked as he handed over his money.

"Errmm... I think its Adam Burns or something; he has a field that people use for this kind of thing."

"Yeah, I know where that is, and its Andrew Bruton by the way, he opens up his land for the public to use. It's a village thing," he said with a shrug. "I've often used it and it's a nice sun trap spot. I hope you have a lovely time, I think we're having a BBQ. My friend Eli likes to gather his family around when the weather is nice and he has a big *family* so it's never boring. We will no doubt have a game of football as there will be enough of us."

"That sounds great, I love BBQ's, the way the smell of charcoal permeates the food giving it that smokey taste, it's the kind of smell that makes you think of summer."

The memory popped into my mind, making the hairs on my arms stand to attention. I tried to hide my giddiness. Were they coming back? I really hoped so.

"Have fun at your picnic." He picked up his bag.

"I hope you win in your football game."

"I always do," he chuckled, winking.

Ayden led the way with a huge wicker basket full of food looped around his forearm. Ayden had whistled under his breath when he'd seen my mother. Judging by the drool slipping down his chin, Ayden had suddenly developed a thing for her and the poor man didn't know what was coming to him. The last victim who'd made advances on her was probably still suffering from the verbal whiplash.

Ayden jumped effortlessly over a small beck, placing the basket down, he turned, smiling at my mother. He didn't even acknowledge me.

Charming.

She graciously took his hand and in seconds was stood snugly against him. He grinned, holding her for a little too long. I watched as she shyly smiled at him. What about the verbal whiplash? Ayden turned his attention to me, but I noticed that he still had one sly arm around my mother's waist. I grabbed his hand and pushed the air to help, the strength in his hand and my element lifted me effortlessly across the beck.

The mid-day heat streamed down on us as we sought a good picnic spot. I wore a vest top with denim shorts and I was still warm. Tabitha, of course, was wearing her sunshine robes and she still looked refreshed and sweat free. Ember had turned up looking like a celebrity wearing a hip hugging dress the shade of pearls and champagne coloured gladiator sandals. Her thick silver hair was pulled back in a long plait.

"Do you need a hand?" I asked.

"No, everything's fine." He turned, bowed.

"It may take a while for me to get used to that," my mother whispered.

"Used to what?"

"People bowing at you."

I'd told him to stop doing it.

I dropped myself down on a blanket and gawped at the food, was he planning on feeding the entire village?

Snatching a loaded egg mayonnaise sandwich, I chewed and watched as Tabitha opened the wine and expertly skipped over my glass.

"Hey! So I can't drink now?"

"You are not of legal age."

"You have to be kidding me? Tab, I'm legal in witch years so this little fact should count for something."

Without much thought, I grabbed the bottle from Tabitha's hand and poured myself some. Ayden roared with laughter and slapped a hand on my shoulder.

"Mature. Very mature," Tabitha chastised.

"Well if you treat me like a child, I might as well act like one."

Silence followed as we waited for her reaction.

"Point taken," Tabitha said.

Ember laughed. "So, whilst we're here I think we need to discuss what we are going to do with the Chattox boy."

"Well, we already know what needs to be done, rather unpleasant and unnecessary, but there you go. We have to protect Cora." Nodding, Ayden pushed the rest of his sandwich into his mouth.

"Of course, we know what needs to be done but we need to set up a training timetable for Cora. Each of us should practice our powers and work with her in developing her skills. This will make our coven stronger when faced with an attack."

"Attack?" my mother squeaked, her wide eyes looked questioningly at me.

I swallowed a large amount of my wine. So, the conversation hadn't come up before, I couldn't exactly bring it up over breakfast: 'oh, Mum, there's this boy who has tried to kill me, twice, and I need to kill him otherwise I die. No big deal.'

It was a big deal, and I still couldn't think about it.

"Jack's coven may *approach* us," Ayden replied, aware that my mother's face had turned a deathly white.

"Mum, I think I may have had a memory today," I announced, changing the topic of conversation.

"Great, what was it?"

"I think I've had a BBQ before. I remember the smell and the taste of the food and I remember that it was a summer night."

"Yes, we've had plenty before."

"At least this is the first step to your memories returning," Tabitha said, her face showing relief.

"I am personally looking forward to working with Cora, your sessions will be fun," Ayden grinned and then licked his fingers as egg mayonnaise ran down them.

"Ayden, I don't think-" Tabitha began.

Ayden cut her off holding up his eggy finger to silence her. "Tabitha, look at her."

All eyes turned to me. I bit back a sarcastic remark. Did they have to stare?

"She's handled this predicament with grace and style. It took me well over a century to deal with my power. She needs to learn how to defend herself. When was the last time you used your power?" he asked me.

"Ermmm... it was at the coven meeting." I refused to look at Tabitha.

"See, she needs to have fun with her power, we did. You don't have to be serious all the time." He winked at Tabitha.

Ayden had such a way with Tabitha, and apparently my mother.

"Now, Cora, show us what you've got."

I looked at Ayden liked he'd developed a hand in the middle of his head.

"Here you go." He picked up a ball and threw it at me.

"What am I meant to do with that?"

He laughed and shrugged his wide shoulders. "Do anything you want."

I lifted my hands. The ball flew right into the hands of Ayden. Who then threw it to another Ayden and then another. I had to admit, his gift was pretty amazing. His face turned from a grin to a grimace of pain as he threw the ball on the floor and yelped. "Tabitha! The ball was bloody on fire."

I spun around and caught Tabitha's satisfied smile. My mother's face was a picture of shock while Ember sat eating her sandwich with a small smile playing on her lips.

I flicked my fingers. My element embraced the ball. I pushed the wind with a little bit of force and watched as the ball crashed against one of the heads of Ayden. With a flick of my fingers, the ball shot off and hit the head of the other Ayden. I could hear the sizzle as the heat singed Ayden's already short hair. I giggled, watching as they turned and ran in every direction.

Cora

Having spent the better part of the afternoon cleaning the shop after the tourist tornado had hit, or the 'witch gawkers' as Ayden liked to call them, I was now sat at the table watching Tabitha wrestle with the cauldron on display.

The cauldron usually bubbled, creating a plume of smoke as customers walked through the door but it had stopped working during the tourist tornado. The poor thing was puffing out smoke left, right and centre.

"Cora, why don't you head out?" Tabitha stopped and looked at me, a screwdriver and a hammer held tightly in each hand.

I knew how mangled the cauldron would look by the end of the shift. "Are you sure, Tab? I can stay."

"No, no, get yourself off. Don't forget you're meeting Ember tonight for your first lesson."

How could I forget? Ember made me more nervous than anyone. "Okay, if you're sure?"

"Of course, go have fun. Sit in the sun and do whatever you young ones do."

Heading into the little room I grabbed my bag and made my escape. As I walked by Andrew Bruton's field I thought of Ember's lesson.

"Cora, what a lovely surprise."

Startled, I jumped. "Hi, Clay."

"I was just making my way to the shop."

"Oh, well, I won't be there as I'm… here." I congratulated myself on sounding so intelligent.

"Yeah, I can see that," he said, his sexy smile widened.

I looked up at him, squinting against the sun. "You can still go to the shop, it's still open."

He shuffled his feet. "It was you I was coming to see."

"Oh."

"Yeah, I just wondered if you wanted to go to the field, perhaps Andrew Bruton's, and have a little afternoon tea."

Did I have the time? I already knew that I'd make the time. Why ask myself that question when I already knew what I was going to do. "Yeah, that would be nice."

"Great," he smiled.

The effects of his smile slammed into my chest, making heat fly into my belly. We arrived at the little beck. I couldn't use my element.

"Hold on, I will jump and then help you across."

Clay placed the blanket and the bag down. In one powerful stride, he landed on the other side. I picked the blanket and bag off the floor and threw them across to him, the bag clattered as he caught it. He wiped his hands on his jeans. "Stretch out to me as far as you can."

I reached towards him and he moved effortlessly, placing his own hand in mine and then shifted his footing.

"You got me?"

He nodded and pulled me quickly over the beck and into his warm body. I blushed and pulled away from his grip. This reminded me of the way my mother was with Ayden.

He walked in front of me and stopped to pull a blanket from his bag. He spread the blanket out and then sat down.

"Sit down, I don't bite," he laughed.

Taking a deep breath, I sat down next to him. My mouth had gone extremely dry. Clay started to rummage around in his bag. Taking two cups out, he set them in front of us. He returned his attention to the bag and brought out two little saucers and placed each delicate cup on a saucer. I laughed, finding it completely endearing that he thought to bring saucers.

He turned to me. "What are you laughing at?"

"I'm sorry, I just think the cups and saucers you've brought are adorable."

His smile was quick and flirtatious. "Well, you haven't seen my secret weapon yet."

He pulled out a white box and then slowly opened it. Positioned side by side were two huge scones, each spilling over with sweet jam.

"Afternoon tea is not complete without scones, Yorkshire folk know that."

I laughed again. "Hot chocolate seems to be a favourite amongst my friends."

"Ah, well I hope you enjoy it." He took a sip of his. "So, why did you come to a small little village in the middle of nowhere?"

"My mum moved here because she got a job and I had to come along because she can't live without me." I shrugged. I didn't really like the lies.

"Do you like living here?"

"I didn't at first, but I love living here now. I've come to think of it as home."

He nodded, taking a bite from his scone. I split the scone and began eating the smaller half.

"So, why are you here? Do you live nearby?" I asked.

"I don't live here permanently. I have a place in Ripon, which is in Yorkshire. I'm only here for a while visiting a friend."

"You will know all about Yorkshire tea then."

He laughed and nodded whilst eating his scone.

"Which friend are you here visiting?"

"I don't think you know him, Eli Yandell?"

"No, but you've mentioned him, the BBQ man."

Clay grinned. "The very same. I'm sure you will meet him in time, it's a small village."

Yes, it was, so how long would it take for him to hear the gossip about Tabitha and look at me and think the same thing? If everyone knew everyone, did that mean he knew Jack?

"How about we do a round of questions?" he suggested. "It's a good way to get to know each other."

"How do we do that?" I pushed the last of the scone into my mouth.

"We ask the first thing that comes into our minds and answer it immediately. You can't think about the answer, that's the rule, no thinking." He pointed his finger at me teasingly.

"Okay," I murmured.

"I will begin. Now then, let me see." He took a bite of his scone and sat chewing it.

My heart zigzagged all over. His eyes watched me, the glint in them making him all kinds of sexy.

"Age?"

"Seventeen."

He hadn't specified which age he'd wanted to know, so technically I wasn't lying.

"Favourite colour?"

"Yellow."

His blonde brows winged up in surprise. "Favourite food?"

"Errmmm... I love food in general. I know my favourite dessert, does that count?"

"No," he chuckled.

"Okay, if I had to pick, and this isn't my favourite food but I like it a lot, it would be sausages and mashed potatoes with onion gravy."

He mused over his next questions whilst chewing. "What music do you listen to?"

"Oh gosh… I don't really listen to that much music..."

"Okay. Skip that question. What was the last thing you ate?"

"A scone," I laughed at the look of mock horror on his face.

He brushed his hair back behind his ears. "Fair play," he said. "But next time you pick such an obvious answer you will face the forfeit round." His eyes flashed with something that made my breath catch in my throat.

"If you could go anywhere in the world, where would you go?"

"Good question. Venice. It seems so romantic." I'd probably been but I couldn't remember.

"I've been *and* it's beautiful. Last question, do you have a boyfriend?"

A pink blush bloomed in my cheeks. "No, I don't have a boyfriend," I spluttered.

"Rather than you asking me the same questions, I know you will want to, I will begin answering my own."

I started to protest even though I couldn't think of any questions to ask him at this moment.

He held his finger. "I am twenty-five years old, and pink."

I snorted, nearly spraying tea out of my nose.

He continued with a smile on his face. "Pizza is my favourite food, I like every topping, stuff some baked beans on there and I will still eat it. Music, I guess anything that has a really good beat. Last thing I ate was a scone, look how much we have in common already, and no I don't have to go through the forfeit round. If I had to pick a place I would probably go to Egypt, because dead people wrapped up in cloth. And…" he paused as the smile on his face stretched wider. "I don't have a girlfriend."

"I do have some more questions to add." I hadn't thought of a question just yet, but I desperately needed to cover up the new flush. "Cats or dogs?"

"Errrmmmm... that's difficult, some people get really offended if you don't pick the *right* one. I would say cats. I love that they are so independent."

I didn't particularly like cats; I knew that was slightly weird for a witch. "Do you have any brothers or sisters?"

"No, I'm an only child."

"Favourite film?"

"Wow, I'm a little bit of a film buff so there are a lot to choose from. I can watch anything, but action mixed with comedy is always great. I couldn't possibly pick, good question though."

"What three words would your friends use to describe you?"

"Jesus, you are good, are you sure you've never done this before?" he asked, teasingly.

"No," I smiled, enjoying his praise.

"Okay, three words... well they would definitely say I'm funny, because I am," he laughed. "They would say I'm kind and also that I'm loyal."

"Do you-"

Our conversation was interrupted by a high-pitched squeal, a noise that sounded like two gerbils fighting. How embarrassing. I hadn't changed my message tone since leaving London.

He smothered a laugh, probably enjoying how much I fumbled. Once I glimpsed the name on my phone, my stomach sank. I clicked to read the full message.

High Priestess, I am at the coven. Tabitha mentioned that you would be here on time for your lesson. I will wait until you get here. Ember x

I faced Clay. "I need to go. I'm so sorry but I'm meeting a friend and she is waiting for me."

"No problem, I should go too."

He made quick work of clearing the picnic. Walking out of the field I found that my exit was blocked by Clay. My heart stopped beating as he moved closer to me. I held my breath, trying to focus, focus on what exactly? His forefinger and thumb lifted my chin as his lips brushed my cheek.

"I'll see you later," he said as he pulled away.

I watched him walk away and then turned, heading towards the shop. I wasn't looking for anything serious, I didn't have the time, but some flirty fun with a good-looking man was something the doctor would definitely order. Because I would make him order it.

Cora

"You're late," Tabitha barked.

I'd run. Desperate times... desperate measures. "I know, I know."

"The door is already open for you," Tabitha called after me.

I ran down into the darkness. My fear of the dark was coming in at a close second to the look I was expecting on Ember's face. I skidded to a stop before entering the small room but was unable to compose myself as Ember was sat at the table with her hands folded, she was looking directly at me.

"Merry meet, High Priestess." As she spoke, she stood and bowed.

"Merry meet, Ember. I'm so sorry I'm running late."

"That is okay, High Priestess."

"It's not okay, and please call me Cora."

"As you wish, High.... Cora," she smiled, gesturing to the chair next to her.

"So, what defence moves will I learn today?" I asked as I sat down.

"You won't."

"Huh?"

"Your power is advancing, I believe when the time comes you will know what to do with my power. If not, I will guide you a little."

Guide me a little. I needed guiding *a lot.*

"I want to talk about me."

"Oh, okay."

"I was born in London on August 3rd 1636," Ember began.

"Oh my god!" Wow. She was old.

"What?"

"Sorry, it's just that I'm older than you. How can I be older than you when you look older than me?"

Ember smiled, and I quickly realised my mistake. "Not that I mean you look old... you always look great," I stuttered. What the hell was wrong with me?

"Thank you," Ember said, as I kicked myself. Ember continued. "I lived with my mother Sarah, my father Charles and my sister Jane. Jane was two years younger. We had a very normal upbringing for that time. We weren't rich, but we managed from day to day. I was known as Mary-" she broke off, probably because of my expression.

Ember had been a Mary? She didn't look like a Mary.

"I can only assume by your expression that you're shocked, I know I don't really *look* like a Mary, but I was Mary Edwards with brown hair and eyes. Life in London was very different to the one you love now.

"Charles, my father, was a tall man, he always looked after his thinning grey hair, his soft whiskey eyes held love and a wisdom learnt over the course of many years. He was the most loving and caring man you'd ever want to meet. I loved him dearly.

"I lost my father to the Civil War in 1642. At that particular time the king and the parliament didn't see eye to eye. The king didn't make use of the parliament and there were disagreements about almost everything, money and control being two important factors. My father sided with the parliament. The first battle took place at Edge Hill, my father was one of the causalities. There were few killed compared to a large-scale war, but he lost his life.

"The house was never to be the same without him. I believe now, as does Tabitha, that this began a change in me. I was very close to my father you see, and now I know why, he was a witch. I cannot believe that he didn't tell me. I don't even know if my mother knew. I've never known the gene to skip a sibling but my sister didn't inherit our father's abilities. I did. Tabitha spent many years researching this, but she didn't find an answer.

"The years after we lost father were very hard for my family," Ember paused, holding her clasped hands together in her lap.

How could Ember be so composed about everything? I'd fainted and laughed hysterically when I'd found out about my life.

"The Great Plague, the one you have learnt about in your history books, hit London in 1665. Human waste and rubbish lined the streets, and the intense heat from a long hot day only added to the stench. Almost immediately after the disease hit, I found my sister had become ill. She had tried to hide it but living in close proximity with each other meant we knew when something was wrong.

"Once my sister's illness became common knowledge, we were subjected to gossip. I do not think badly of my neighbours, they were simply trying to survive. Our home was closed, and we were unable to leave. I can only assume they believed this would contain the disease. How wrong they were." She shook her head. "In a matter of days Jane had become delusional. The plague, I knew, was slowly killing her. Before Jane had become ill we'd heard about this plague. How it ate away at you. Hearing and seeing are two completely different things. I hate to remember my sister like that.

"One morning she told me that father had visited her and I knew then that her time was coming. I hope that father was there for her at the end. Mother was constantly at Jane's side, we hadn't slept, each taking it in turns to nurse her. But we could do nothing to help her. Jane was lost to us in July of that year."

Her voice weakened with the memory.

"My mother had reached an age many never dreamed of for the times, disease and standard of living usually took those people we consider young nowadays. Our home was still under lock down when my mother could no longer hide the disease. She lay where Jane had, also losing her fight. I was so angry with her at first, she'd covered the bulbous swellings even in the heat so as not to worry me. I hadn't noticed until it was too late, her black fingers gave her away. Now, after all these years, I understand that she loved me and she only tried to lessen the hurt. I looked after her until the end. She left me on the 3rd August 1665. That was my twenty-ninth birthday."

I felt tears sting my eyes. "I'm so sorry for your loss, I truly am."

"Thank you, Cora, but I've had years to deal with my grief."

Ember gave herself a moment before continuing.

"The night my mother died was the night that changed my life. I believed I was dying from the plague, although I didn't hold any of the signs, the pain I felt was excruciating. I lay on our dirty floor alongside the bodies of my sister and mother believing I was going with them. I'm not ashamed to admit this, but at that moment I wanted to be with them. I closed my eyes ready for my lovely father to come for me.

"I was awoken in the night by sounds. The men with the carts had come for the dead and I knew I only had a matter of minutes before they realised there was still one survivor remaining. I hid, and when there was a free second I made a run for it. I stumbled upon an empty house several streets away from my family home. This was the best I could do; it was either live in this house or on the streets.

"The next morning, I made my way down to the Thames and was careful to avoid the ones who knew me, they would know about the plague you see. I washed myself trying to clean away the death and the dirt wondering why I was spared. I thought I wasn't worthy of death. I was jealous of my mother, sister and father. They'd been picked and I had been left. How silly of me to think that because I know that life is a miracle and we are so blessed to have what we have.

"I was stood knee deep in other people's filth when I doubled over as the most horrendous pain surged into every part of my body. I gasped as the brown of my hair just fell out in my hands. The brown just fell away with the water. I looked at my reflection and was shocked to see that it was silver. I nearly screamed but biting my lip saved me. I then saw my eyes, they felt like they were suddenly on fire. I rubbed at them and tried to rinse them, but nothing worked. I was petrified. I didn't know what else to do so I ran back to the house and locked myself away, afraid that people would take me away because I'd changed my appearance. Silver hair was no doubt a sign of madness.

"Some time later the officials came knocking at the door. I rubbed mud into my hair, but they were enquiring about my name and whereabouts. I gave the name Ember Smith and I told them I was from Scotland and had travelled there before the plague hit. They were too busy to question this so went on their way. I lived in that house and made it a home whilst learning my new skill. I lived there until the dreadful night in October 1666 when the Great Fire hit. I made it out of the inferno rather quickly but many perished. I left London and made my way up here. I met Tabitha some time during the 1670's and I haven't looked back since. Tabitha has taught me everything I know today."

Knowing this helped me see Ember in a different light.

"Why did your hair change?"

Ember shook her head. "We honestly do not know. Tabitha had never heard of it and it's never happened since. I think I may have been a unique case."

I agree. Ember was definitely unique.

"Since meeting Tabitha I have found a new family, one I have come to love. I watched you with the Hunt family. I watched you in London." Her grey eyes softened. "I consider you family, although you may not remember, I did occasionally visit you during your birthdays. I hope the green bag has been of some use?" she asked.

My much-loved bag had been a gift from Ember? "The bag still goes everywhere with me."

"I hope you understand me a little better? I wanted you to know about me now that you are no longer under the charge of Tabitha and your memories will remain with you."

"Thank you."

Ember nodded and stood.

We opened the door to the shop which stood in darkness. Ember turned towards me and smiled as she gently kissed my cheek.

"Goodnight, Cora."

"Goodnight."

I watched Ember leave.

"You've learnt a lot tonight I gather?"

I turned, too emotionally exhausted to even jump. "You could say that."

"Do you want to come up for a drink?"

"Okay."

I followed Tabitha and stepped into her living room. I'd been in Tabitha's flat before, but I would never get used to its quirkiness. A soft grey corner sofa faced the chimney breast that still held the original brick of the house. The cauldron shaped mirror reflected much need light into the small space. The walls on either side of the fireplace housed large bookcases and both were brimming with their heavy loads.

Tabitha pottered around in the kitchen, a breakfast bar the only thing dividing the two rooms, held a rather unique fruit bowl in the shape of a witch's hat. I made my way over to a stool and dropped heavily on it.

"I take it the session with Ember weighs heavily on your heart?"

"I really don't know how she can carry on with everything after what she's been through."

Tabitha nodded and put a hot chocolate in front of me. "Time heals. It is a term that is perhaps over used but one that is never wrong. You cope because you have to."

I blew on my hot chocolate. The kitchen was a great little room. The walls, a lovely toffee shade created warmth, the cupboards were white, the counter tops were granite as white stars twinkled from within the depths of the black. The small fridge reflected Tabitha's personality, it was green in colour. A door next to the fridge led to the bathroom and the bedrooms.

"Please tell me Ayden doesn't want to explain his life story? I don't think I could take two in one week."

"No, your training sessions will be combat training."

I felt relieved and guilty, but my heart couldn't take any more loss at the moment.

"Did Ember become a member of the coven once she found you?"

"Yes. She was never lucky enough to meet your mother; she was born a few decades too late. Once she was initiated, she was told the history of the coven and she felt somewhat compelled to protect you, hence her visits to London."

We sat in a comfortable silence as we drank. I really didn't know what to do with the information I'd learnt tonight. We'd all lost so much. I didn't even know about Tabitha, not really. And I wouldn't push. She needed to feel comfortable to tell me. I would never force someone.

I put my cup down, still half full and sighed. "I'm tired, Tabitha, I'm going home."

"Yes, it has been a trying evening for you."

Tabitha pulled me into a hug. "Goodnight, Cora."

"Night, Tab."

Tabitha held the door open for me, but she didn't follow. That was one great difference between Tabitha and my mother, Tabitha knew when I needed to be alone.

Cora

It was Friday, thank God. The little bell tinkled as I began procedures for closing up. I turned to see Clay sauntering up the steps towards me. My heart skipped many important beats. Smoothing down my hair, I smiled.

He walked right up to me, and brushed his lips against my cheek. "Hi."

I breathed through the flutters in my chest. "Hi. Do you want something from the shop? I'm about to close up."

"I actually came here to ask if you were doing anything later."

"Oh, I have plans with a friend tonight." Disappointment sat like lead in my stomach.

"Okay, no problem," he smiled. "We can arrange something for another night. Do you mind if I walk you home?"

"No, of course not, let me get my things."

I locked up and followed Clay outside and shivered as a

gust of cold wind slapped my face. I pulled my jacket tighter around my body.

"Here, let me do that."

Clay pulled me under his arm and into his warm body.

My God, he was smooth. And very clever.

"So, I guess you'll be busy for the next couple of weeks, what with Halloween around the corner?"

"Yeah, we have lots of bus tours coming in. You know what it's like this time of year, the excitement about the supernatural."

"So... what do you think of the supernatural and stuff?"

I laughed, trying to hide me discomfort. "I think it could be possible. Look at Harry Potter; he's done well for himself."

He laughed, pulling me closer into his body. "When are you free?"

"I don't work Sundays and sometimes I can have Saturday afternoons off."

We stopped at the entry way to my house.

"Okay, it's a date," he confirmed.

With that comment, I watched him walk away and felt disappointed that he hadn't kissed me. He also hadn't specified a day for this apparent date, it would be something nice to look forward to.

I opened the door and found Ayden stood on the step, a grin stretched his lips. I cast a dubious glance at his attire. He was wearing navy blue cord jeans and a white shirt. Who would wear white if they were going to get their arse kicked? Yes, that was wishful thinking on my part, it could happen. I'd had decided on navy blue and black, so the mud wouldn't show.

"Hi, may I come in?"

"Sure. Mum, Ayden's here."

I turned to see her already stood in the doorway, grinning like a school girl with a crush.

Ayden turned his deep ocean blues on my mother. "Laura, it is always a pleasure. Thank you for having me in your home."

He gently brushed his lips against her cheek. I watched, horrified, as a deep red exploded in her neck and cheeks.

What the hell was going on?

"Of course, you are always welcome here. I will leave you two to train. Would you care for a drink before you start?"

"No. We need to get started, but thank you."

Ayden started leading the way to the back door. How did he know where the back door was? I shook my head, it didn't matter. I felt excitement dance giddily inside me. This was going to be fun.

Cora

Ayden walked down the wooden steps, past the lounging chairs and into the middle of the garden. He stood for a moment, his back to me as if he was looking at the shield of trees that surrounded us. Then he turned and faced me. Even from this distance I could see the flash of excitement in his eyes. What would he teach me first? Defensive moves? Attack moves?

"Right, give me what you've got."

A jolt of surprise shot through my body. "Ayden?"

"I want to see what you've got without training. I need to know how powerful you are and what we need to work on."

I could tell him what I'd got, a fat lot of nothing.

"High Priestess, attack me!"

I jumped. I couldn't hurt this man, I knew him, I liked him. Well, I had up until this point.

"Cora!!"

I lifted my trembling hands and stared at him. I couldn't do this... my hands dropped dejectedly back down to my sides.

A blinding pain exploded in my shoulders, the act forcing me to the floor. It happened so quickly that I didn't have time to put my hands out to stop my face from hitting the grass. A shocked cry escaped my lips as my chest took the brunt of the fall and my head smacked heavily against the ground.

Gathering my senses, I coughed and moved myself up. The pain in my shoulder was so immense I actually forgot how to breathe. Was Jack here? I was sure I'd heard the faint whisper of his laugh. I pushed onto all fours, standing wasn't going to happen just yet. Breathing in another lungful of air, I felt like I was ready to stand up, and then a sledgehammer crashed straight into my side, crunching heavily against my ribs.

I wheezed.

Before I could suck in much needed oxygen, something yanked my ponytail from behind, ripping any thought process clean out of my mind. I lifted my hands in an attempt to grab the person, but they were suddenly pulled awkwardly and painfully behind my back. My wrist screamed as the tension became too much. I panted, breathless with pain, as I felt my bones creak with the effort to stay in one piece.

I screamed and then bit my lip, thinking of the danger my mother could be in. I thrashed in the little space I had to manoeuvre, and then the bone in my wrist exploded.

Instead of pain, I felt power.

A torrent of wind surged around me and the hold on me was gone. Pushing myself to a crouching position on my good hand, I turned around and found them.

One attacker stood on the grass but he was already pushing himself to his feet. The other must had smacked hard against the house as he lay face down against the wall. I focused on the man who was stood with his back to me, but something didn't look right. I jumped back and gasped as the attacker turned and faced me.

Ayden.

What the hell was going on. I placed my hands down beside my body. Ayden had quite clearly lost his bloody mind.

"Put your hands up!"

I obeyed immediately, pain soared up my arm affecting the function of my lungs. I held my breath as the pulse in my wrist intensified.

Ayden stepped closer.

The wind laughed joyfully as I threw it at him. It lifted and flung him aside like an unwanted carcass. I stood, braced for what came next. I blinked and in that one second another Ayden was stood in front of me. A crunch sounded behind me, making me turn. I lifted my arms but knew it was a feeble attempt to block an attack. This was why he should be teaching me defence moves.

A blinding white light exploded behind my eyes as his knuckles connected against my cheek. I fell. The hard smack on my body made me wheeze. Enough was enough. If Ayden wanted to see what I had; he was going to get it.

Thunder boomed as the sky darkened and the ground responded almost immediately, rippling from my anger. Ayden ran at me, my element flew at him, picked him up and tossed him aside. Another Ayden appeared and I did the same thing. I was panting with the effort as two more ran towards me, a growl escaping his lips. I lifted them together and sucked in a deep breath, feeling the pain in every corner of my body. I dropped them to the floor.

"Enough."

Ayden stepped out of the trees and looked exactly the same as he had when he'd arrived. How could Ayden look so perfect? I probably looked like I'd been through a war. I slumped to the floor and felt Ayden lift and cradle me against his chest. "Cora, drink this." Ayden thrust something into my hands.

I clumsily drank it.

When I opened my eyes, my mother and Ayden were peering down at me. Both had two very different expressions on their faces. My mother looked like she was going to cry, worry lines were etched deep around her eyes. Ayden was smiling; it looked like he was happy with the training session.

Nothing about that whole experience had been pleasurable.

"I have to say, that was fantastic. I set out to push you and you did exceptionally well. You are already in tune with your power, you feel... it feels. It was amazing. The thunder was something new." His eyes sparkled as the words rushed out of his mouth.

"Glad you enjoyed the show." My sarcasm made his grin stretch wider.

"I tested you and perhaps I did wrong by duplicating myself. You wouldn't make a move until I attacked you. You must understand that sometimes you face people you know, your friends, people you trust, they may turn against you and you must be prepared to defend yourself. You do not think, you act."

"Aren't you hurt at all? I feel like I've been through a war and you look...normal."

"I feel pain the same as you. You slammed me against the house. But we learn to control our pain, it is something you will learn in time. I know I have a few cracked ribs but nothing I can't sort out. With intense training you will also be able to recover quicker and hide the injuries you do have."

Right now, I didn't want any more attacks to recover from.

"I must leave you, will you be okay?"

"I guess so," I huffed.

"I've left some remedies with your mother. Have a lovely weekend."

If this first session was anything to go by, training was going to be one big pain in the arse.

Literally.

Jack

The last few weeks had been absolute bliss, well apart from the times I'd been dragged to several boring coven meetings. Clay and Eli persisted in telling me how to handle *her*. I didn't need advice because I could handle that girl perfectly fine.

Lying on the sofa, I stuffed my hand into the big packet of crisps that balanced precariously on my chest. Grabbing more than a handful, I forced them into my mouth. I muttered at the person sat on the stage on a re-run of a *Jeremy Kyle*. These people were seriously messed up.

Eli was shuffling around in the kitchen and I held back my frustration. I loved Eli like a brother, but that man had pushed my patience, even the sound of his feet made me angry.

"Jack, the weather is lovely outside, you fancy having a training session?"

Speak of the devil. "I don't need to learn anything, Eli."

Eli was about to say something else but was interrupted as Clay walked into the living room. Something was going on with him. I'd caught him on more than one occasion smiling to himself.

"Clay, would you like to do a training session?"

Eli had cornered Clay and for a second Clay looked like a rabbit caught in blinding headlights. Rather impressed, I observed the way Clay brushed aside this momentary lapse and smiled. "Of course."

Even though I wouldn't mind finding out what was putting the smile on Clay's face, I didn't want to do any training. "Nah, I will watch some more of our Jezza Kyle."

Clay and Eli exchanged a look as Clay walk towards the kitchen. I knew what the look meant; it infuriated me that they did it in front of me, like I couldn't decipher their code.

"I don't need you to keep nagging at me about using my power. When I face her, who is by the way only one small little girl, I will be ready."

"You've not practised your gift, Jack. I can tell you that fighting for your life is very different to playing around with your gift if, and when, you please. It is of great importance that you train with each of your coven members. Without this, we won't be able make sure you survive. You are our High Priest-"

"Yes, I am your High Priest, Eli," I snapped, trying to hold back my temper, "which means you need to follow *my* instructions. I don't want to practise right now and will tell you when I am ready!"

Eli's face held shock, but he took a step back and looked me straight in the eye as he very slowly bowed. Guilt definitely sucker punched me.

"Of course, High Priest, please let your coven know when you are ready to begin training.

Bowing again, Eli turned and headed to the kitchen.

Chuffing brilliant! I'd royally screwed that up. I cursed. I knew I had to train, but one thing held me back. I didn't want to look stupid. I didn't feel good enough to be the High Priest and I knew that I would shame my coven. But wasn't it easier to look stupid in front of my coven rather than Cora? "Eli?"

Silence followed, and it felt like a fist to my heart. I'd taken things too far. I needed them. He was my family.

"Yes, High Priest?" Eli walked slowly back into the room.

I held back a sigh. "Can you cut it out with the High Priest crap? I'm just Jack, your brother in law. So," I paused, "I'm sorry for being a dick. When do we get started on this training business?"

"Right now, if you want?"

"Sure."

I brushed my hand through my hair and followed Eli outside. Whilst I was mastering my gift, maybe I would find out what was putting that smile on Clay's face.

Jack

"Clay, Jack wants his first training session; shall we show him what we've got?"

"Sure, I'm up for a challenge," Clay threw me a wicked grin as he stood up and followed us into the middle of the back garden.

"It is important you know how to defend yourself. I will start by throwing a few things your way and see how you handle it."

I nodded.

Before I was able to prepare myself, I saw something move, a blur of black and white. I didn't have much time to react as the thing smacked me on the top of my head and bounced a few times on the floor. A football. Eli had cheated. I hadn't been prepared. I opened my mouth to shout at him then realised I'd look stupid if I did. When you're in a fight you don't just stop and say, 'by the way, I'm going to hit you now, just so you have a heads up.'

Something winked mischievously at me as it caught the rays of the sun. My heart jumped up into my mouth. I made a conscious effort to grab my power, but I couldn't feel any sort of stirring in my gut. What I felt was pure, undiluted fear.

I could see that the gleaming tip of the fork was close. I was a dead man. I looked down, bracing my body for the pain. The fork would slide through my skin like a hot knife in butter. Why had I worn a perfectly good top today of all days? I closed my eyes and waited for the blow.

It didn't come.

"You're not ready, now can you see why you need to train and prepare yourself?" Eli's shout eventually registered through the pounding of the blood that was pumping around my head.

I opened my eyes, the fork sat on the ground near my feet. I wiped my hands over my face. "Okay, what do I need to do?"

"You need to build and hold your power, even during times of fear."

"Okay."

I focused on breathing and then nearly whooped with glee when I felt the rush of power.

"Are you ready?"

I gave a curt nod.

Freezing water smacked me hard, knocking the air out of my lungs. I made a huge mistake and opened my mouth in an attempt to breathe. Thousands of razor blades attacked my mouth and throat. I couldn't open my eyes; the water was coming at me too fast. It was too strong.

This was a test. I knew that I needed to get out of the way, but the lack of oxygen wasn't helping. Grabbing the power, I held my arms out and was instantly rewarded with the lightness. I didn't know how far I could go. I pushed up. The water subsided, making my lungs cry joyously as air reached them. I spluttered and opened my eyes.

I had to be suspended at least thirty feet in the air. I'd never been afraid of heights but the only thing that stopped me going head long into the floor was my ability to control my element. That wasn't what you would call great odds.

Eli laughed. "Come down, Jack. That was really good. Took you long enough to figure out what to do, we thought you'd grown gills."

I wasn't finding this whole experience funny. I slowly descended. What worried me the most was what happened now? Not once since I'd developed this power had I landed without some sort of thump. My heart pounded with each decrease in height. At around fifteen feet I felt my element sneakily retreat. I flapped my arms hoping that would keep me afloat.

Fat chance.

I felt the intense pressure of gravity crush my body and I couldn't do a thing to stop it. I hit the floor, my legs crumbled beneath me. Pain exploded in my head and then I was blissfully engulfed by darkness.

"Christ, do you think we need to take him to the hospital?" Eli's voice was filled with worry.

"Right, Eli, and how would we explain what happened to him? Well Doc, he was levitating and fell out of the sky."

"Clay, you don't have to be a smart arse all the time. He hasn't moved at all."

I could hear them bickering through the buzzing in

my head.

"We need to do something."

"Jack."

I felt hands grip and shake me.

"Eli, I don't think you should do that. You could cause more damage."

"What else do you suggest?"

"Let me think? A doctor, like I suggested before."

"Jesus," I mumbled. "You two could wake the dead with your bickering."

"Not funny. Where are you injured? Can you feel your legs?"

"My legs are fine but the fireworks exploding in my head are my main worry."

"Right, let's get you inside, Clay?"

I opened my eyes and looked at Clay, I caught him glancing at his watch. "You got somewhere to be? Who is the lucky lady?"

Clay blushed. I hadn't realised the man was capable of blushing. Clay had a different woman every week, to see the man blush over one woman made things a little more interesting.

"Oh, you like this one, do we know her?"

"Some other time, eh?" Clay said and smiled as he helped me stand.

He sat me on the sofa and grinned. "Right, I'm heading out. Is there anything you need from the village?"

"No. Just go and have a good time."

Pain lanced through my arm, making me hiss. This is what I got for training, but it meant I wasn't good enough, yet. When I was ready, she'd better watch out.

Cora

So far, and it was only 11.15am, I'd dropped two cups of hot chocolate, skilfully avoiding burning myself, five big books, one book nearly falling on a customer's feet, three bottles of multicoloured sand, a bag of dried daisies and a cat ornament that had quite literally flown off the bookcase as I'd cleaned it. My wrist, having been snapped in two last night, was throbbing angrily. Ayden's miracle juice hadn't taken away the pain.

Tabitha's usual welcoming smile transformed into a scowl when I'd walked into the shop looking like the walking wounded. It wasn't like I wanted the training session to end in pain.

I made my way over to the display window. My next job was to stock the more popular items. I leant over the waist high banister that enclosed the display. My fingers brushed the mat. Bending further, I grabbed the mat and felt my rib crack. I cried out as stars winked in my vision.

"Cora, what are you doing?" Tabitha snapped.

Gripping my side, I panted. My lungs wouldn't function properly, had it punctured one? The world turned too quickly, making me cling onto the banister.

"I... needed to... restock..." I gasped.

"That injury has caused so many problems today," Tabitha sighed. She slid her arm around my waist and helped me to the table.

The bell above the door rang. I willed Tabitha to move so I could see who it was. Although I didn't know how I would begin to explain this to Clay. I didn't need to worry as fire sparked out of Tabitha's hands, the heat from them licking hungry at my sensitive skin.

Ayden stood at the top of the steps, his expression blank. The scene in front of him didn't look good. I was panting, holding my side. He had to know something was wrong, yet his face gave nothing away. Well, apart from the eyes, they were ice blue and dared Tabitha to bite. He looked deadly serious and judging by the increased heat in the room, Tabitha wasn't exactly playing around.

I moved awkwardly in my chair. The temperature had become so hot that my trousers were sticking to my arse. Tabitha brushed past Ayden without saying a word and stormed to the door. She snapped the lock shut before turning. I was way too hot, but my complaints stayed firmly in my mouth.

"How *dare* you injure our High Priestess during lessons which are meant to help her, *and* you didn't tell me. I watched Cora walk in here this morning looking like that!"

I sat very still. I didn't look great, I knew, but there was no reason for her to blatantly state it like that.

"I don't want another injury like this again! I cannot mend

everything, Ayden. She's sat there because she has no doubt cracked a rib leaning over the banister doing her job, which she's been poor at all day!"

"Hey!" I felt the sting in my pride.

"Sorry, Cora, but it's true."

I slumped lower in the chair and ignore the angry lick of pain.

"Tabitha," Ayden's voice was low, dangerous. "I understand it was a shock to see her like that, although I did give Laura some remedies to help with the injuries. Cora did exceptionally well last night, and I am very proud of her."

Hearing his praise made the dent in my pride slightly smaller.

"It was still unnecessary. You did not need to go to such extremes to show her this."

"We need to get her ready, Tabitha!" Ayden snapped. "We cannot skirt around the issue anymore, she is our High Priestess and she must be responsible for her coven. She wouldn't defend herself last night, so I had to take the necessary actions."

Tabitha stood with her hands on her hips.

"Errrmmm... can I say something?"

They both turned to stare at me; neither of them spoke, I assumed that was my green light. "Considering you're both talking about me, and I am sat *right here,* I think I should be able to speak for myself. I feel Ayden is right in some ways-"

"But you are injured, how can that be-" Tabitha began.

"Tab, listen to me," I pleaded.

Tabitha fell silent.

"Ayden is right. I need to be prepared for whatever comes and learning to fight is important. I have injuries, yes, that *really* hurt, but I have them because I'm not good enough." I stopped to take a breath because the pain was only allowing so much oxygen to pass into my lungs. "Ayden stopped the battle when he saw I was weak, but I know Jack won't stop."

Tabitha's face was hard, her leaf green eyes ablaze with fury.

"I have to do this, Tab," I urged, "you can't carry me through everything. If I have to learn the hard way, then so be it." I hardly felt like smiling so the painful grimace I gave them both would have to do.

"Very well, High Priestess." Ayden bowed at the waist.

Tabitha's eyes were focused on me. "If you're sure, then I will follow your wishes." Tabitha cocked her head to the side, studying me. "But, do not come complaining to me if you are hurt and need medication. I will no longer give you it. You want the injuries; therefore, you must learn to live with them."

"I will," I sighed; if that was a victory then I would take it. "Tab, does it still count if I was hurt before this conversation ever took place? Because it really hurts and I could use something to help before I pass out."

Tabitha clucked her tongue, but she moved towards the little room behind the counter.

"I'm so sorry you are hurt, Cora," Ayden said once Tabitha had disappeared. "I thought the drink I made you would help. I will take better care next time."

"No! I don't want you to be careful." I took another shallow breath. "I want to win these training sessions because I'm good at it, not because you treated me like a girl."

"That told me," he chuckled.

Tabitha sauntered over to the chair with a steaming cup in

her hand. "Drink all of this, every single drop of it," she demanded.

I lifted the cup to my lips trying to ignore the rancid smell of sulphur, warm mouldy cheese and sweaty feet. I wrinkled my nose in disgust, looking up at Tabitha.

"I never said it was going to be nice," she informed. "It might teach you to take better care of yourself next time."

With a triumphant nod, Tabitha walked back behind the counter and into the little room. Holding my breath, I took tiny sips. It tasted as bad as it smelt but I could already feel it working on my rib.

Ayden stalked over to the little room and closed the door behind him. It was going to be round two in there pretty soon. I could already hear the muffled voices from behind the door. The liquid was too hot and it was definitely a drink that needed to be down the hatch in one go. Holding my hands around the cup, I instructed the wind to cool it and swallowed the now tepid drink.

I lifted myself slowly out of the chair and approached the room. Knocking, I opened the door. "Can I just put this in the sink?" Without waiting for a reply, I edged past Ayden. Tabitha was sat in a chair, as I passed, her hand gently touched my arm.

"Did you drink it all?" Tabitha asked.

"Yes, it tasted like crap. Thanks."

"I'm glad you liked it," she said as a smile played on her lips. "The remedy seems to be working if you have your sense of humour back. Take the rest of the day off and come in on Monday ready to work."

I felt no urge to stay in the shop and listen to them fight. I picked up my bag and coat and then shut the door.

Cora

I almost stumbled back when I saw Clay stood in front of my door. His back was to me, so he hadn't seen me approach. I hadn't expected him to be here. Was this the date? Jesus. How was I meant to hide my injuries?

Taking a deep breath, I had no other option but to face the music. "Hey," I called.

He turned and smiled. Holding back a wince as my footing slipped on the gravel, I kept the smile plastered on my face.

"Hello back at ya," he said, smiling as he walked towards me.

His lips nearly brushed the corner of my mouth as he gave me a cheeky kiss on the cheek. He placed his arm around me and tucked me into his side, I hissed before I could stop it.

He pulled back and looked at me. "Are you okay?"

I'd already failed the test. *Brilliant.* "Yes, well, no, but it's not a big deal."

His finger brushed my cheek. "What did you do to your cheek?"

How could he see that? "I had a mishap at work but I'm fine, really." That excuse came pretty quick for a very bad lie. "Do you want to come in for a drink?"

"Sure, I would love one."

I stepped around him to get to the front door and held my breath as I pushed the key into the lock. I walked to the kitchen and heard him follow. "Do you want some tea?"

"Yeah, that would be great."

"How do you take it?"

"Milk, no sugar."

He sat down at the kitchen table, but I knew he observed me. I moved slower than I usually would. I shuffled over to the fridge and reached to get the milk, I bit back the curse as a quick jerk of pain stole the air out of my lungs.

"So, did you have a nice day at work?" he ventured.

I stopped for a second, and then continued like he hadn't asked the one question I didn't want to answer. Pouring the milk, I stirred his. "It was a normal day at the office. Customers came in and I did some re-stocking."

I placed his cup in front of him and then holding my breath, I sat.

"So, are you going to tell me what you did?"

My hands stilled with the cup mid-way to my mouth. I knew I would have to tell him something, and I knew it would be best to stick to the truth as much as possible.

"I was leaning over the banister, our bestsellers live there," I sighed. "I couldn't quite reach and I..."

He sat up straighter.

"I leaned too far and cracked one of my ribs."

"Christ!" he cursed. "You can't just crack your rib like that, it would take more force. Had you hurt it before today?"

Okay, was he a rib breakage expert? "I was tidying my room last week and I stupidly leant over the computer table. That side hurt for a while, I guess I must have made it weak or something."

His mouth looked like it was chewing hard metal, his jaw popping with the effort. I kept my gaze steady.

"I *wish* I could help you." His brow furrowed as his teeth clamped together. He looked frustrated.

"I'm fine, really."

"Nice try Cora, but I can see your pain."

I shrugged. What else was I meant to do? The less I said, the less likely I would put my foot in it.

"Cora?" My mother's voice drifted into the kitchen as the front door clicked shut.

"Yeah, I'm in the kitchen."

She waltzed into the kitchen and stopped when she saw Clay.

"Mum, this is Clay…" I stalled, realising I didn't know his last name. I cringed, that was embarrassing.

"Clay Barnes." He held his hand out. "Hello, Mrs Hunt."

"Oh, that makes me sound old, plus I'm not married," she laughed. "Please, call me Laura."

She looked at me with concern. "Cora, you don't look so good. Are you feeling better?"

I glared. If Clay had doubts before, he definitely knew something was wrong now.

"I'm looking after her, Laura."

He *definitely* knew something was wrong. Tabitha was going to kill me if our secret was out.

"Good. Are you stopping for lunch, Clay?"

He glanced at me. My response was a shrug.

My mother laughed. "Chicken salad okay for you?"

"Yeah, that's great. Do you need a hand with anything?"

"No, no. I'll call you when it's ready."

I made an escape before she said anything else that further damaged my weak lies. I held my breath as I sat on the sofa.

"Have you been ill?" he asked. "I just thought with your mum asking if you were feeling better..."

"I have been ill, just some headaches and feeling sick. But I'm better. Well, apart from the rib. What have you been up to?"

"Nothing much. I've been at home with Eli, we had a water fight."

"Yeah? I bet that was fun." A water fight had to be better than an actual fight.

"It was." He looked at me, the intensity of his eyes made me squirm. "Are you sure you're okay?"

"I'm fine."

Silence followed, making it awkward. Then my mother called us for lunch.

This has to be the strangest date ever. Had I ever been on dates before? My God. A date. In the kitchen. With my mother there.

"This looks lovely, thank you."

"Oh, there's no need to thank me." She waved her hand to brush off Clay's compliment, but I noticed it had already touched her cheeks.

"So, Clay," she mother said, "what brings you to this little village?"

I started eating the salad and waited for Clay's answer.

"I've moved here to be with my friend Eli. I've known him

many years and he needed me back home. Family emergency." He shrugged his shoulders.

"Nothing serious, I hope?"

"Nothing that we can't handle," he answered and smiled.

It was good that parents were so nosey. I could find out things.

"So, Laura, what do you do?"

"I'm a school teacher."

"You must have a lot of patience."

"I love my job, so patience isn't needed," she said, stabbing a red pepper. She popped it into her mouth and chewed it before continuing. "The good kids make it all worthwhile and the bad ones make my day interesting. No day is the same."

"I can imagine your days are interesting," Clay said, a smile playing on his lips.

He speared a tomato and popped it into his mouth. We continued to eat in silence.

This wasn't awkward at all.

Cora   Jack

"I have to get home," Clay announced with a yawn as the rolling credits of the film began.

"Yeah, I'm sure people are wondering where you are."

"Eli will probably send out a search party," he laughed.

I walked with him to the front door, before I could take a breath and say something awkward, his soft lips were on mine.

It was warm.

Nice…

Should it be more though? Had I really just described a kiss as warm and nice?

He pulled back, his eyes tracing the line of my lips like he wanted to kiss me again.

"See you later." His finger gently brushed my bruised cheek before he left.

I lay back on the sofa with my feet in the air as Eli paced. Clay was late, which for some reason angered Eli. Eli stomped out of the room and out onto the front porch.

"Sorry I'm late." I heard Clay's apology before I could step next to Eli in the doorway.

"Come on, Eli, leave the man alone, he's here now."

"I'm sorry, High Priest. I didn't receive your message."

"It's all right," I smirked. "You were with this new woman. Have your fun while it lasts, I'm sure you will move on next week."

I hadn't known Clay very long, but in the time I had known him, I knew that he liked the company of women.

"No, she's different."

"Whatever, I reckon you will find a new one next week."

"I won't, and I would rather you didn't continue with this line of conversation because you won't like my responses."

Clay's tone suggested a challenge and I found that I would like to see how far I could push Clay. "Oh, you like this one?" I stepped closer to him.

"Yes."

"And does she have a friend?"

"She's new to the village so she doesn't know many people."

"Where does she live?"

"Down by Andrew Bruton's field. She has a job in a shop in the village."

A little bell rang in my head. It couldn't be? It would be too much of a coincidence, surely? "What's her name?"

I already knew. Clay looked at Eli in confusion. I lost hold on my patience. "What's her bloody name, Clay?"

"Why does it matter what her name is?"

"It matters," I spat.

"Her name is Cora, but I don't see why you should-"

"You stupid-"

"Jack, step aside." Eli placed his hand on my shoulder, moving me away from Clay.

I moved, but my eyes remained locked on Clay's face. This was her game and she was playing me for a fool. I would make her pay. She wouldn't win, not this way. I'd been sat on my arse, literally, and she was already pulling my coven away from me.

"Clay, do you know who she is?" Eli asked, his voice deadly serious.

"No." He shook his head.

"You know that Alizon Device has a daughter?"

"Yeah."

"Cora is Alizon's daughter."

"But Alizon's daughter lives in York."

"No, she moved to London and then moved here. You didn't know?"

"No."

Screw this; I didn't like Eli's way of questioning. It wasn't getting the answers I wanted.

I pushed Eli and stepped towards Clay. "You knew. Oh, you knew! Did you think you could overpower me with that *bitch*?"

"I didn't know!" Clay stepped into me, his hands fisted.

I shoved past Clay, hitting him hard in the shoulder and started sprinting toward the village. I could hear Eli shouting, demanding that I stop. Feet stomped close behind me. Before I could run faster, ice cold water washed over me, pulling me under. Dazed, but ready to keep going, I jumped right back up and came face to face with Clay.

"You're not going anywhere, Jack. You need to tell me what the hell is going on!"

I charged at Clay. My shoulder smashed into his stomach. I heard the air wheeze out of Clay's mouth as I landed heavily on top of him. We tousled on the floor, but I gained the upper hand, punching Clay. Before I could pull my fist back, I felt two hands grab me and drag me away from Clay.

"Jack, what the hell are you doing?"

"I'm doing what needs to be done, Eli; I will do the same thing to you if you stand in my way."

Eli froze in shock. I didn't waste time; I turned and ran in the direction of the shop.

I'd only run several feet when water grabbed me and swept me aside like I weighed as much as a feather. My chest slammed heavily against the concrete. I rolled over onto my back and the world moved in slow motion as Clay pulled his fist back. My cheek exploded as the taste of old coins spilled into my mouth.

Swallowing the warm red liquid, I waited for another blow. It didn't come. Clay stood and ran. Grinning, I wiped the blood from my mouth and sprinted after him.

I picked up the DVD and headed to the bottom of the stairs. "Do you want to watch a DVD with me?"

"Yeah sure, which one are you watching?"

"Sex and the City."

"Oh yes, I would give up anything to watch Mr Big."

I almost heard her sigh. "I'll wait until you come down. I'm getting a drink first."

She gave no reply so I headed to the kitchen to get two cans of coke. Thunder boomed hard and heavy against the front door. I jumped as I put the cans down and edged slowly to the door. The banging persisted.

"Cora!"

Clay's shout made me walk quicker. I opened the door and Clay pushed his way into the house.

"Cora, listen to me..." He shut the door behind him.

"Clay, what happened?"

He doubled over, trying to get his breath. I'd noticed that his lip was bleeding. Had he been fighting? What the hell was going on?

"Cora, you need to listen to me, something has happ-"

"Cora, you bitch, get out here!"

I gasped and stared at the closed door. How had he found me? Clay was shaking his head and grabbed my shoulders, trying to hold me back but I brushed him off. I wouldn't back down from him.

"Please, don't go out there."

I opened the door and came face to face with Jack.

"Come out here and face me. I know you thought you could get Clay on your side, but it won't work. You're mine now and I finish this today!"

I stepped out of the front door, walking towards him. I didn't have a clue what I was going to do but I wouldn't hide. "What are you talking about?" I shouted over the sudden noise of the wind.

"Clay is mine. He will never join your coven. He belongs to me!"

Clay belonged to his coven? Before I could think about this, I watched Jack levitate and braced myself.

The ground fell away beneath me. I was flying and not in a good way. I took a breath as the ground crashed into me. Clay shouted my name but it was cut short. I looked up to see Jack holding Clay suspended in the air several feet away from me. Jack lifted his arms and flung Clay against the nearest tree.

I jumped up, ignoring the pain in my side as the wind laughed excitedly. I pushed it and had the pleasure of watching the powerful currents pick him up and pound him into the ground at his friend's feet.

I felt a moment of satisfaction before something hit the side of my face. I lifted my hands just before the onslaught came. What was that? My arms, my legs, my entire body screamed from the onslaught and I couldn't grab my power. I held my breath; and then it suddenly stopped. My arms continued to shield my face, just in case.

A light spray of water sprinkled against my arms. I cautiously dropped them and gasped. Clay was stood in front of the tree he'd hit but my eyes rested on his hands which were held in front of him. Water, actual water, was coming out of him.

Clay was a witch?

"Cora, get in the house!" Clay's shout was almost washed away in the roar of the wind.

I tripped as I moved towards the house. The ground shook violently beneath me.

Earthquake?

The floor continued to move, I fell, unable to keep my balance.

"Clio, what are you doing?" Clay snapped.

"Protecting Jack."

I managed to stand and turned in time to see Jack charging towards me.

Jack

She didn't have time to react, which was perfect. I felt a trickle of blood run down my cheek from my head wound. It didn't bother me.

A little spilt blood was worth it.

My head connected heavily against her stomach. I pulled back my fist and let it fall heavily against her face. She didn't cry out, she only looked at me, and then she smiled before she spat at me. Wet mucus hit my cheek. Anger flooded my chest as she jerked beneath me. I heard the whistle of the wind and then I flew through the air.

I grasped at my element, but it failed me. I tried again but it wouldn't come. I hit the floor.

"Time to play with the big boys!"

I was dragged over the grass by the scruff of my top. Before I could gather my bearings, it must have been only seconds, I was slammed to the floor again.

"Get up!"

I turned over and looked at a heavy-set man whose eyes were the colour of dangerous ice.

"Get. Up!"

I wobbled to my feet, felt the earth dip and sway. The man grinned. Before I could do anything, a sharp pain hit my back, forcing me to my knees. Air whooshed out of my lungs. The man pounced, pulling my arms behind my back. I screamed as my shoulder blades protested under the pressure. Before I felt them pop, something kicked me hard in the side. My mouth opened and closed but my lungs had stopped working.

"Enough!"

A woman's voice echoed around us. I fell to the floor and the freedom sent my body into overdrive. I sucked in air too quickly which resulted in a coughing fit. I rolled over on to my knees and wiped my mouth before I looked up.

Eli, Clay and Clio were held by the man who had attacked me. There were three of the same man. I shook my head, wondering if I was seeing triple rather than double. Cora was sat on the grass guarded by the man-*again*- and a woman. Tabitha was also stood at her side. I stood up slowly.

"Do not think of doing anything, young man. It will be the last thing you do."

"I could kick your arse if I wanted to!"

She laughed. "I'll believe *that* when I see it."

Barely sparing me a glance, she walked past me and stood in front of Eli.

"What is the meaning of this attack?"

"It wasn't an attack, it was..." Eli's explanation drifted off because it was an attack.

Tabitha, obviously bored with Eli, turned her attention to Clay.

"And, who might you be?"

"Clay Barnes."

From this distance I saw Tabitha cock her head to the side. "I've not had the *pleasure* of meeting you yet."

"I'm a newer member of the coven. I am in Jack's coven but-"

"Then you were involved in this attack?"

"No, Tab, he wasn't."

My head whipped to Cora. She looked at the woman at her side and then slowly they moved together.

"Cora, don't move." Tabitha's protests fell on deaf ears.

Cora brushed off the woman's words as she walked past me, she didn't look at me, but the woman's cold steel eyes glared. Cora shrugged off the woman's help and gave a quick nod to the man holding Clay. He let go and stepped back. I looked around the group. Several faces showed confusion at this. They hadn't know either. That meant Cora had been keeping secrets. Tabitha turned her attention back to Eli.

"I will repeat my earlier question, why did you start an attack?"

Rage popped inside my chest. "Eli isn't the leader of this coven, I am!"

Tabitha turned to face me. "You will accept the consequences of your actions, but first I want my question answered."

I looked from one face to another and refused to be ignored. "She," I said, pointing my finger at Cora, "she thinks she can take a member of my coven away from me. She thinks she can make them all turn against me. I will kill her before she does that!"

"I will kill you before you touch her," Clay snapped.

"See! He's already on her side."

"I haven't taken anyone. He isn't on any side... I didn't

even know about Clay and your coven. He never told me," her voice became a whisper at the end.

"Keeping secrets already," I mocked.

"If it wasn't for Eli, our coven would have fallen apart ages ago. You are nothing but a-"

I lifted Clay like a feather in the wind and launched him against a tree. Within seconds I felt the blast of cool air hit me in the chest. I flew back, landing on my arse. I was instantly up, levitating. Powerful bursts of water were fired at me, but I continued to move even though the speed exhausted me.

"Enough!"

Heat encased my body. I screamed, dropping like a brick to the hard ground.

"Clay, perhaps you could cool off your High Priest."

My body was hit by freezing cold water.

"Ayden, you may let the other two go."

"Eli," Tabitha began, "I want you to take your High Priest and leave. If you enter this property again, you will be dealt with. We will need to discuss this event at a later date."

Eli nodded and moved towards me, giving me a look to tell me to be quiet. Eli took one of my arms and dragged it over his shoulder. I felt Clio take my other arm and we slowly moved away from Cora's house.

"Clay." Eli stopped, turning around to Clay. "We need a coven meeting. You need to be there."

"Wait."

I watched in disgust as Clay approached Cora.

"Cora, I didn't know. I would never-"

"I suggest you leave," Ayden snarled.

Clay let his hands fall dejectedly by his sides and watched Cora walk away.

Eli helped me walk away. Okay, that hadn't worked out the way I'd hoped.

I was injured.

Eli was pissed at me.

And that Tabitha woman was rather scary.

I had to do better next time. Next time, Cora would see what I was made of.

Cora   Jack

With Ayden's help I hobbled into the house.

"Are you all right?" Ayden asked me.

"Yeah, I'm just great," I whispered so Tabitha couldn't hear me complain. "My rib hurts, *again*, I swear it's punctured my lung. I have mountains forming on my body from whatever that man pelted at me. My knee feels like someone has put a cheese grater to it, and the only man who took an interest in me turns out to be a member of Jack's coven."

He smiled. "It's good to see that you still have your sense of humour."

"Huh," I groaned as pain shot down my leg.

"Sweetheart, are you all right?" My mother ran to me and threw her arms awkwardly around us both. "Ouch, Mum, my rib."

"Sorry, love," she apologised as she shyly smiled at Ayden.

Ayden helped me on to the sofa.

"Would anyone like a drink?" my mother asked, playing host.

"I think we could all do with some tea," Tabitha said.

Tabitha faced me, and the look could freeze water. Oh Christ. "Cora, you need to explain yourself."

"I don't need to explain anything," I replied smartly. I didn't. My life was my life. I could see whoever I wanted. Although, Clay and I weren't seeing each other. One date with my mother present wasn't such a big deal.

"Do not get smar-"

"I think what Tabitha is trying to say," Ember interjected, "is that we are deeply concerned with what has happened here. We would like to hear why this event has happened."

"Fine, since you ask so politely, I met Clay whilst I was working in the shop just before our picnic in the field-"

"Bloody Jesus!" Ayden's outburst made me jump.

"Ayden, let her speak," Ember chided.

"I swear I've only seen him a few times and he stayed for lunch today."

"I never would have let him stay if I knew it would cause trouble."

"It's not your fault, Laura. Without you, we could be facing a different outcome."

"Why?" I questioned.

"Your mother heard the commotion outside and rang me. Ember used her ability to project here. She made sure you were safe until we arrived."

"Safe? How is being thrown across the drive, safe?"

"You were very impressive, Cora," Ember assured me.

I hadn't felt impressive.

"Anyway, please continue."

"Clay left saying he had to get home. Around ten minutes later there was pounding on the door. I opened it and Clay came in gasping for breath. He was trying to tell me something, it was at that point that Jack shouted me. I really didn't know Clay was part of the other coven. He didn't know I was a witch either."

"I could have killed him!" Ayden shouted.

"No, Ayden, you will not lay a finger on him. Clay tried to help me before you arrived."

"Do you like this man?" Tabitha questioned.

"It was very early days. I'll admit that I liked the attention, who wouldn't? Have you seen him?" I paused but received silence. So, no one else was going to comment on his good looks?

Fine.

"We didn't know each other; it was at the stage of it being something fun."

"Before this happened, Ember and I were preparing a spell to put over an area in which both you and Jack could... you know..." Tabitha glanced cautiously at my mother. No one wanted to state the obvious in front of her. "We had that particular area sorted; unfortunately, this attack has taken place in the open."

"Oh, well, *sorry*, the next time he comes knocking at my door I will cower behind the sofa."

"Cora," my mother warned.

"That amount of magic and the emotions behind it were bound to be noticed," Ayden pointed out.

"Commoners notice when wind, water and people fly into the air," Ember noted.

I swallowed. They did have a point, but when faced with it, you just deal with it and then think later.

"Instead of a government, we have a law of our own. They make sure the rules are followed."

"Who are they?"

I didn't want to know because it already sounded ominous.

"The Corenthio Coven. The current members of this coven are Varick, Akina, Melitta and Evander. They are much older than Jack and your coven put together, with age comes more power."

"Enough doom and gloom for now," Ayden interjected, the smile on his face slightly forced. "We need to decide what we are going to do with the other coven."

"Cora will need to speak with the High Priest whilst we are present."

"Are you joking? Jack can't string two words together let alone have a conversation about something so important."

"Good one, Cora." Ayden slapped me on the back, making me wince in pain. "Oh, sorry."

"Cora, you have a responsibility now. You are in charge."

Why did I have to be in charge when the shit hit the fan? Why couldn't Tabitha lead on this one. Jack and I had serious anger issues when it came to each other, I wasn't sure we could actually have a conversation.

I slumped on the sofa, ignoring the shouts from various places in my body as Eli paced up and down the room with his hands rammed in his pockets. Clio was stood at the door next to Clay, they both remained silent. I closed my eyes and tried to focus on something other than the pain.

"Why didn't you tell us that you were with Cora?" Eli asked Clay.

"It was none of your business. I may be part of this coven

but you're not my parents, I don't have to answer to you. Plus, I honestly didn't know that this Cora was the same Cora."

"Jesus, Clay. How many clues do you need to be given? I mean, she works in a bloody witch shop; how can you not know!?" I snapped.

Clay shrugged, which added fuel to the raging fire inside of me. "You are no longer part of this coven, get out."

"Jack, you can't make a decision like that!" Eli protested.

"I don't give a damn. Get out!!"

I glared at Clay and caught the look he gave Eli. "Get out!! I'm the High Priest, you follow my orders!"

Clay bowed and left the house. Clio watched him leave, her eyes drifting to the floor as Eli resumed pacing around the room.

"Jack, we need to do something about the other coven. It is dangerous that we should face each other like this. It can have repercussions. If the other coven find out, it will lead to-"

"I can handle it, Eli." I had to deal with Cora first.

"No, it's not something you can handle. They are-"

"I don't care." My head throbbed after being thrown around a few times. "I need to lie down."

"But Jack... what about the other coven?"

"I will handle it."

Cora

It had been more than a week since hearing anything from Jack or his coven. The radio silence from Clay also helped me think a little clearer. The bell above the door rang, signalling yet another customer. I walked into the shop and did a double take as he pushed his hand through his short hair, the green and blues of his eyes studied me.

"Hello, Cora."

"Eli, what can I do for you?"

It was thanks to this man that my arms looked like an abstract art of black and blue.

"I've come to talk about what happened."

I nodded. Tabitha had expected this. "Shouldn't I be speaking with Jack?"

A blush appeared in his cheeks.

"He doesn't know you're here, does he?"

"No, he doesn't. Jack has been somewhat *engaged*."

Engaged...? Meaning he was being the idiot I'd come to know.

"We can talk, but I don't have long."

"That will be fine."

I watched him sit down in my usual seat and stopped myself from grinding my teeth.

"Can I offer you a drink, Eli?" I slid the bolt on the door.

"No, thank you."

I sat down.

"I need to talk to you about what happened in 1612. I don't think you know the *right* version."

"When you say *right* version, you mean your version."

"The only *right* version is the Chattox version-"

"Don't." I stopped him by raising my hand. "You won't come in here and tell me your side. I know what happened in 1612. My mother was murdered."

"And so was my wife."

Wife? Eli had been married? That shocked me into silence.

"I was married to Jack's sister, Anne." He took a deep breath. "Your mother was a murderer-"

"Hold on just one damn minute!" I shouted. "How dare you come in here accusing my mother? It was your family who sent my mother to her death. It is quite obvious that *certain* traits run through your blood line. You should have words with him. Without his anger, this would never have happened. He attacked me first." My voice dipped dangerously low. "I want you to leave."

He stood, crowding my personal space. "If this situation isn't resolved, we're all in imminent danger!"

"Well, you just tell your High Priest to get his arse into gear then!" I shouted at his back as he slammed the door behind him.

Each and every member of his coven was stark raving mad.

"I have to say, he was right."

"Jesus Christ!" I jumped.

"Sorry," Tabitha apologised as a smile played on her lips.

She wasn't sorry. "What do you mean he's right?"

"I don't think he is right about your mother, but we need to resolve this situation."

"Well, Jack doesn't make that easy. Neither did Eli coming in here saying bad things about my mother."

"After all this time he still grieves for his wife."

It didn't make what he'd done, what he'd said, right.

"What happened to the two families, Tab?"

"I don't know. I understand that one rumour may have led to another, but for rumours to end like that. Have you found anything in your family book?"

I blushed guiltily. "I haven't had time to look at it. Don't stare at me like that. What with working here and doing the training, there's been very little time for sleep, let alone reading the book."

"And seeing Clay in your free time," Tabitha added.

"Yeah, that too. Are you mad about that?"

Tabitha hadn't said much on the topic which, reading between the lines, meant she wasn't happy about it.

"What can I do about it now? It is done. Have you heard from Clay?" Tabitha asked.

"No."

"I'm sure things will turn right in the end, but you still need to resolve things with Jack."

"I know. I just don't see why I have to make the first move."

"Because you must be the sensible one in this situation." Tabitha tucked some of my loose hair behind my ear.

If I was going to do this then I needed to do it now before I thought about it and convinced myself I shouldn't. Tabitha smiled as she walked down the stairs. She knew what I was going to do. I pulled my phone out of my bag and sat in the little tea room as I liked to call it.

A white note was stuck to the fridge with Tabitha's lovely neat handwriting on it. The two words under the number read 'Jack's mobile.' I didn't want to know how Tabitha had got that number.

Taking a deep breath, I picked up the note and started punching the number into my phone.

"Hello?"

"Jack, its Cora... don't hang up."

"Give me one good reason why I shouldn't?"

"Because you will regret it?" I couldn't help the jibe.

"Oh, yeah?"

"Jack, listen to me."

"No, you listen, you bit-"

"Shut up!" I snapped.

Silence followed.

"You hate me and I hate you, that much is clear. Our parents died, they are no longer with us because of this hatred. Now, we could continue to play the blame game, or we could focus on the here and now and sort this."

"When and where?" His voice was cold and straight to the point.

"Meet us on Andrew Bruton's field at midnight on Monday."

"Halloween night?"

That had totally slipped my mind. "See you there."

He hung up the phone without responding.

"So, it's done?"

"God, Tab, you have to stop doing that."

"And you need to listen with your ears a little better."

"Yeah, it's done. We're meeting at midnight on Monday. I forgot it was Halloween."

"No, that's a good thing. If Jack loses his temper again, which is a high possibility, then we can cover up the magic with the atmosphere of the night. Go home for the day. I'm sure we will be rushed off our feet tomorrow. We have three more coaches coming in, and a primary school."

"Oh God! Why? Bring them to me, I will take great pleasure in telling them how horrid it is being a witch."

Tabitha laughed. "You wouldn't change it for the world." Tabitha's leaf green eyes danced with her amusement.

"Humph." I shrugged into my coat. "See you tomorrow."

"Be safe."

"I'll try," I smiled.

I stepped out of the shop and was greeted by a lovely cool breeze. Regardless of what I'd just told Tabitha, I loved being a witch. It was just hard luck that my first month as a witch had royally sucked.

Cora

I sat on the little stool behind the till watching customers pick up the half price deals Tabitha had put on after lunch. It surprised me that people were still fighting for bargains, after tonight they wouldn't use the things again.

The shop looked the part for the night ahead. My favourite item sat on the end of the counter. It was a medium sized black cauldron with a little stirring device, similar to the one in the window that was forever malfunctioning. This one exploded after a customer bought something.

There were several real brooms, Lord knows where Tabitha got them, hanging from the ceiling. At the entrance a black cat perched on the end of a broom. If you went up to the cat and stroked it, it purred. The kids loved that. Ghostly pumpkin faces grinned within the layer of smoke in the window.

A few loud, smoke filled explosions later and a hushed silence fell over the shop. Tabitha was in the coven room arranging a meeting after work. The meeting before I saw Jack tonight. Butterflies attacked my chest.

"Have the customers gone?" Tabitha asked as she came up the stairs holding two cups of hot chocolate, somewhat a tradition now.

"Yeah," I said, sliding down from the stool behind the counter to join Tabitha at the table. "We don't have much stock left over. You could put what we have left on the website."

"Good idea. You can do that tomorrow morning." Tabitha raised her eyebrows.

I held back a groan. It was so old and so slow it would take me the entire day to upload the items with the pictures, prices and save it. I preferred to be dealing face to face with customers, even Mrs Rogers who liked all the love spells. "So, what is the itinerary for tonight?"

"That's up to you. This is your meeting."

"Are you joking? You made me do the meeting, which by default means it's your meeting."

Tabitha laughed. "I'm afraid it doesn't work like that."

I groaned. "If I have to sort this meeting then I'm going to need food."

I grabbed my phone, punched in the number and listened to it ring. The bell above the door sounded. I turned to see my mother struggling through the doorway with a huge picnic basket.

"Mum..." Cancelling the call, I jogged over, taking some of the weight of the basket. "I was just ringing home for some food supplies."

We dropped the basket to the floor. What was in that thing, a whole cow?

"Well, I knew it would be a long night for you all. Ayden had mentioned something to me earlier. I wanted to make sure you were all-"

"Ayden told you earlier? What do you mean?"

The instant blush in her cheeks told me everything I needed to know. Something was going on.

"Well... we..."

She was interrupted as Ayden walked in with a huge smile on his face. "Well, well, well, my three favourite ladies."

I eye balled Ayden as his hand slid around my mother's waist. To my shock he leaned in and gave her a loud kiss on the lips.

"Does anyone want to explain *that* to me?" I pointed at the two of them. The action had been more than explainable, but still.

"I was going to tell you-"

"But you thought taking part in tonsil tennis right in front of me would be the best way to explain this?"

"Cora," Ayden warned. "We didn't tell you because we wanted to see how it went. It's been only a few weeks. We wanted to make sure it was right before we brought it up. Plus, your mother has irresistible lips," he added and kissed her again.

"Will you two stop swapping saliva!" I was only half joking. Seeing it was quite disturbing.

"Cora," my mother warned, giving me the *look*.

"Mum, you're dating a member of my coven. I have every right to not like the situation."

"Cora is correct. I'm sorry, I should have asked but I'm asking now. Is it okay?"

I looked at them and knew it was already too late to say

no. And I didn't think I could have. "Fine" I sighed. "Give me the food and all is forgiven. Where's Ember, Tab?"

I saw the quick exchange between Tabitha and Ayden and knew something was happening and they weren't telling me.

"She was caught up with something. She will be here tonight for the meeting in the field."

Although I wanted to know what that look was between them, I wouldn't get a straight answer. It was really hypocritical of them because they demanded to know everything I did.

"Right, if Ember isn't coming until later then we should get started."

I followed Tabitha down the stairs and left Ayden and my mother to say goodbye in whatever way they wanted, without seeing it. Tabitha knew what to do without me having to say. A small flame surrounded Tabitha's hand, so I pushed the wind, licking up the flame. A soft glow lit the entire tunnel as we walked, and my thoughts drifted to tonight. I didn't know what was going to happen but at least I would have my coven with me this time.

Cora

We walked across Andrew Bruton's field in silence. My mind raced with defence blocks, attack moves and sarcastic retorts. Just in case. Tabitha walked to my right; Ayden to my left. They walked with their backs bolt upright, shoulders square, faces solemn.

Tabitha halted, her arm snapping out. I looked around but couldn't see anything. We were surrounded by dark shadows, the little hairs on my arms stood upright in anticipation.

"Hello, Cora."

Jack shot forward at a startling speed and landed with a heavy thump. He remained upright, wobbling unsteadily on his feet in front of me.

"Jack."

"You wanted to meet. Start talking," Jack said and lifted his hands in invitation.

I ignored his rudeness, being the adult that I was. "I think we need to find some way to live peacefu-"

Jack's hysterical laughter cut me off. "Peaceful! You started this, and I intend to finish it."

"Jack won't touch you whilst I'm here."

I looked over as Clay stepped out of the shadows. I understood why Jack wouldn't want him here with the coven, but he had to think like an adult. Tabitha, Ayden and Ember were my family, I couldn't understand why he didn't feel the same way about his coven.

"You have no say in this, Clay. Cora, shall we finish what was started?"

"There will be no fighting tonight."

I whirled around to see Ember walking towards us. A silent conversation played between Tabitha and Ember.

"Cora, I need to intervene in this meeting, may I do that?"

"Yeah... of course." I stepped aside, feeling nervous by the look that had occurred between them.

"I have received grave news. Ember was sent by me, without Cora's knowledge, to find out what was happening within the Corenthio Coven. I'd believed word may have reached them regarding your little *meeting,* and I'm afraid it has.

"According to Ember, they've heard a few mutterings regarding magic, screams, and unusual things occurring here. They have discussed their options at great length," Ayden laughed but Tabitha continued "A repeat of 1612 would be disastrous for our kind and considering the families resided here, they will be extra cautious. The Corenthio Coven are set in their ways and resolves these types of situations by doing one thing..." Tabitha looked at me, her leaf green eyes portraying something I couldn't decipher.

"How could we solve this? How can we talk to them without it heading in their favoured direction?"

"Talking isn't on their agenda," Ayden scoffed. "They didn't think it over. It took them less than three bloody weeks!" Ayden shouted.

Jack looked confused, but he always looked like that. He was staring at Eli who looked like he'd aged twenty years in seconds. I turned to my coven. Ember, the bearer of the bad news, looked unaffected. Tabitha had edged closer to me. Ayden appeared to have another outburst ready.

"What is the Corenthino Coven?" Jack asked, breaking the silence.

Tabitha hissed in frustration. "Eli, what have you actually taught your leader?"

"The boy doesn't want to learn, apparently he knows everything there is to know," Clay sneered.

"Shut your mouth, you arsehole," Jack growled at Clay.

"Do you want to come over here and say that?"

I didn't look at Clay but I knew there would be a smile on his face, tempting Jack to bite.

"Enough!" Eli shouted, holding Jack back. "It is true; I have found it *difficult* to teach him."

Jack wrestled against Eli's strong hold. "I don't need your help; I will deal with this new coven by myself."

"And you will die before taking a breath," Tabitha barked.

"Is there no way to survive this?" Ayden asked, rubbing his hands over his face.

Jack slumped against Eli, perhaps understanding for the first time the severity of the situation.

Survive? Was that really what we were up against?

"No one has ever come away alive when the Corenthio Coven set their mind to it," Ember declared.

"Everything is happening again. I'm sorry; I keep trying to save you..." Tabitha whispered.

My heart squeezed painfully. "You *have* saved me. Please don't do that. Don't blame yourself."

I looked around at the people gathered on the field and realised that I had to make a decision, one that would save my coven. "Jack, we need to join together to face the Corenthio Coven. I know that we cannot face them alone."

"I believe that would be our only option, Jack." The woman next to Jack spoke.

"Cora's coven has my support." Clay edged towards me.

"It is the only way Jack, we-"

"No! No! No!" Jack shouted. "It's not the only way. We can do this without *her*."

"Clay and Clio believe it is the right thing to do. I do too. I will stand with them to save our coven."

I actually felt guilty which was ridiculous considering we'd come here to…to what? Fight? I was making him choose and his options weren't appealing. If the roles were reversed, I would be pissed at Jack too.

"Jack, when we face the Corenthio Coven, the covens will be equal."

Jack's chocolate brown eyes glared at me. "If we must do this, I have no choice." His voice was dead with defeat.

"Fine, we will talk later."

I turned and walked away. The emotions playing across Tabitha's face told me how serious this was. My chest tightened. Would I die because of this? The expressions on their faces didn't give me positive vibes.

"Cora! Cora, we need to talk."

Clay ran up ahead, stopping us.

"I don't want to speak with you tonight, Clay. I have too much to think about," I sighed.

I also believed there was nothing to discuss.

"She will deal with this tomorrow," Ayden said, his words were ice cold.

We continued walking away from Jack and his coven.

"I'm so proud of you, Cora," Tabitha whispered.

"I don't feel like I've done anything for you to be proud of. If I could have just kept my anger in check or stayed away from Jack-"

"You will never berate yourself over this," Ember interrupted. "You have given up your role as High Priestess to work with Jack, a boy who has done nothing but attack you. You are the most selfless person I know, and I couldn't be prouder."

My throat felt thick with emotion. I nodded as Ember placed her arm around my waist. Ayden walked in front of us, protecting us from any unknown threat that may lurk ahead. Unfortunately, we knew the threat, and we would have to deal with it.

Jack

Clay was stood off to the side, brooding with his hands in his jeans pockets, his face was set in hard lines, his eyebrows were pulled together in frustration. I watched with delighted glee as Clay kicked his boot into the frost-bitten dirt. Whilst venting his frustrations, Clay never took his eyes off Cora. I almost laughed. That man needed to get a grip.

I shifted my attention to her. I still didn't like the girl, but it was something that I had to put up with if I was going to survive; because surviving would mean I could seek revenge at a later date.

I caught Cora's exaggerated sigh as she finally discovered her little audience of one. As far as I knew Clay and Cora hadn't spoken since the meeting. I could tell because Clay was a ball of pissed off energy. Yesterday I'd watched Clay sprinkle water over her and I'd caught a smile, a very small smile playing on Cora's lips. I'd also seen her quickly cover that smile with a scowl just in time for Clay to see.

I saw everything.

The group were stood in the woods near my cottage which wasn't too far from Cora's house. Ironically. Tabitha was striding around, barking instructions at Eli and Cora, her long green flowing robe lapped at the hard ground as long black hair was pulled high on her head, away from her face and those hardened green eyes. It pissed me off that Eli looked as happy as a child on Christmas morning.

I lay slumped on the floor, I was freezing but I'd sat down and hadn't wanted to appear weak by standing up. I could curl up my coat and use it as a pillow. A few minutes of sleep would do the job and energise me. I'd made it perfectly clear that I wanted no part in this whole arrangement.

I closed my eyes.

A scream made them pop open.

My focus shot straight to Cora. Had she already started the attack whilst I'd been sleeping on the job? She leaped towards a large tree trunk that was suddenly lying in the middle of the training area. When had that got there? Clay was no longer brooding as he had rushed forward, trying to grab a chunk of the tree that lay on the ground.

The scene played out in front of me in slow motion. Clay tried to lift the trunk without success, his fingers slipping off the rough bark. Cora flung her arms high, trying to control her element; I felt the wind gather, cold and powerful. I looked back at the trunk and realised the tree trunk had flailing arms underneath it. I scanned the area, I couldn't see Eli. I leaped up, rushing towards the tree.

Grabbing the trunk, I shifted my weight to the back of my legs and pushed. It felt like I attempting to lift a bus.

"Lift it!" Clay shouted.

"Cora, use your element!" Tabitha ordered.

Cora lowered her hands and closed her eyes. Clay was pulling the trunk. I tried lifting it again, but my fingers slipped on the rough bark, blood oozed from the cut. Eli was still moving around under it. Why wasn't Eli using his power? Why was he under the trunk to begin with?

I reluctantly let go of the trunk knowing the weight would drop back onto Eli. I pushed my panic aside as I grasped at my element. I felt Cora's power glide up against mine. Adrenaline pumped through my body, my panic was stopping my element from fully developing. My left foot was levitating whilst my right remained rooted to the floor. My brother needed me, and I'd frozen.

I closed my eyes.

"Jack, come on!!" Clay snarled.

"Shut up, Clay, I'm bloody trying!"

A warm hand filled mine. My back went rigid as my eyes shot open and found Cora stood at my side. I pushed her hand from mine. "Don't touch me!"

She sighed. "We need to work together, Jack."

"Get. This. Thing. Off. Me!" Eli's muffled shout filled the area.

My attention moved from Cora to Eli. "Fine," I snapped.

I closed my eyes and felt her hand slide into mine, she squeezed. It felt warm and clammy. My element glided playfully with Cora's. I opened my eyes and was shocked to see the smile on her face. Wind whipped around us but not one hair on my head moved. I was stood in the eye of the storm.

I felt the lift, felt the weightlessness. She was levitating with me and for a second I felt a smile play on my lips, I'd done it. Sickeningly, she'd helped me. Was I thankful? There was something in my chest that didn't feel right.

Shaking my head, I shook off the unwanted feeling. I had a game plan and I was sticking to it. I didn't need to think about the way a beam of light caught the deep brown of her eyes, making them swirl. I didn't need to think about the way the sun cast a ray of light that seemed to kiss her face, making her pale skin shimmer and glow. I didn't need to think about the fact that she seemed familiar to me at the very moment.

I focused on the scene in front of us. Eli had stopped moving beneath the trunk. Our elements twinned together and then the trunk moved, rocking against the pressure we created. The trunk gave one final shake before it flew off Eli, hurtling towards the trees.

Eli rolled over and coughed. We floated back to solid ground.

It was the first time I'd done it and found my balance as my feet touched the ground.

"Good job," Eli said, and he then stood up like nothing had happened.

"Why are you grinning?" I asked.

"You passed the test," Tabitha said.

"What test?" Cora asked.

"We needed to get you two working together sooner rather than later. We thought sooner would be best. You did brilliantly by the way," Eli praised, whilst wiping dirt from his jeans.

Red mist exploded in my vision.

"Jack, don't," Cora commanded.

I felt the tug on my hand. I was still holding Cora's hand? Her grip tightened, pulling me towards her, *and* I allowed it.

"Jack, they were looking out for us. You can understand that our safety is their number one priority. We eventually needed to work together, but…" She stopped and scowled at Tabitha.

Tabitha glared at Cora, her eyes narrowed into slits. I'd seen the look many times and I didn't like it. Tabitha could actually kill you with such a look.

Cora seemed to ignore it and continued. "Tabitha, it was a stupid way to do it. You could have discussed it with us like adults. To put someone Jack loved in danger was wrong."

My breath shot out of my lungs. Cora had hit the nail on the head. Before I could respond, Cora was tugging on my hand again. I still hadn't let go.

What the hell was wrong with me?

"Look what we did together," she said and smiled.

I considered it. They looked happy and Eli looked cautious. He knew my moods. Was I that bad?

"We did a good job." I swallowed.

I felt her grip my hand tighter and then let go. The cold air hit the area she'd kept so warm. I clenched my hand into a fist.

Cora walked to Tabitha's side. I studied them as they both moved away, already engrossed in a conversation and laughing. Cora's hair had fallen from the bobble that had secured it. Delicate wisps of her hair had fallen across her face, I watched as she brushed them back behind her ear. I turned to Eli, the grin reached his eyes.

"So… you had that all figured out?"

"Yeah." Eli slapped me on the back. "My master plan worked a bloody treat. Come on, let's go, Cora's mum has offered to feed us and I can never pass up on free food."

I trudged behind him. Eli was chatting about his training session with Cora. He sounded excited, alive. I couldn't remember the last time Eli had sounded like this. Cora had forced me to focus, by doing so she'd helped me. I hated that I owed her something.

Was this our life now? Where we relied on Cora and her coven to help us? Had Eli forgotten what her coven, what her mother had done to our family?

I hadn't.

I clenched my fist.

Jack

"Jack, concentrate!"

"I'm bloody trying!"

I glared at Eli, trying to blink through the sweat that was dripping down my forehead. Eli was pushing me beyond my boundaries. I was currently suspended in the air with Clay and Clio elevated beside me. I felt my limbs shake under the pressure of holding them. I didn't want them to go crashing to the ground. Well, apart from Clay.

"Keep it up, Jack!" Cora shouted encouragement from below.

Cora had suggested taking people up with me. I hadn't wanted to look stupid in front of everyone, in front of her. I looked down at her and my concentration lapsed. We plummeted rapidly out of the sky, I heard a gasp escape Clio's mouth.

"Whoa, Jack!" Clay shouted.

I regained my balance, holding them both. That had been too close. I fought the internal battle that was making a mess of my insides.

"Jack, you stay up there!"

"Eli, I can't do it!"

"Keep it going!" Eli urged.

My stomach rolled. I was going to throw up if I stayed up here, and I was sure Eli wouldn't appreciate *that* shower. I dropped slowly to the floor.

Over the past week I'd managed to work on the landing. Now I was smoother. I concentrated on keeping Clay and Clio in the air, even on the floor, the pull on my energy was taxing.

"Come on, you can do this." Cora knelt down beside me.

"I can't, it hurts. I feel so drained," I moaned. I couldn't care less if I appeared weak. I'd seen her weaknesses.

We'd spent every day working together. I had, rather surprisingly, felt great about the training sessions, even in the presence of Cora. It had been a hard week, but what had made it harder was my lack of sleep. Each night for the past week I'd had the same horrendous nightmare.

In these nightmares I always started in the same place, instantly surrounded by people, the roar of a large crowd created a noise that battered my ears. There were so many faces that they blurred, the heat, the smell of rotten food, stale breath and sweat hit my nostrils and clung to my body. That wasn't the worst part.

The iron cuffs that bound my hands made my skin crawl. Long thin strips of rusty metal grazed my vulnerable skin, always on the verge of breaking through. No matter how many times I consciously tried not to move my hands, I always did. Every single time I felt the *pop* and sickening sting as the sharp rusted spike slid into me.

It was at this point that I woke up, rubbing at my wrists.

I hadn't told Eli about them. I felt stupid. He didn't need to know about some stupid dreams.

"Start again." Cora's voice cut into my thoughts.

"Okay," I took a deep breath and rose to join Clay and Clio in the air.

Midnight was drawing in when we finally stopped. I'd managed to lift myself and the entire coven.

"Jack, perhaps you should work on your levitating with Cora," Tabitha suggested, "It's imperative that you both use your elements together against the Corenthio Coven. We have no way of defending ourselves when on the ground unless you help us."

"Yeah, sure that's fine. Is everyone going to be there so I can try levitating them?"

"No, I need to work with Ayden and Clio."

"Right, so who will be there?"

"Cora."

I stopped breathing. In the weeks of training, I'd never been *alone* with Cora. I didn't actually know if I could be trusted. I pushed back my anger when we were training because the others were there to control it. But on my own...I didn't know.

"I heard my name."

I looked up as Cora approached. Her hair hung loose, falling over her shoulders. Her brown eyes focused on me. Even though the weather was cooling as it neared December, she wore only a thin t-shirt over tattered jeans. I wore similar gear; it was hard, sweaty work learning new techniques.

"I was just telling Jack that you two need to focus on your

skills and working together. It is you two that are the most important."

"No, Tab, we all want to protect each other. I don't want to be saved before everyone else."

I watched as lines of frustration gathered on her forehead. For once we agreed on something.

"I understand that, but we can use our skills we have been using them for centuries. You still need to master yours."

"So, who will be there?"

"You and Jack."

I watched a puzzled expression cross her face that had, I imagined, only seconds before flickered across my own.

"Fine, when is the best time for you?" She looked at me.

"Any time is fine with me; I can practise better at my cottage."

I caught the uncomfortable shift in her footing. "Or would that be a problem?"

"No, no problem. What about tomorrow after work?"

"Cora, you can take the day off work."

"Great, we can have a full day at it," I said eagerly, pushing her into an uncomfortable decision.

"Sure, see you around ten?" Cora asked.

"Okay."

She walked away arm in arm with Tabitha. That pair always seemed to be whispering about something. Clay was stood talking to Eli, I couldn't see Clio.

"Where did Clio head off to?" I asked.

"She needed to go. She said to get in touch with her if you needed her for more practice, but she will be working with Ayden at some point."

"I know, Tabitha just told me that I'm going to be working with Cora tomorrow at the cottage."

"Oh, good, are you going to work on your levitating?"

"Hmmm, but I will be working only with Cora. I don't know how to do that. How can you forget everything that girl has done to our family?"

I hadn't forgotten. There was a new unease in my chest and I put that down to this new treaty. I wanted to deal with things and then get back to what was important.

An expression, one that screamed protective and jealous, crossed Clay's face. What the hell was he jealous of? Me and Cora? There was no me and Cora.

"You will cope because that is the best thing we can do. We have to adapt to the situation," Eli instructed. "So, I ordered some newel posts and spindles that are piled up in the back garden, you can use them."

At least I knew that Eli hadn't forgotten. "Okay. Will do. Come on, let's head home. Tabitha and Cora have already gone."

Clay shot one last brooding look in the direction of Cora's house and headed to the cottage ahead of us, his feet stomping on the hard ground. I knew that Clay didn't like that I was working with Cora alone. I didn't like it either, but I liked teasing Clay with it.

Cora

"Tab, I had the dream again."

"Are you okay?" Tabitha asked, concern deepening her tone of voice.

"Yeah, I think so."

Ever since I'd found out that the Corenthio Coven were coming, I'd had dreams involving my mother. With the phone against my ear I looked at the old photo Tabitha had given me.

"What happened in this one?"

"She tried to tell me something about family, Jack's family or my family, I'm not sure. Images were flashing so quickly they became more of a blur and then I woke up. I've only just managed to understand that the flashing images are coming from her and now she wants me to learn them faster."

Tabitha sighed, frustrated. I felt exactly the same. I wanted to understand her meaning behind them, I also wanted to feel happy about seeing her, but the whole situation was making it stressful.

"Have you asked Eli? Is Jack having dreams?"

"I've asked but Eli said Jack hasn't mentioned any dreams to him."

"If he was having them I'm sure we would know about it. They're horrible. On the one hand I'm so happy to see my mum in the weird crazy way that I am, but on the other hand, it frustrates me when she can't tell me what she needs. When she opens her mouth, nothing comes out. She came to tell me something and I'm not hearing it."

"You will, Cora, please don't worry."

"I can't help it. She was mouthing the words 'see the truth' but by the time I'd managed to lip read she was flashing images in my head. See what truth?"

"I don't know, Cora, but you will find out. Perhaps approach the subject with Jack today?"

"Sure, because we have such great conversations already. In the middle of training I can just turn around and say, 'oh Jack, what lovely weather we're having, by the way have you been having conversations with your dead mother in your dreams?"

"All right, Miss Sarcasm," Tabitha laughed.

"I'm not comfortable with this training session at his house. Yeah, recently he's acted okay, but to be on my own with him? He could start something, and I won't sit back and take it."

"If he starts something, contact a member of your coven. We will deal with it."

I would deal with it myself.

"I know this whole situation is hard for you, but this is something we have to do to make sure you are both protected. Eli wants Jack to be safe, and we want you to be safe. This is the only way. Now, stop whining about it and get on with it.

Ring me if you have any more thoughts on your dreams. Love to you."

"You too."

I slid out of bed and pulled a t-shirt over my head. My phone buzzed softly on the duvet. I glanced at the screen and sighed.

"Clay."

"We need to talk," he asserted.

"We talk, Clay. We talk nearly every day."

"I mean properly."

"We have nothing to say." We didn't. Why did he want to drag this out?

"I want you to just listen to what I have to say."

"Okay."

"Okay... okay, what?"

"Okay, I'll listen to you."

"When?"

"After I've finished the training session today." I heard him growl before I've even finished saying it.

"I don't trust him."

"I'm capable of looking after myself, Clay." I didn't trust Jack either.

"Fine. I'll see you tonight."

I ended the call. Why had I answered the damn call to begin with?

I opened the waist high gate, making my way up the multi-coloured brick path to the front door. Colourful plant pots littered the little porch area. Standing in front of the royal blue door, I took a deep breath but before I had a chance to lift my hand and knock, Jack opened it.

"Hey, come on in." He moved aside, allowing me room to enter.

I stepped into a small living room. The brick fireplace was the main focal point of the room. It was similar to Tabitha's, which was strange to think about. The rustic brick contrasted beautifully with the crimson paint on the walls. A television sat on a stand in the corner nearest the window whilst a wide book case holding a mixture of books and DVD's stood against the other wall. I spotted the black leather book on the small coffee table. A book that was similar to my own.

"I thought we could practise outside, at least it's nice and cool." He opened a door into what looked like the kitchen.

I shuffled behind him and out into the garden.

"Eli said we could use the decking posts. I've tried to lift some this morning and so far my magic number is six. I can lift them around twenty feet in the air whilst I'm stood on the ground."

"How much do they weigh?"

"I'm not sure. I started with one then worked my way up. Eli left pretty early this morning so I made a start."

"Right, shall we get started then?"

"Yeah... do you want a drink or anything?" He pushed his hands through his hair; his eyes looked wider today, more alert. They stood out on his pale face, large dark buttons that were now looking intently at me.

I shifted my feet. "I think we should get started first."

He smiled then headed to the mound. "Right, I think I'll do seven now."

"Yeah, then at least we know what to work with. Perhaps you could go up with them?"

He wouldn't be able to do it. I knew he would find it difficult. Jack nodded and then jumped straight into the air, just like that. Posts from the pile started rising up to him. Lifting my hand to shield my eyes against the bright winter sun that was dipped low, I watched as the posts circled around him.

"Now, can you pick up a few more of the posts?" I didn't need a reply as three posts lifted in unison. They joined the circle currently dancing around him in the air. He was making this look easy.

I lifted a post and judged that three or four posts would make up the average weight of a person and he had the equivalent of two people up there with him. That would be the same as Clay and Clio yesterday. He wasn't really pushing himself, not yet.

"How about you pick up four more?"

Lines creased his forehead. I knew exactly what he was feeling, the way muscles rippled in protest when they were flexed to their limit. It made you want to scream with the effort. The four posts lifted rather more steadily than the previous ones. They stopped swirling around him, now they just hung like dead sticks. I tried to hide the smirk on my face.

"Something funny?"

"No." How had he noticed? "I was just wondering how much more you could take up there."

"I could take you."

That single comment froze the breath in my lungs. This was what I'd been trying to avoid, the constant power challenge between us. How could I respond without appearing weak?

"Cora, may I use my power to levitate you?"

Well, Jesus. If someone asks politely, how could you say no? "Sure."

I felt the pull, the feeling of cling film encasing me. On previous occasions I'd not felt this sensation, having had little time to think about it before crashing into something hard.

The pulling stopped. My legs dangled. I bobbed in the air fifteen, maybe twenty feet up. It wouldn't be wise to anger him at this moment in time. Glancing up at him, I could clearly see the strain.

"I'm struggling. I can't get you to the same level as me."

"Yes, you can. Pull the power to you, feel it inside your body and build it."

Who was I to tell him how to do it? I hadn't mastered my own element yet. The pull returned and then I felt a force pushing me down. The ground zoomed towards me and I collided with hard dirt.

I rolled over, taking the weight from my ankles, fearful they would snap on impact. Shit. That hurt. I looked over as Jack descended. He thudded down next to me.

"Cora, are you okay? I'm sorry... I couldn't hold it."

A post crashed to the ground, narrowly missing me by inches.

"Sorry." Jack leaned over, shoving the post away.

"It's fine, no one got hurt." I grimaced. "I was thinking."

Well, I was trying to think, but his intense gaze was really putting me off. "Well, you could do that again with ten posts and I could join you, but I could add my element into the mix."

His eyes traced the lines of my face. "Okay." He shrugged. "Are you sure you're okay?"

He stood up holding out his hand to me. I looked at it and accepted his help. His hand felt warm and sweaty as he pulled me up, but my ankle gave way. He grabbed my arms, without his support I would have fallen on my face.

"Have you hurt your ankle?" he asked.

"I just fell on it too hard when I hit the floor, it doesn't matter."

"Come on, we can go inside to get some ice on it."

His arm slid around my waist, pulling me against his lean, rather deceptively muscular body which created a heat I didn't entirely feel comfortable with. My heart palpitated, the beats worrying me. My reaction to him was wrong. He wanted to hurt me, and I was breathing heavy over the feel of his body next to mine. What the hell was wrong with me?

He placed me gently in a chair and walked to the freezer. Taking out a bag of frozen peas, he moved towards me.

"Here, put this on. Do you want a drink?"

"Sure, what have you got?"

He turned towards the fridge. "CID, what drinks do we have?"

Who was Sid? I opened my mouth to ask him but shut it when I heard a mechanical monotone voice:

'The fridge holds two Dr. Peppers, one beer, the light variation, and two bottles of spring water. You need to restock cans of coke, this is your favourite variety of drink.'

The mechanical voice ended. I expected balloons or party poppers to come shooting out of it.

"So, your choice is Dr Pepper and water."

"I'll have a Dr Pepper please. That thing has a name?"

"That was CID, the Content Identification Device. Eli built it so we could restock when things get low."

What was wrong with just opening the fridge and having a look yourself?

"You can also select favourites. It's pretty cool."

I accepted the can as Jack slumped down on the chair next to me. He popped the top and started sucking back long drags; he was probably just as warm as me. It was a cold November day but working and straining every muscle in your body kept you warm.

I sneaked a glance at him whilst he drank. His dark hair, cut into a jagged mess, moved in one wave on the top of his head. His Cupid's bow lips sucked at the opening of the can, dragging the liquid into his mouth. My eyes continued their journey and followed the line of his neck. The muscle taut, pulling, as his throat pushed the cool liquid down. His top was a darker shade of blue, wet from exertion. Defined abs were highlighted by the closeness of material. I bit my lip and quickly averted my gaze to the bag of frozen peas.

Again, what was I thinking?

"Jack..." I began, "have you been having... weird dreams?"

His eyes popped wide with shock; his cheeks had lost the healthy glow from training. The can was held halfway to his mouth. "What did you say?" His voice was ice cold.

"I've been having weird dreams, my mother comes and..."

The thunderous look on Jack's face told me to stop. The can crunched under the strain of his hard grip, spewing its contents all over his jeans and the floor. He ignored it.

"Your mother's been in your dreams," he snarled, his voice

dangerously low. "Your mother has come to see you. Well, what a lovely, *happy* reunion for you both!" He lurched to his feet, his tall body casting a strikingly cold shadow over me.

"Jack, it wasn't like-"

"Perhaps your bitch of a mother will give you tips on how to kill me?"

Why was he suddenly so mad? I wasn't trying to goad him, for once. "Jack, I-"

"She never shows herself; but I feel her pain, the way the long metal spikes slid into her skin if she dared to move just an inch. I can hear the noise; can taste and smell everything."

"Jack, I..."

My God, I hadn't realised. Why didn't Eli know? I wanted to help him, shocking myself with such a thought.

"Get out, Cora, get out and don't come back."

I numbly stood. I didn't know what to say. Was he seeing his mother the day she died? Why? I placed the frozen peas on the table and limped to the kitchen door that led through the lounge and outside. Jack's loud frustrated curse followed me down the brick path.

Cora

I opened my front door and was instantly greeted with a high-pitched feminine laugh followed by soft murmuring.

That was code for loved up.

Did I really want to enter and see?

Sighing, I headed towards the kitchen and nudged the door open enough to see my mother stood at the sink washing up. Ayden had his arms around her waist with his chin resting on her shoulder.

"Hi, I'm back," I said, "Just letting you know."

Before you did something that I didn't want to see or hear.

"Wait! Cora! Why are you back home so early?" Ayden asked.

I paused on the stairs. "Jack freaked out and then kicked me out of his house."

"Why?"

"I've been having these dreams that involve my mum, my real mum." I held up my hand, stopping Ayden's questions.

His eyebrows had shot so high up on his forehead that he was in danger of losing them. "I've told Tabitha about them, but I asked Jack about them. He told me to leave and never come back, which I'm more than happy to comply with."

His bright blue eyes searched my face. "Have you looked in your family book?"

Oh crap. "No, Tab told me a while ago to look in it. I don't have the time, Ayden." My voice had taken on a whiny tone similar to that of a five-year-old.

"I suggest you look at it. It may hold the answers you need. As for Jack, let him cool down. He will realise he needs us, and Eli may talk some sense into him. Don't worry."

"Oh, I'm not worried."

I wasn't, something else niggled at me when it came to him. I worried my lip as I hobbled into my bedroom and knelt down on the floor to look under the bed. Lying flat on my belly, I wriggled and felt the sharp sting in the lower part of my back as the wood ripped off a layer of skin. Sucking in a breath and lots of dust, I pulled the book towards me and wriggled out, reminding myself to stay low.

I coughed and sat on the bed, propping the pillows behind me. Opening the book to the first page, letters curved together. I could see the beginnings of a tree. Each name looked like a branch which then sprouted off into other branches of what I could only assume were sons and daughters. I flicked the thick smooth paper over and found blank pages, some had names on the top, ones I recognised from the family tree. I pulled my phone from my pocket.

"Cora?"

"Hey, I'm looking through my book and the pages are blank."

This statement was greeted with silence.

"I don't know why the pages are blank. I thought it might have been different for you," Tabitha murmured.

I flicked through the pages as I listened to Tabitha, and then my heart stopped. My mother's name was printed in huge bold lettering; the page was full of writing. I flicked to the next page and the one after that.

"Cora?"

I could vaguely hear Tabitha's voice above the buzzing in my ears. Underneath her name were two names. Alivia and Roane Device.

"Cora?"

"I've found her page. I've found my mother's page. But-"

"It is blank like the rest of them. I know," she said. "I've tried every spell to see if the writing would appear, to know the truth. I'm sorry, I thought-"

"Tab, shut up, I was trying to say that there are pages full of notes about my mother... it's all there."

A sob rose in my throat. "My mother's birthday was 3rd April? This is the type of thing I would like to know. Who are Alivia and Roane?"

"Oh my word, you can see all that?"

"Yes."

"Alivia and Roane were your mother's parents."

My grandparents. "What were they like?"

"Alivia was the soul of the family, small in height with bouncy grey curls; eyes the colour of olives. She was the magnetic pull of the family." I heard the love and admiration she had for them as she spoke. "They weren't killed in the witch trials, but they fled the country. Your grandmother died a hundred years ago, your grandfather passed three days later.

He couldn't live without her... Are there still blank pages in the book?"

"Yeah, someone called Katia had a name at the top and nothing written underneath."

"Katia was your mother's cousin. I wonder if only imminent family can read the pages? If this is the case, then history will be lost without those here to read it."

"I will call you back with information."

"Make sure you do."

I took a deep breath and prepared myself to read the details of my mother's life.

Cora

My eyes scanned the first page that read like a fact file.

3rd May 1587-

Element became more powerful. Fully aware of her growing power. Parents introduce Alizon to the world of witchcraft.

8th August 1588-

Small family hut was blown down due to her growing powers. Family move to Millsteeple.

12th November 1588-

Device Family and Chattox family live within the same area. Alizon befriends Anne Redfern and Tabitha Preston.

23rd July 1594-

Attends Anne Redfern's marriage to Eli Yandell.

7th November 1594-
Anne Redfern confides to Alizon that she is pregnant with Eli Yandell's baby.
She miscarries, Alizon is the only person who knows.
Anne Whittle also falls pregnant.

Oh my God. Anne had lost a baby? That meant she would have been pregnant at 11 years old. My word. People really did have babies so young. I couldn't even remember if I'd started period at that age. TMI, I know. But it was too young for such a loss. They were all so young to have to deal with what they were dealing with.

15th December 1594-
Alizon is pregnant with child.
Father is banished from the village.

My heart stopped beating as blood rushed to my head. What? But there had been no mention of a man in previous entries. I flicked back a page to make sure. There was nothing there. Why wasn't he mentioned?

10th August 1595 -
Alizon delivers Anne Whittle's son at 10:32am.
Son named Jack.
Father unknown.

23rd September 1595 -
Alizon's daughter born at 5.43 am
Alizon tells Anne Redfern the father is Nathaniel Sadler
(Commoner banished from village)

Marriage is forbidden.

Nathaniel...so that had to be my father... I pushed my head in my hands and pulled in deep breaths as I fought my body's urge to hyperventilate. I had to read on, I had to know more. I pushed the intense ache to one side and continued to read the page.

17th May 1609 -
Alizon sits with Anne Redfern who is taken ill.
Noah Thomas, the village healer, visits the Chattox home and bleeds Anne fearing an infection.
The infection persists in weakening her. Alizon stays with the Chattox family to try home remedies for Anne. Tabitha Preston is also present.

Where had it started to go wrong for the two families? Why was Anne present in this book? We'd been friends with them. More than friends. Family. I needed to know Tabitha's side of events, but I couldn't speak with her yet, I didn't know how to form the words without sounding like I was demanding the details. I sent her a text and continued reading.

29th May 1609 -
The magistrates visit Alizon regarding an incident reported to them involving Noah Thomas. Thomas claims he was bewitched. She denies all knowledge of it.

17th July 1609 -
Alizon visited by the Corenthio Coven. The matter of

bewitching was addressed and is currently under investigation. Tabitha Preston is apprehended when trying to defend Alizon.

19th June 1610 -
Alizon attacked in her home. She seeks refuge at Chattox household with her daughter.

Anger flooded me so quickly that it stole my breath and my head developed a pulse. Someone had attacked my mother? Had I been present at the time? Tabitha had been apprehended? The wind howled, responding to my emotions.

For several moments I listened to the wind, enjoying the power and the calm state it brought me. I exhaled, dispelling the turmoil swirling around in my chest. I continued scanning the page ad was disturbed as my mobile bleeped. Picking it up, I read the text from Tabitha:

The spell cast on your family book works by stating the life events of your mother; no person who tells it. It's like a kind of narrative. Also, regarding your second question, if Anne appears in your book as much as you might suggest, then she must have had a massive impact on your mother's life. That is the only thing I can deduce from what you have told me. X

Anne Redfern and Anne Whittle obviously played a big part in my mother's life. Was this part good or bad?

17th July 1611 -
Thomas, Smith and Ward families lead the villagers to the Device household.

Alizon hides her daughter and Anne's son. Alizon, Anne Whittle and Anne Redfern are immediately detained and dragged through the village.

9th November 1611 -
Anne Redfern acquitted of witchcraft charges.
Alizon took full responsibility of the charges of witchcraft towards Noah Thomas.

Oh. My. God. A fist grabbed my heart and squeezed. I had a name... but it wasn't the one everyone believed it to be. We hated each other, for no good reason. Jack and I had brought back the coven because of a belief that had been so wrong. What had we done?

11th November 1611 -
Alizon Device found guilty of witchcraft.

25th December 1611 -
Anne Redfern tried on a second charge of witchcraft.
Detained until punishment is served.

Anne was taken? Why? My mother had taken responsibility so why would they also take her? Did this mean she'd chosen to die to save her friend and her friend had died anyway?

20th August 1612-
Alizon Device and Anne Redfern hung at Lancaster Prison.

1st September 1612 -

Cora, daughter of Alizon put into the care of the Hunt family.

End of record for Alizon Device.

Jack

I stood with my hands on my hips, breathing in and out and trying to kill the anger that was burning in my gut. She knew about the dreams. How? Dropping down on to the sofa, I closed his eyes. An image of her shocked face popped into my head as my phone rang in my jeans pocket. My hand hit the wet patch, cursing, I rummaged for it. "Hello?"

"Jack, it's me, please don't hang up."

"What do you want? I don't wan-"

"Jack, have you looked in your book?"

"How did you… it doesn't matter. Why do I need to look in the book?"

"It holds all the answers. Every answer you ever wanted to know about your life, your mother Anne, and your sister. Just read the damn book... please."

The line went dead. I leant over and picked up the family book from its resting place on the end table. Something in Cora's voice made me tear through the pages in search of these so-called answers. There were pages and pages of nothing, just blank pages with names on the top. What the hell was she playing at? For one stupid moment, I thought I would get the answers I desperately needed.

Just as I was about to give up, the pages of the book started flapping crazily, each turning too fast for my eyes to follow. I moved my hands in the air, letting the book know that I surrendered, and then one name flew up at me.

Anne Whittle.

My mother.

The wavy, perfectly sculptured words, battered my heart. I turned the page and read. My eyes dropped to the bottom of the page, reading the words.

I stopped and then re-read them slowly.

A cold steel hand smashed through my rib cage and encased my heart. Before I could catch my breath, the pages moved erratically again. My sister's name, Anne Redfern, was written in huge swirly writing at the top of the page. Again, I got to work on scanning the page. My breath caught as my eyes stopped on a paragraph.

Who knew that one single paragraph could change life as I knew it?

I fumbled for my phone, my hands suddenly taking on the not so sturdy properties of jelly. I found the number of the one person who would understand what I was going through. "I need to speak to you. Meet me at the training spot." I waited a moment. "I'm sorry, Cora."

A person I'd disrespected beyond any hope of forgiveness.

What had we done?

The icy wind whipped around me as I walked. The day was

dull, cold and wet. Everything I hated. I knew that I deserved everything she was about to throw at me. I would take it without a word of complaint.

Three bullet points were etched into my brain, ones that would remain there until my dying day. In summary, Cora's mother had tried to help my family, but had only added to the death count. My mother had stepped forward and taken the blame.

There was another bullet point. A bullet point that was still too difficult to even think about at the moment. A single line that was so real, so brutally crushing, that I couldn't breathe if I thought about it.

There was a possibility we were going to die because of my stupidity. I should have read that stupid book long ago. I shouldn't have given up after looking through empty pages. I wouldn't let anything bad happen. I would repay her, I would repay her mother.

I jumped up and down on the spot trying to keep warm. I looked up at the sound of approaching footsteps. Her hands were rammed in her coat pockets as she walked closer. Her hair was stuffed snugly under a bobble hat and her cheeks were flushed a deep red from the cold.

"Hey."

With that one word I felt something click into place. After everything I'd done and said to her, she'd greeted me like nothing had happened. I deserved anger. I deserved a punch to the face. How could I really apologise for what I'd done?

"I'm so sorry. I was wrong about everything-"

"Jack, I don't want an apology. What did the book say?"

Her words weren't harsh; the wind wasn't flying around

like it usually did when she was mad. Her eyes squinted up at me; the dull light of the day hit her face.

"Actually, scrap that, I'm freezing. We can go back to mine. The folks are in so we won't be alone."

My eyebrows shot up in surprise. Why was I surprised by her kindness? Since we'd started the sessions she'd been nothing but kind. I'd made things difficult, I'd been the annoying, arsey one.

"Sure, we can go back to yours."

She knew how I felt about all of this, so we walked in silence. To have someone understand this feeling without having to describe it, it made all the difference. Any trace of anger dropped out of me, another feeling surged to the forefront, one that I'd been fighting against for weeks, those feelings hadn't felt right before but now… I sighed. I felt more at peace than I'd been in a long time. I was finally here, the moment of truth, and I was glad Cora was the one here with me.

Jack

Ayden was going to kill me the second I walked in the house because I'd made Cora walk home with a swollen ankle. I wouldn't stop him, I deserved it.

She shouted to her mother as we stepped through the front door and I felt the sharp pang of jealousy. I'd never had that. I'd never had a family who cared if I was home or not. Not until now. And I'd kept Eli at arms length…

Laura opened a door and smiled, her large hazel eyes danced as she pushed back her nutmeg curly hair. I knew Cora's mum, but I hadn't really spoken to her. And then Ayden walked in. I shifted my gaze from the intense ice blue eyes to the smiling hazel ones.

"Mum, this is Jack, you know him but I'm introducing you officially."

I managed a lame hand wave.

"Will you be staying for tea, Jack?" Cora's mother asked.

Invited for tea? Surely this woman knew what I'd done to her daughter? Cora was looking at her mum with eyes the size of saucers. A silent conversation seemed to pass between them as I awkwardly stood in silence.

"I'm sure he can stop, can't you, Jack?" Ayden slapped a heavy hand on my shoulder. It felt like a boulder had dropped there.

I swallowed. "Sure, if it's okay with Cora?"

"It's okay with Cora. Don't mind her; she has moody fits *all* the time."

"Mum!" Cora hissed and looked mortified.

Little flecks of pink brought colour to Cora's otherwise pale face. The infusion of pink made her skin look softer, less harsh.

"Thank you, Mrs Hunt."

I couldn't recall ever being invited to someone's house for tea before.

"Oh, none of this Mrs Hunt business, what is it with your friends, Cora? They persist in calling me that," she said, laughing, "It makes me feel like an old married lady, you can call me Laura."

"You don't look like an old lady, you are more of a..." Ayden whispered close to Laura's ear, drowning out the comment.

"Oh my God, please stop," Cora moaned and received a smirk from Ayden. "Jack, you can head to the living room. I'm going to get my book."

She strode up the stairs stomping on each step. She seemed annoyed at Ayden and her mother. I assumed she wasn't exactly over the moon about their relationship. Studying her, I saw the line that had formed between her eyes. No, annoyance wasn't it. I'd watched her for weeks and felt like I knew her. I felt like I could read her expressions. She wasn't mad, I realised, she was worried.

"Would you like a drink, Jack?"

I averted my gaze back to Laura and found those hazel eyes watching me in fascination. I blushed, realising I'd been watching Cora walk up the stairs. "Urrrmmmm... no, thanks, I'm okay."

"Nonsense, I'll get you something."

She walked off leaving me alone with Ayden. I glanced once in his direction but a fire within the ice of his eyes made me look down at the carpet.

Ayden grabbed the collar of my coat and pulled me forward, the brute strength nearly lifting me off the floor.

"You will be careful with her," Ayden whispered. It hadn't been a question. "You will be careful; otherwise you will have me to deal with. If you put one foot out of place, even your little toe, you won't recognise your face when I'm done with you, understood?"

I nodded.

"I assume you remember where the living room is?"

Without waiting for my reply, Ayden dropped my coat and followed Cora's mum back into the kitchen.

I'd just eaten my own heart. Jesus. But again, I'd deserved it. I walked, rather shakily, to the door and opened it. I liked the warm coffee colour splashed with beige in this room, I'd seen it before and now knew it suited Cora's mother. I sat down on the cream sofa, pushing the coffee and orange dusk coloured cushions to the side.

"Right, I have my book, obviously you didn't bring yours, but I guess we can talk about what you did read."

She dropped the heavy book on the little oak coffee table and crouched down, tucking her feet under her bum on the floor. I leaned forward to look at the book, it was blue instead of the black one I had and, as I bent down closer to Cora, I was engulfed by the sweet smell of strawberries.

"So, what did you see in your book?"

I composed myself and tried to ignore the way the strawberries made my mouth water. Where was I meant to start? Which news should I tell her first? It was all bad news anyway. The door swung open as Laura entered. Laura pushed Cora's book to one side, ignoring Cora's protesting tut, and placed the tray on the table. Several cans of pop, a plate loaded with biscuits, slices of what looked like angel cake and two packets of crisps were piled high on the tray.

"Just a little snack to keep you both fuelled," Laura said and quickly left the room.

"She calls that a snack?"

She shrugged. "Yeah, she likes to make sure people are full when they leave the house. Full... sick, same difference."

I smiled and picked up a can. Cora ripped open a bag of crisps and stuffed a handful in to her mouth whilst she mulled over a page in the book. I smirked behind the can and watched her eat. Her eyes were flicking back and forth reading.

"Can I see what entries are on your page?"

She nodded. I crouched down next to her, the smell of strawberries making me breathe in deeply. What did she use to make her smell this way? She moved the book across the little table so I could share. I looked at a blank page. "Cora, are you actually reading this?"

She swallowed the last of what she was chewing and looked at me. I couldn't judge the expression. I knew some of her expressions but not all of them, yet. I tried to hold back a smile as I spotted a lone piece of crisp hanging on for dear life at the corner of her mouth.

"Yeah, why?"

I thumbed the crisp away, and then froze. What the hell had I just done? Her eyes pinged wide in shock. I quickly pulled my hand away. I spoke to divert the attention away from what I'd just done. "I can't see anything on the page, Cora. There are no words."

She looked at me, her cheeks a deeper shade of red, her full lips open, her eyes wide. "You can't see anything?"

"There are no words."

She grabbed her phone from her pocket and dialled.

"Tab, yeah. Jack is here and we are looking at my book and he can't see anything...yeah, even though there are things in it about him..."

Cora knew things about me from her book? Why hadn't she said anything? Did she know the worst of it?

"That is what you said. So, what do we do? Okay, see you soon." She hung up and looked at me. "Jack, you need to ring your coven. Tab said she needs all of them here and then we can sort this out."

I'd had Eli's number since moving here, not once had I used it before this moment. Eli picked up on the first ring.

"Jack?" he answered, surprised.

"Eli, I'm at Cora's, I need the coven here as soon as possible."

"Clay?"

"Yeah, him too."

I still didn't want Clay to be part of the coven. It niggled at me, the way Clay looked at her. It had annoyed me before all of this…now, it bothered me.

"Right, we will be there as soon as we can."

"Okay." I clicked off the phone and picked up the can.

"Mum!"

Pop sprayed out of my mouth.

"Sorry," she apologised, smiling like butter wouldn't melt.

I mopped up most of the spill. Laura popped her head around the door. "Yes, love?"

"Tab, Ember and Jack's coven will be coming over at some point this afternoon. You may need to do more for tea."

"That's fine, love. Ayden, you need to go and get some more..." She left the room.

What was it like to have a parent who was so giving? Who altered their plans to suit their child's?

"You want to watch TV? There's no point in discussing things now and then later when everyone is here."

She understood. And I nearly sighed with relief. She wouldn't make me repeat the nightmare story more than once.

"Sure."

I knew how hard it was going to be telling everyone the news when it came to it. I wasn't ready, but having Cora here, knowing someone fully understood it, it helped.

Cora

The kitchen had never been as busy. I was almost sat on Tabitha's lap as we shared one small chair. Tabitha, Ayden, Jack and Eli were also crammed around the small table, a table that was advertised as *comfortably* allowing seating for two people. Well, it was right; there was nothing comfortable about cramming an extra three people around the pine table.

Ember was leaning against the counter. She looked out of place in her flowing copper dress with her silver hair pulled back into a high messy bun. Little wisps of hair had escaped, cupping her beautiful face. Clio and Clay were sat on pillows that my mother had taken from the front room.

We really needed to start talking, otherwise we could be here all night. I cleared my throat which made everyone look at me. "I think we should really start discussing things?"

I looked at Jack for confirmation but noticed that his face was now bloodless. His eyes were downcast. Ayden, the man of the house, walked to the cupboard, took out all the small plates and started slicing the cheesecakes. My mother loved feeding people, even during times like these when eating was the last thing on our minds. I would try to eat, for her.

"When I first looked through my family book I thought every page was empty. I haven't really looked at it since Tab first gave me it. But today I found my mum's page." The loaded plate landed in front me. I popped a strawberry in my mouth and ignored the gag reflex. I continued. "The book has all the facts about everything that happened in her life, including the witch trials. It reads a little like facts, not a story, but you can piece everything together because it appears in chronological order.

"When Jack came here, after I told him to look in his book, he tried looking at my book, but he couldn't read it. This confirms what Tab said about the book only being read by the descendants of the family. Does that sound about right, Tab?"

"Yes," Tabitha agreed.

"So, anyway, I figured if anyone has any questions after we've spoken about both our books then we can answer them the best we can from the information we have. I think Jack wants to say something first."

A fork dropped to the table. The shock on Eli's face was clear. Jack was staring at his untouched piece of cheesecake with sudden interest.

"Jack?" Eli spoke after swallowing. "Have you found something in the book?"

"I...urrrmmm. I looked at the book today, after Cora rang and said the book had all the answers, I wanted to see if it was true. I thought she was trying to mess with my head," he smiled at me and shrugged. "Sorry, but I thought you had a bigger plan to get at me... anyway, I've not really gone that far into the book before."

Tabitha tutted. I nudged her. It was hardly fair considering I hadn't looked at the book before today.

"We have been rather busy, Tabitha," he scowled. He looked at Tabitha, maintaining eye contact. "Anyway, I found out some different information than Cora. It corresponds to the same events, I'm sure. The book describes their last days, my sister's and my mum's. It also describes how Cora's mum helped." Jack stopped and looked at me now. "Cora's mum, Alizon, was the one who tried to save my sister, your wife, Eli. It said in my book that Alizon and my mother were imprisoned because they took the responsibility for the crime held against my sister. It didn't work; they stood and faced death together on that platform."

I grabbed Tabitha's hand. I knew this information already. It was also written in my book, but to hear someone else say it meant that it was real.

"Jack, what are you talking about?" Eli asked, looking rather perplexed.

I looked between Jack and Eli. Everyone else in the room was holding their breath or, if you were Ayden, still eating the cheesecake.

"Eli, it means that our covens are not enemies. It means that we should be friends, our families were friends. How can we be enemies when Cora's mother died to save her friend? She sacrificed a life of her own, a life with her daughter, because she loved her friend so much. My mother also gave her life to save her daughter. God, it's so messed up," he sighed, pushing his hand through his hair as he looked intently at Eli. "Eli, how did you come to the conclusion that we hated one another when we were friends before?"

Eli continued to shake his head back and forth. It looked like he didn't want to accept any of this. Eli had spent his entire life hating me, having someone to blame for the death of his wife, his mother-in-law. Where was his outlet now? I could understand his confusion, his hesitancy in believing this.

"There had to be a reason why she died, my wife... my beautiful wife. She was not a killer." He slammed his fist on the table. "But Anne was taken, taken to be killed... only Alizon could do that. Only Alizon could have her outcast as a witch." Eli's body was shaking. "I thought... I thought she had told the magistrates that Anne was also guilty. We tried to hide, it was Christmas day when they came and took Anne back."

There was silence in the room. Clay and Clio quietly sat, looking at the faces sitting around the table. Ayden, who'd finally stopped filling his mouth, appeared to be shocked. Ember's feelings remained under lock and key. Tabitha's face was ashen, the deep leaf green of her eyes standing out on her ghost white face. She squeezed Tabitha's hand harder.

"But when you both met, the hatred, the power within you was ignited. Why?" Tabitha asked.

"I don't believe it was hatred that we felt," I explained. "I've thought about it this afternoon. There's a fine line when it comes to emotions, and clearly pain and confusion blur these lines significantly. I can't understand why I felt so angry all the time; I can only guess that our bodies were trying to warn us. You suppressed our power and I believe because of this when we met, this triggered our elements."

"Can you explain the anger?" Clay asked.

"We were told we were the reason our families had died… it was an anger that was passed down to us."

Tabitha nodded. "We understood it to be anger; we believed the families were to blame for the other's deaths."

"I'll admit that I felt angrier when I was told that Cora's mother was responsible for my mother's death. Obviously, now we know that isn't right."

Now that I knew the facts it felt wrong to hate him. There was silence as everyone tried to digest this information.

"How can we know if you aren't lying?" Eli stood up, his body shaking with emotion.

I flinched away, if he hit me I wouldn't react. He was grieving. I understood his mixed emotions.

"Eli, I understand this is difficult-" Tabitha began.

"Difficult! I lost my wife. The woman I will love until my dying day. I lost my whole family, what did you lose? A bloody *friend*!"

Tabitha gasped, her body sagging. I was about to stand up but Jack beat me to it.

"Hang on a damn minute!" Jack shouted. "I've seen what happened, the flashbacks tell me enough to understand why you've reacted the way you have, but you do not-"

"What flashbacks?" Eli interrupted, confusion forcing his brows together as lines hounded his forehead.

"I'm sorry I didn't tell you, I've not been handling them very well, obviously. In these nightmares I've witnessed everything. You told me what happened on that day so I know what I'm seeing is the final steps of their lives. My mother or my sister, I'm not too sure as I see it and feel it through their eyes."

"Why didn't you say anything?"

"It was too much for me to handle. What with everything else I just didn't know where to begin. Cora knows. She's been having them too."

I sensed everyone's attention latch onto me, but I continued to watch Jack and Eli.

"She could be lying. This could all be some part of her plan."

"Eli, shut up for just one damn minute!"

I was shocked for a second time. Eli put his head into his hands, trying to muffle the beginning of his sobs. Tabitha gripped my hand tighter.

"I'm the High Priest and you will believe what I say. The flashbacks, the facts, they are true, they match. Now, I can go get the book if you want me to and I can read the bloody exact date and paragraph. In fact, Cora and I could read it together, would you believe us then? The past cannot be changed no matter how much we want it to. I'm so sorry for what has happened, but we now have a chance to change our future and we have to change it together, like our families would have wanted."

Tension hung heavily in the room.

"Eli, today we accept Cora's coven as our allies, in fact we must treat them as family. From day one I set out to hurt Cora, I've treated you so awfully." He turned towards me. His eyes pleaded. "I'm so sorry."

There was nothing to forgive, I hadn't acted innocently either. "I forgive you. I hope you forgive me?"

"There's nothing to forgive. Everything that has happened is my fault."

"No, *you* didn't do it, Jack. Someone else did it. So, who did it? Who caused their deaths, who caused the breakdown of these two families?" Ember asked.

"Thomas. Noah Thomas," Jack announced.

I heard sharp intakes of breath. Noah Thomas had been the village healer. He'd started the rumours within the village. It was the answer each of them had waited centuries for.

"That bastard!" Ayden roared.

"I can't believe it, why?" Tabitha whispered.

"People didn't like those who were different…" Ember murmured.

Jack coughed, clearing his throat like he was ready to say more. "Eli, there is something else that the book mentioned, something that I feel you should know, it shouldn't be kept from you."

"What?" Eli asked, his voice was raspy with emotion.

"I don't know if I can say it..." Jack's voice broke.

Jack was hurting, and I found myself hurting with him. To show such vulnerability, it pulled at my heart.

"What is it?" Eli cried impatiently.

"Your wife... my sister died..."

"Yes? Jack, tell me!"

Jack opened his mouth and then dropped his head as the sobs erupted.

I patted Tabitha's hand and moved out of the small cramped space. I approached Jack who was lost in his own personal hell. His head hung down as if he was ashamed of his tears. I took his hand which was warm and soft and squeezed it, trying to give him some comfort.

"Jack, would you like me to say it? You could tell me and I could say it for you."

He squeezed my hand back. "No, I need to do this."

I held his hand whilst he took a deep shuddering breath and looked at Eli. I braced.

"Anne was pregnant. She was carrying your baby when she died. I think that's why Alizon tried to save her, why my mother stepped forward as well."

Tears pricked my eyes. Ember moved to Tabitha who was now crying. Jack had his head bowed again; his eyes were closed as glistening tears pushed through the sweep of his thick lashes and then slid down his face.

Eli had tears running down his face. My entire chest ached; my throat was on fire as I tried to stop the onslaught of tears. Eli slumped against Jack. Jack's hand jarred in mine and then let go.

"Eli...?" Jack's muffled voice came from underneath Eli.

Eli cried out and fell to his knees, taking Jack with him. Jack held onto his brother. My hand brushed his shoulder as I nodded towards the living room. They needed time alone.

"I can't believe it," Clio whispered as I took a seat next to Tabitha on the sofa.

"It doesn't seem real," Ayden said sadly.

"Oh my word!" Tabitha exclaimed.

"What, what is it?" I jerked.

"Jack. I know why. What a big mistake we made... it never... I didn't know."

"Tab, you're speaking in riddles."

"Jack, he was placed with the Thomas family."

"Oh God," Ayden whispered.

"Will someone tell me what this means?" I demanded.

"Thomas, Cora. Jack used to live with them, they must be descendants. It must have been a weak family tie when I placed him. I researched; I would never do that intentionally... I just wanted you both to be safe."

I didn't know much about his family, but Jack had never stood a chance of having a normal upbringing, a normal family if that family had a hatred for witchcraft.

"We don't tell him," I pleaded with them, making the decision there and then to at least keep this from him.

I looked around the room. "Tab, we don't tell Jack, agreed?"

"Don't tell me what?"

I turned to see Jack, red eyed and puffy faced, stood in the doorway looking at me.

Cora

"Tell me what?" he repeated.

"Jack, I... we..." I stammered, unable to find the right words.

"No, Cora, I will take care of this. Jack, the Thomas family that I placed you with, it was the-"

"Same family who were related to Noah Thomas. I know," Jack interjected.

Tabitha's mouth moved but no words came out.

"I kind of put two and two together. It wasn't your fault, you didn't know."

"I'm still very sorry."

"You have nothing to be sorry for, you didn't know."

His ability to forgive Tabitha made my heart melt a little.

"I should be sorry, Tabitha. I've often acted like an idiot, but in the past few months I took my stupidity to a whole new level. Without you and Eli, I would be dead, Cora would be dead. You did a wonderful thing by sacrificing your right to a life in making sure we were cared for."

"Thank you, Jack, that is very understanding of you."

"No, thank you."

"Right, I must be going," Ember announced.

Everyone else stood, making their excuses until there was just Ayden, Jack and myself left in the room.

"I will see you kids later." Ayden left in search of my mother.

"I better get going too. Eli still wants to speak with me. I guess I will see you tomorrow?" he asked.

"You know where I am if you need to talk."

"I can't tell you how much that means," he sighed.

I watched Jack leave. My heart felt like it had swollen in size and no longer fit inside my chest. My phone vibrated. Pulling it out, I groaned.

"Clay."

"Cora, we still need to talk," Clay demanded.

"No, we don't."

"We had something, or the beginnings of something. We could continue with that."

"We didn't have something, Clay. It was fun. That was it, and we don't really know anything about each other."

"That's the whole point of dating…"

"We can be friends," I insisted.

"I don't want friends."

"That's all I can give you. Goodnight."

After everything that had happened, I knew that the thing with Clay had been a bit of flirtatious fun. I'd enjoyed the attention, anyone would have. Now, I knew that he obviously understood it to be something more, yet I hadn't done anything to make him believe that. He needed to move on.

I dragged myself to bed. This day needed to go away. I

wasn't sure tomorrow would be happier. We all knew what had happened, and now we knew what would happen. A repeat of 1612 was heading our way, and we were powerless to stop it.

Cora

I was glad to see the back of some very busy weeks of work and training, and I was feeling every bit as tired as I looked. I couldn't believe that there was only two weeks to go until Christmas.

I did like one thing about Christmas, the shop. The little semi-circle display in front of the window housed two medium sized Christmas trees, sweet pine was now the smell I loved. Deep purple organza ribbon cascaded from the top of the trees, swirling around several branches and dipping to the floor. Little baubles in the shape of witch hats, brooms, cats, and wands were strategically placed around the tree. They were for sale in the shop. Soft emerald coloured presents covered the wooden floor, piled precariously under each tree. The bell jingled above the door.

"Hey."

I turned at the sound of Jack's voice. He dropped his head to one side and studied me, which made me pat my hair self-consciously. Why did he have to study me like that? A smile was already settled on his Cupid's bow lips. His smile expanded to a grin which pushed the two dimples deeper into his cheeks. I felt *tiny* little flutters in my chest, but I brushed aside the feeling.

"Hey," I said, smiling back at him.

Without another word, he grabbed the duster and started working. He'd done this every day since the revelation, so he knew what he was doing. I heard the approaching footsteps of Tabitha up the fake staircase with three cups of hot chocolate. Of course she also knew that Jack would be here.

"Hot chocolate is ready when you want it." She placed two cups on the table and wondered around the shop sipping from her own.

She walked around me, switching off the Christmas tree lights and turning the sign on the door to *closed*.

"How is the levitating going, Jack?"

"It's going pretty well." Jack stopped dusting and smiled at her. "I can now lift Cora, Laura and Ayden around... what was the height again?"

"It was about thirty feet, wasn't it?"

It was an experience I didn't want to relive. I nodded.

"Yeah, it was amazing. I can feel it getting stronger. I'm going up myself next time and then I will grab everyone else."

"Good, just let me know when you need me for a guinea pig."

"Will do."

"Right, well, I have business to attend to."

What business? I had a horrifying feeling that Tabitha was purposefully leaving us alone.

"I will be upstairs if you need me." Tabitha walked up to her flat above the shop.

Jack took the duster and the brush he had been using back to the storage room. I breathed deeply. Things were changing between us. I could feel it and I didn't know what the hell to do about it. My feelings had gone from intensely hating him to intensely... what? God. I needed to stop overthinking it.

"So, what are we doing tonight? Training?" I asked.

I watched him walk across the shop towards me. His jumper, a coral blue, sat snug against his toned, lean body. He looked different today, but I couldn't put my finger on why he did. I watched as he lifted his hand to sweep his hair to one side. And then his eyes locked on mine. I swallowed, feeling too hot all of a sudden.

Things were definitely changing.

"I thought we could give training a miss tonight." He sat casually next to me and picked up his mug. He blew on it to cool it down and lifted it to his lips.

"Here let me."

I knew that he didn't like his chocolate too hot. I moved my hand and placed it around his cup, our fingers touched, sending sparks of electricity running down my spine. His eyes were focused on me.

"Cheers."

"So, is it a night of freedom then?" I smiled, although my insides squirmed nervously from the contact.

"Well, I was thinking we could just... hang out?"

A little flutter flapped in my chest. "Urrrmmm... what do you want to do?"

He shrugged his shoulders. "I guess we could go to my place and just chill. I know Ayden will be at yours and he still gives me the creeps. That man hates me, and I haven't got a clue what I need to do to prove myself to him."

"Ayden's just protective. He doesn't want to see me hurt, that's all."

"I won't hurt you, Cora," he said, his eyes blazing with the truth of it.

My heart banged hard, stopped, and then started again. "I know that. He will see that eventually, you're no longer the Jack we first met."

"Yeah," he sighed. "It takes a while to forgive, I can understand that. I like that you trust me now."

"We trust each other."

"Yes, we do." His jaw tightened and pulsed as he looked intently at me. "Well, we could watch something on the box and get some food...I mean... only if you want to?"

Why was I making a big deal out of this? We were friends, and I enjoyed his company. He was funny, without really knowing it; he could pull the best facial expressions that would make me laugh at inappropriate times. Tabitha had been very unhappy on numerous occasions during training sessions. He was caring, even though he wouldn't admit it. He was always consciously aware of people's feelings and how they were during training sessions. More often than not he would place his jacket around my shoulders when it was cold.

I was so glad I'd been able to see this side of him and not the moody, hurtful side. He wasn't really that person.

He was staring at me now, his brow furrowed together in concentration or confusion. Had I been quiet too long? "Sure. I'll just call Mum and let her know that I won't be heading home straight from work."

I stood too quickly, and awkwardly, and moved towards

the little back room. I tapped my foot as I listened to the ringing.

"Hello?"

"Hey Mum, just wanted to let you know I'm going to Jack's for tea."

"Oh, how *lovely*..."

"Mum," I sighed

"What time should I expect you back? Oh wait... you *are* coming back, aren't you? Not *spending* the night."

"Oh, good God, Mum!" I spluttered and listened to her laughter. "Mum, you're the adult and you've just jokingly asked your daughter if she was staying the night at a man's house. Do you know how wrong that sounds?"

She continued to laugh. "Okay, I'm putting my parent hat on now. Don't be home too late. Have fun."

My stomach did somersaults as I approached Jack.

"Mum has okayed it."

"Eli, will be out, he just text me. Clay and Clio will also be out."

We would be alone? Oh lord. Now that made it ten times worse.

I gathered my things as Jack pulled on his coat, hat, scarf and gloves. It was cold out now and I really wished for a white Christmas morning. The icy wind, sleet and occasional snow had not been enough to actually sit on the pavements and roads to make it look pretty and idyllic. I could change the cold, but Tabitha had warned me against it. Apparently, it wasn't great to change the weather at will.

As we walked, I was more aware of Jack next to me, where his hand was in relation to mine. Butterflies exploded in my chest and made it difficult to breathe. I coughed. Jack looked at me, which ensured my cheeks exploded from embarrassment.

Great.

Jack smiled and then diverted his attention to his feet. I stuffed my hands into my pockets and forced myself to ignore my thoughts and focus on the pretty surroundings.

Jack

I opened the door and stood aside, letting her walk in first. Was I having the beginnings of a heart attack? My heart was palpitating like mad. It had been happening a lot recently. "Do you want a drink? Or shall we pick the food first?" I asked.

"I guess we could pick food and then we could watch something..."

It wasn't usually this awkward between us, and Cora had definitely acted different on the walk home. Our friendship was the most natural thing in the world, other than today where there was a weird vibe between us. I felt more at peace, more at ease when I was with her. I felt like I'd known her a lifetime, which I had, but I couldn't remember it.

I opened several cupboards and noticed that each of them was filling nicely with dust. Cursing, I kicked the lower cupboard. Eli seriously needed to go food shopping. I pulled my mobile out of my pocket and rang the only option I had left.

As I pushed open the door to the living room, I found Cora sat on the sofa with her legs curled to the side and her sunshine socked feet tucked under her bum whilst she was flicking through the channels.

Something tugged in my chest.

"So, tea is sorted. What are we watching?" I rubbed my chest.

"Well, we have *Shark Attack,* or there is a comedy that starts in half an hour?"

"What's the comedy?" I pulled off my trainers and sat next to her.

Strawberries, sweet and fruity, swamped me, taking away any sort of normal thought process. I took a deep breath and fought for concentration.

"It's about some detective that gets shot and then he is partnered with a man who is scared of bullets. Why would he become a cop? Maybe that is the comedy bit." She shrugged.

"It sounds good though."

"So, what's for tea?"

She pulled her hair free of its bobble and shook it. Her thick brown hair fell like liquid around her shoulders as she forced her hands through it, brushing out the kinks with her fingers. My fingers twitched and I felt the urge to push my hands through the soft, melted chocolate. The bobble hung out of her mouth, her lips sealed around it, holding it while she got her hair ready.

I was staring at her.

And now she stared at me.

My pulse quickened but I couldn't move my eyes. I tracked the contours of her face, the sweep of her long dark lashes that framed inviting eyes. The warm raspberry in her cheeks made her face glow.

Shit.

I focused on the television.

"Jack...?"

"Mmm..."

"Tea... what's for tea?"

The knock on the front door made me jump. I smiled and stood up. "Tea is here."

"What?"

I made my way to the front door and knew that she followed, she hated not knowing what was happening. I opened the door and found Ryan holding two large newspaper packages with a huge smile on his face. He was still wearing his apron that was smeared with chip fat.

"Thanks Ryan, what do I owe you?"

"Nothing man, it's on the house," he said, winking.

"I'll speak with you later." I started to close the door aware that Ryan had seen Cora behind me.

"Don't do anything I wouldn't do." Ryan whistled.

I hurriedly shut the door. Damn it.

"So, that's what you call tea," she teased.

"These are the best chips around, I'll have you know"

"They are the only chips around,' she laughed.

That was true, but still. She followed me into the kitchen and hoisted herself up on the counter. I put the bag down and fumbled with the stack of plates. I heard the rustling of paper and looked around the open cupboard door to see that she had a chip mid-way to her mouth.

"You know, if you keep gobbling them like that you won't have any to put on your plate."

She stopped chewing as she cocked her head to the side. "I don't gobble..."

I dropped an even amount of chips on both plates, handed

her the salt, vinegar and utensils and headed back towards the room. "Sure you do."

I liked the way the heat in her cheeks deepened.

"So," I said, popping a very salty, vinegary chip into my mouth. "Have you done your Christmas shopping yet?"

"Uff! No, I haven't! I'll have to get it all online now and Ayden is constantly hogging the laptop. It's becoming a bit of a nightmare. Have you got anything yet?"

"I have actually!" I admitted smugly. The scowl on her face made the ache in my chest tighten. "Hey, don't hate me because I've found some time. I've found one great present for Eli, you've seen the kitchen so you know he is obsessed with gadgets."

"Yeah, you have the Content Identification Device, and that's why we have to wear those weird things during training."

Eli had produced tiny little ear gadgets so we could talk to each other as a team and attack as one unit. Tabitha and Eli stalked the side lines barking instructions into our ears. They were annoying, but probably important too.

"I've got him a watch that practically does everything but tell the time."

"What's everything? Does it tell him that he has a stupid kid brother?" she teased and then squealed when I threw a chip at her.

"The watch wouldn't tell him that, it doesn't tell lies." I enjoyed the sound of her laughter.

I leant over and wiped the vinegar from her face. It was an action I hadn't thought about, but she sucked in breath, or had I imagined that?

I tried to ignore the way she looked at me. "Do you want to buy some things before the film starts?"

"Yeah, that would be great, but no peeking."

I pulled the laptop from under the sofa and passed it to Cora. If I wasn't allowed to peek did that mean she was going to buy me something? Should I buy her something? There should be a rule book for this. I had never bought Christmas presents until I'd moved in with Eli.

I watched as she sat with the laptop balanced on her lap. Her face was a picture of concentration as her teeth pulled at her lower lip and nibbled. My heart jack hammered as my mind raced. "I'll just go and wash up."

"I will give you a shout when I'm done and when the film comes on. Thanks."

"Not a problem." I needed a drink anyway because my mouth suddenly felt dry.

The plates didn't take more than two minutes to wash but I waited in the kitchen, messing with Eli's little gadgets. It was a big no-no to mess with Eli's gadgets.

"Hey, little bro. What you up to?" Eli called as he walked into the kitchen, lugging shopping bags.

I quickly pulled my hand back, trying to look innocent. "We're waiting for a film to start. You finally got food?"

"Yeah, the cupboards were looking at bit bare." Eli dropped the heavy bags to the floor.

"You're telling me. I got some food from the local chippy, thanks to Ryan. You can watch the film if you like?"

"No, no. I will leave you to it," he winked.

"Eli!" I sighed and pushed him. It didn't help that I was teased over spending time with her.

But I couldn't deny my reaction to her. Because she made me react. I felt things I hadn't felt before.

"Jack, I'm finished, and the film is just about to start," Cora shouted.

"Hello, Cora!" Eli shouted whilst stood on his tiptoes. Did he think that would elevate his voice in some way?

"Hey, Eli," she called back.

"Speak later," I muttered, trying to ignore yet another wink.

"Do you need a drink before the film starts?" I asked as I stepped into the room.

"Nope. I'm good."

The opening credits started rolling accompanied by a high screeching rock ballad. I didn't have a clue who was in the film, or what had happened so far. My attention was focused on how close her hand was to mine. I glanced at her face which was animated with all sorts of emotions as she watched. She licked her lips and smiled. I clenched my fist and stuffed it roughly in my pocket. This was going to be a very long film.

Jack

I trudged towards the shop, sinking into my coat and scarf to escape the artic conditions. I reached the cluster of houses and could see that the shop was crowded. A little mini bus was parked outside and people were either boarding or dawdling near the window talking in little groups.

Cora was stood in the middle of a group of women and a lone man, the sight of her created a warmth that flooded my chest. She was wearing her grey coat that hugged the slim lines of her body, but her hair was pulled back into her usual ponytail exposing her neck to the cold wind.

Gritting my teeth, I walked towards her already taking off my scarf. I stepped alongside Cora as she said her goodbyes and promised more goody bags for their next visit. She turned towards me.

"You had a good day's business?" I asked as I wrapped the scarf around her exposed neck. I tried to ignore the way my fingers brushed against her soft skin.

"Yeah. That was our second mini bus today. I've given out over seventy goody bags, I made up ninety this morning, I very nearly didn't but I'm glad I did. What have you been doing?"

We stepped inside the shop as she pulled off her coat, revealing a teal coloured jumper that highlighted her curves. She kept my scarf on.

"I've practised but I still don't feel confident enough to get everyone up in the air. What if I drop someone under the pressure?"

"Jack, you won't drop anyone, I know because *you* won't allow it."

"How can you be so...so *calm* about this?"

"I'm not calm. I'm anything but." She put her hand in mine.

The feel of her hand sent electricity buzzing through my body. I fought to concentrate on what she was saying.

"If I think about it, I could throw up." I pulled a face and stepped back, but I didn't let go of her hand.

She laughed. "Seriously, I'm scared, but what good would it do to sit here and wait for them to come? We have to do something. We can't just give up, not after everything we've been through."

"Jack, how are you today?"

I reluctantly pulled my gaze away from Cora's face to Tabitha. Cora let go of my hand.

"Fine, Tabitha. I was just telling Cora that I've been practising today but I still don't feel confident enough." I tried not to feel dejected that Cora had dropped my hand.

Tabitha wrapped her arm around Cora's shoulder affectionately. "Well, Jack." Tabitha's leaf green eyes danced. "It's a good job we're having a practice session tomorrow."

"Are you being serious?" Cora said looking sternly at Tabitha.

"Yes, I'm being *serious*. Why?"

"Tab, it's Christmas Eve tomorrow, which means it's Christmas on Sunday. *Christmas*... does that mean anything to you?"

Tabitha laughed, grabbing Cora tighter and crushing her into her body. "Well, we could do it tonight in the freezing winds." Tabitha paused, brushing some of Cora's hair behind her ear. "We could make a day of it tomorrow and then leave training until the New Year?"

"But-"

"Cora, sshhhh," I interrupted. "We can do tomorrow."

I grinned at Cora who stuck her tongue out at me.

"Fine!" Cora snapped. "We can do tomorrow but, Tab, no bruises, no aches and no pains." Cora listed them off on her fingers. "I want to be able to rip open my presents without groaning in pain." She playfully poked Tabitha in the ribs.

"I can't stop a few bumps and bruises, plus, you give out as much as you get."

I was about to agree with Tabitha but the hard look from Cora told me to keep my mouth shut.

"Jack, stop smiling," she chuckled, playfully hitting me.

"Right, I will leave you both."

"What time are we meeting tomorrow?" Cora asked Tabitha.

"That's up to you; we can do whatever time you want."

Cora looked at me, waiting for an answer. I found myself engrossed by her face. My fingers itched to trace the lines, to brush her bottom lip with my thumb. I shrugged, having lost the use of my tongue.

"I guess we could make it early-ish so then we have the rest of the day to do what we want?" Cora suggested.

I nodded.

"That's fine, but what time is early-ish?" Tabitha prompted.

Cora looked at me again. My tongue had tied itself into knots.

"10 a.m.? Then we can train and hopefully still have some of the day left. At least it should be warmer than early morning temperatures."

"Let the two covens know," Tabitha said and smiled. "Have a lovely night. Jack, see you tomorrow." She kissed Cora on the cheek and squeezed my arm.

"So, what do you fancy doing tonight?" I asked. At least my voice seemed to be back to normal. My heart wasn't.

"Oh, so he has a voice!" she remarked. "I don't know. I guess we could just hang out. I'm really tired after the hectic week, do you mind coming to mine?"

"No problem."

I hissed in frustration when a freezing gust of wind slapped my face. The street was deserted. Little lights flickered from within the houses as the street lights cast a mournful glow along the pavements. Nobody in their right mind would come out in this weather. "Can't you control this bloody wind or something?"

"I can, but I don't want to," she replied and grinned.

I groaned as we took a quick left onto her drive. Laura's

car was sat in front of the garage which meant she was home and wherever Laura was, Ayden was sure to be.

I liked Laura Hunt. She was what I considered to be the typical mum. She had a friendly smile. She never shouted. She fed you when you were hungry. She had this infectious laughter which made Cora laugh. It was something I always loved to see and hear.

I hadn't grown up with laughter.

Maggie Thomas, my mother for all intents and purposes, was tall, skinny and incredibly pale. Her thinning, ginger hair was always pulled back into a bun on the highest point of her head, forcing her face to look pinched and harsh. Her blue eyes were cold, dark pools of nothingness. When I thought about it now, I couldn't actually remember seeing those thin lines you call lips ever breaking into a smile. She was a hard, stern, law abiding woman.

I was everything she hated.

Victor Thomas was a rotund man with eyes the colour of rusty iron that sat too small on his big face. His receding salt and pepper hair had always been combed in odd places to hide the ever-growing bald patches. Victor worked in construction, the job keeping him from home six days a week. For six whole days I'd lived a somewhat normal life, if normal meant not speaking to your mother, eating food when she was out and living in your bedroom.

The trouble in my life reared its ugly head on Sundays.

It was demanded of me that I sit with the *family* during Sunday dinner. For two hours I was forced to sit down at a table in silence. One murmur from me would lead to a severe beating. I'd had been my father's punching bag for years. Eli hadn't known, but once he'd found out he'd taken the initiative to bring me back to Millsteeple.

The day that changed my life happened on a Wednesday. As I'd walked down the street, I'd been given a sheet of paper. The leaflet had stated there was a room to rent, the rent depending on the income of the person. I had thought it was slightly strange that someone would be willing to let someone live with them rent free if they didn't have any income.

I hadn't known, but the man had only handed one leaflet out that day. That man had been Eli. Without Eli's help I wouldn't have left the Thomas family.

I wouldn't have met Cora.

"Jack, how lovely to see you again!" Laura entered the hall from the kitchen.

I grinned at her, I couldn't help myself where Laura was concerned.

"Mum, you only saw him yesterday and the day before that and the day before that," Cora grinned as her mother hugged her and then hugged me.

"Are you trying to say that you're sick of seeing me?"

"No, I'm just... it's..." Cora blushed and shrugged off her coat, ignoring her mother's quizzical glance.

Ayden entered the hall from the living room.

"Ayden, there's a training session tomorrow at 10 a.m. I couldn't make my mind up about the time and Jack couldn't make a decision, so I did."

"You're stopping for tea," Laura said.

Cora grabbed my hand and led me to the kitchen. My heart stumbled as I enjoyed the feel and look of our hands entwined. Did she know what she did to me? How she made me feel? How would I ever tell her?

Jack

I trudged through the woods listening to the wet crunch of thawing leaves and twigs beneath my feet. I could hear Tabitha and Eli talking; I just couldn't see them yet. Laughter filled the air around me. I stalled, I knew the laugh.

Five Ayden's surrounded me. I didn't want to admit it, but the man still made me nervous.

"Nice of you to join us, Jack, we've been training for a while now," Ayden remarked, flashing his trademark smile.

To any other it may have sounded like a playful joke but to me, it was criticism. "It's not even ten yet, Ayden, so technically, I'm early," I replied smartly.

The five Ayden's didn't say anything, they turned and walked in another direction. I entered the circle, heading towards Eli and Tabitha. The training ground, otherwise known as the woods between our houses, had been purposely built for us.

Eli had put several axes to work which had chopped away at the trees and bushes. Clio had shaken the ground, thus opening up the mess that Eli had created, allowing Tabitha to ignite everything. For an hour or so the circle was a graveyard. The smouldering remains hadn't smelt nice but they'd made great obstacles. Well, I'd thought so, Tabitha hadn't.

The circle had remained that way until Clay had washed all of it away creating some sort of barrier around the circle. Now we had a huge circle in which we could train openly without anyone seeing us.

"Hey little brother, you made it," Eli announced.

What was *with* everyone today, I wasn't late. "Hey," I said, shoving the irritation away. "So, what's happening?"

"Cora, you have five minutes," Tabitha whispered.

I looked around just to make sure she wasn't in the circle. She wasn't there, I would have known. Who was she training with? Ayden? Cora's scream echoed around us. A primitive growl rumbled in my throat. I surged forward but before I could do anything, a hand clasped tightly onto my arm and I was quickly jerked back.

I whipped my head around to see what was obstructing me. Tabitha held my arm. She shook her head, it was all it took; not a single word was spoken. Tabitha projected enough conversation in that one look. I stepped back but only because I could still feel Tabitha's fingerprints engraved into my skin. If I heard another scream I would go. No matter what.

Seconds passed but it felt like hours before I finally heard the crashing. The ground trembled beneath my feet. A second later, Cora came bounding out of the woods and into the circle. I felt some of the tension lift, but I couldn't see who she was with.

She stood with her hands by her sides, her posture telling me she was ready for something to happen. Where the hell was her coat? Her hair, having fallen free of its bobble, was streaked across her face. She was focused on a part of the wooded area, the part she'd just come from. I started unbuttoning my coat and then a tidal wave of water hurtled from within the depths of the woods, bashing against the barrier that Cora held.

It was truly amazing to see. She stood, a woman on her own, fighting off tonnes of pressure. She must be freezing. I'd been hit by Clay's water and knew how cold it was. The wave battered harder against her hold, I could see that she was slipping. The mini tornado that swirled around her was slowing down.

I ran, not caring if Tabitha tried to stop me. She didn't. Cora's right foot slipped but she realigned herself so she could control her shield. The strain clearly showed on her face, her lips were set in a tight line, her brow was furrowed. A hard hit of water took my feet from under me; it felt like a speeding car smashing into my legs.

"Cora, let me in!" I shouted above the roar of the wind as I scrambled back to my feet.

There was no way I was going to step into a tornado.

I felt the energy move, sucking me in rather than pushing me out. Standing behind her, I placed my arms around her waist. She was drenched, her clothes dripping with water as her body shook uncontrollably. I swallowed a growl and held her tighter. I moved my mouth closer to her ear, trying to ignore the smell of her, the feel of her body so close to mine.

"Cora, work with me," I whispered.

She gave a slight nod of her head as her hands pulled me closer. Resting my chin on her shoulder with my cheek touching hers, it distracted me for a second. Taking a deep breath, I pulled my element and felt the two join. As it joined the circling tornado became an iron wall, forcing the water into a vertical position. It stood between Clay and us like a river trapped between two invisible beds. It sloshed around within the tight constrictions.

"Now." My lip brushed against her ear.

I could feel the energy it took for her to push with me. The water roared in anger as it flew towards Clay, encasing him.

Cora's breathing was raspy; I could already hear the beginnings of a cold leeching its way into her chest. I held her tighter, trying to give her my warmth. The wind moved around us, waiting for its next command. I caught a blur of blonde to my left. I turned us both as Clay came bounding out of the woods, firing balls of water.

I worked with Cora and lifted Clay off his feet. Using her power wasn't the same as using mine. With hers you could see the energy cast. The lines of the wind that should be invisible to any normal person weren't invisible to me. The water was still spewing out of his hands, cascading down like a waterfall as he floated in mid-air. Cora took in a deep breath which made her back brush against my body, sending a shiver down my spine.

Clay flew higher and stopped. All too quickly he crashed down his own waterfall and landed heavily on the floor.

"Enough!" Tabitha shouted.

Clay stood up and snarled at us, and I knew it wasn't the end. I braced, the water whipped against our combined elements, knocking the breath out of us. With a growl, I lifted Clay off the floor pushing him higher and further away from us.

"I said enough!!" Tabitha instructed, striding closer.

The wind fluttered and then died. I couldn't bring myself

to move away from her. "She needs warmth!" I called as I half turned towards where everyone stood.

Dragging off my coat took an important second. I tucked it around her and instantly pulled her back into my body. Lifting her chin so I could look into her eyes, I moved her hair out of the way. Her face was pale, her lips blue.

"You okay?"

"Yeah, jus...just... co...col...cold," she stuttered.

She was breathing deeply, trying to calm the chattering of her teeth. I looked around, still holding Cora tightly to me. Ayden and Clio were stood at the far end of the circle. I had the satisfaction of watching the realisation hit Ayden as he pieced together what had happened. This was definitely a training session that had gone wrong. I couldn't wait to see what Ayden did to Clay.

Tabitha was talking to Clay who stood looking at the floor like a child would when they'd been told off. What had Clay wanted to achieve by hurting Cora?

"Jack, no," she spoke softly.

"He took things too far," I snarled.

"We were training, it had to be realistic." She lifted her head so she was looking at me. I fought the urge to scoop her up and take her home.

"They could do far worse to me," she sighed into my chest.

They would have to kill me first.

"Cora, I'm sorry!" Clay shouted from where he was stood.

"It is fine, Clay," Cora said, though her words were muffled by my shirt.

"I will ring you tonight."

He would what? Were they talking again? I ignored the disappointment that dropped heavily inside of me.

"Jack, wait here a moment, we'll be back." Tabitha slid her arm around Cora, taking her away from me. The cold instantly hit where she'd been.

"We need to regroup, Jack," Eli spoke, placing a hand on my shoulder.

I was led towards the middle of the circle. Ayden and Clio followed. I walked faster, all the more eager to get to Clay.

"Clay, that got out of hand, you *do not* get back up and attack. Tabitha declared it was enough and don't pretend you didn't hear her!" Eli shouted.

I clenched his fists.

"Jack, this is not the time or the place. As much as I would love to see your fist connect with his face, we have more work to do," Ayden growled.

"Right," Eli said, ignoring the tension. "Tabitha and I have arranged the teams that we are going to work in."

"We're working as a team? I thought we were doing one on one?" I asked.

"Yeah, well, you just worked one on one with Cora so what difference does it make?" Eli smiled.

I caught the disgusted look on Clay's face. So that was it? The second attack had been aimed at me. Clay was jealous. I grinned as Clay clenched his fists.

"The first team consists of Cora, Jack, Clay and Ember. The second team is myself, Tabitha, Ayden and Clio."

I tried to focus, when we went up against the Corenthio Coven we would need to work together.

"We can begin!" Tabitha called.

I turned. There was some colour in her cheeks, probably

thanks to Tabitha who could warm anyone in a second. She was also wearing new clothes with her now dry hair pulled back into a ponytail.

"Cora, I'm so sorry."

I whirled around and glared at him. If he took a step towards her, just one tiny step, I would have him.

"Clay, it's fine, really. No big deal."

Cora made her way over to me and stood at my side.

"Right, here you go." Eli handed out the little ear pieces. "I have adjusted these as I know we were having some difficulties with hearing and buzzing last time. All being well, they will work."

"Now, you must work together in your teams," Tabitha instructed, looking at Clay and then focusing her steely gaze on me.

What? I was all for team work.

"Use the ear pieces to instruct your team members. My team will be the enemies. You must deflect our advances. Treat this like the real thing, understood?"

I walked with Cora, putting the little ear piece in place. Was it against the rules to knock your team member around a little? Cora looked at me.

"No funny business," she warned.

"Me?" I said, flashing a wicked grin, "I'd never do such a thing."

She scowled, but she couldn't hide the little smile that played on her lips, not from me.

Jack

"Right, we know that they are going to hit us good and strong. Like Tabitha said, lets treat this like the real thing. So I suggest we do what comes naturally to us."

"When you say naturally, does that mean you have no plans at all?"

I turned my attention to Ember. She was wearing a bright white dress which seemed to glow with her hair. She would stand out a mile in battle. This training session was going to be a failure from the start. Clay was already a dead man, Cora would be exhausted from earlier and Ember stood out like a lighthouse. That left me, and my attention would be on Cora.

"Have you got any better ideas?"

"No," she said, her voice devoid of emotion. "In fact, I love it. The freedom to do what I want, when do we begin?"

The tree exploded above us, sending shattered pieces of bark pelting down.

"Now!" I shouted.

We spread out just as a large ball of fire rushed inches past my head. Cora stayed close to my side.

Good.

Ember headed west. I spotted Clay running straight ahead. With a little grin, I pulled my element and sent it flying. Clay was lifted a little off the ground and then dropped on to his arse. Clay turned, glaring at me. I sent him a lopsided grin. I felt better already.

"Jack, Tabitha is to your right and she can see you." Ember's voice was as clear as a bell in my ear.

I ducked just as another fire ball smacked into the tree. Another rocketed to the floor in front of me. Cora rustled up closer, her arm touched mine and ignited little shivers. I couldn't think straight when she was this close to me.

"Clay, what's your position?" I asked, speaking quietly into the ear piece.

"I headed north. I'm trying to come around on them. I saw Clio, she ran past me, but she didn't see me," he whispered.

It was all business now; my issues with Clay were pushed to one side. The ground shuddered underneath us, knocking me off balance. A ball of fire came from the right without warning. Cora lifted her hands to shield her face. I leaped towards her but before I could do anything, the ball turned to ice and dropped to the floor with a heavy thud.

"Jack, did you see that?" she squealed in excitement.

"Yeah," I chuckled, "but if you squeal like that again we're going to get caught."

The ground violently shook. Ember suddenly appeared at my side. "Crap, Ember, don't do that."

"Sorry." I knew that she wasn't sorry. "Ayden is coming up around the back of us and Clay is lost by the looks of things."

A sound from our left made us turn. Ayden grabbed Ember

from behind. Before we had a chance to act, Ember looked at me and then Cora, smiled and then disappeared. Ember's projection was no longer here so Ayden lurched towards us.

I grabbed her hand and threw my element around her. She levitated beside me, her warm hand in mine. A fireball whizzed past us, skimming my hair. I looked to Cora who had her eyes closed.

"Sorry about this," she whispered.

"Sorry about what?" I asked.

Heavy, torrential rain bucketed down. This woman amazed me with her strength. No wonder my heart swelled everytime I saw her. The wind swirled, firing the rain in all directions. A crack of thunder rumbled overhead. The wind twisted, building in speed and strength until a tornado formed. It wasn't a very big tornado but it was powerful. The high pitched whistling was deafening. The tornado burst from her hold and lapped at the ground thirstily.

"Clay, tornado heading your way, where are you?"

"I'm nearing where we first started," he shouted.

"Wait there!" I instructed and then looked at Cora. "You stay here."

"Got nowhere else to be," she giggled.

I ducked lower, concentrating on keeping her up there. I felt I'd got my energy just right but if there was a blip she would go crashing to the ground. I shuddered at the thought. The smouldering trees from the fireballs made visibility hard which meant they couldn't see me, it also meant I couldn't distinguish who was who. I peered down and could just see Clay underneath the cloud of smoke.

"Clay, stay where you are and put your hand in the air," I whispered.

I reached for Clay. Cora's mini tornado was crashing around with balls of fire whizzing around within it. We needed to think of another plan.

"Ember, are you there?" Cora spoke into her ear piece.

"I'm here, sort of, my other self is somewhere safe."

"Ember is fine but we need a plan of action."

"I was thinking, I've never frozen one of Tabitha's fire balls before but I guess it could work on anything. The idea has never come to me before and we might as well learn what we can do and push ourselves now before they come. Isn't that the whole point?" she asked and without waiting for a reply, she continued. "Anyway, Clay, I could try and freeze your water and create a barrier around us."

As she spoke I noticed the way Clay looked at her. His eyes roamed every angle of her face, following the curve of her cheekbones and then coming to rest on her lips. How did I look at her? Her warm brown eyes, they weren't just brown to me, they were a soft fawn flecked with bronze that popped out at you from underneath the heavy curtain of thick dark lashes. Her lips enticed me, the bottom one just asking to be nibbled. I knew every line of her face, what every crease in her forehead meant, what her eyes were telling me without her words.

I shook my head. "I think this is the day to try new things," I agreed. "Right, we need to get somewhere safe."

We descended and ducked down, within seconds I could hear knocking sounds. Eli was up to his usual tricks.

"Clay, now," Cora hissed.

Clay ducked as low as he could and let the water flow. The ripple of crystal blue water cascading out of his hands was something I may never get used to. The water travelled, covering the floor space quickly. The air around us stilled. Two deep lines formed between Cora's closed eyes.

I watched as the water stopped moving and started to become solid. The water cracked and groaned against the pressure of the cold air. My breath puffed in a white cloud around my head. The ground around us became an ice rink.

Ayden appeared. There was a pop and another Ayden joined the first one. They stepped onto the ice. I held my breath. One Ayden slipped and fell, the other Ayden moved tentatively. The wind picked up, sending the second Ayden falling on the floor.

"Clay, I need water."

Clay produced the water. The water became ice much quicker than before. A five-foot wave formed with deadly shards protruding, creating a dangerous obstacle. Ayden's lips moved and within seconds the ground shook. It felt like a small vibration at first and then it escalated becoming a major earthquake.

"Ember, where are you?" I spoke into the ear piece and instantly lost my footing.

"Right here, Jack," she whispered as she appeared beside me.

"Any suggestions for what we could do next would be great."

Before anyone could answer, heat surrounded us. I looked over the top of the barricade to assess the situation. Tabitha was stood next to Ayden and Clio. The ground shook as Tabitha's heat thawed the ice.

"It's not going to last, Tab's melting it," Cora said.

"Yeah, they are going to get through sooner or later. What do we do now?"

"Go out there fighting?" Ember suggested.

I looked around our small group to assess the situation and formulate a plan. "Okay, Ember you stay here and when they get close enough you can zap back to your body, where is that by the way?"

"It's at Cora's house laid up on the sofa," she said and grinned.

"Does my mum know?" Cora looked surprised.

"Yes," Ember laughed, "she keeps giving me chocolate when I go back."

"Charming," Cora sniffed. "Well, when you go back bring me some."

"Focus, ladies. Right, Ember, you wait here. Clay, Cora, you're with me. We are going to go behind them and attack. That's all we have left. Ready?"

They nodded and moved swiftly across the tops of the trees. Ember made as much noise as she could to divert attention away from our floating figures up above.

"Jack, Ayden is nearly here, I'm going to go real soon. You ready?"

"Almost," I whispered back.

We hovered above the tree tops with a view of what was happening. Tabitha was melting the ice as multiple versions of Ayden surrounded the area. Clio stood to one side occasionally stomping her foot which sent actual ripples across the ground. Where was Eli?

"Ready?"

"Yeah," Cora whispered.

I lowered us behind the others. Clay took the right, I took the left and Cora remained in the middle. A blow to my right shoulder sent me flying to the ground. Another blow hit me in the leg. I grabbed my leg, trying to squeeze out the pain. "Jesus Christ!"

Eli appeared in front of me with a smile on his face. Another rock came hurtling towards me but it suddenly darted off in the opposite direction.

"Come on."

I lifted Eli high enough to make him squeal; the drop was a long way down. Fireballs flew overhead, igniting the bark as they hit with an almighty *thud*. Several blasted against the trees as one hit the floor, ricocheting into a bush beside us. It burst into flames and died almost as quickly as it started.

I ran towards Ayden, my energy quickly lifting Ayden into the air. Another Ayden came bounding towards me from the left.

"Clay!" I shouted into the ear piece as water fired at Ayden.

I quickly glanced at Cora who was dealing with Tabitha's fireballs like they were annoying flies buzzing around her head. I cast my energy and lifted several Aydens in the air. A yelp of pain stopped my heart. I turned to see Cora on the floor, holding her hand. Tabitha had another ball glowing in her hand ready to throw. All thoughts of this training session not being real flew out of my head. I just had one thought, to protect.

Tabitha threw the ball of fire at Cora's face.

The ball of fire slowed and came to a stop, mere centimetres in front of Cora's face. She barely held the ball suspended between both hands. I skidded to a stop next to her. A surprised expression moved across Tabitha's face.

Suddenly, and then Tabitha laughed. The sound made Clay come out of cover to see what was happening.

"Training is over," Tabitha ordered. "Cora, where did you learn the ice trick?"

"I just thought of it, why?"

Tabitha shook her head and I noticed sadness touch the greens of her eyes. "I used to know someone who could do that."

Cora touched her arm but said no more. Judging by the sadness, the person was no longer with us.

Eli came out of hiding just as I heard a faint pop and felt my energy return to me. "That was fantastic! Jack, you were brilliant. Cora, that was amazing!" Eli praised as he slapped me on the back.

Cora looked across at me and smiled. Her hair was a mess; her face looked tight and drawn. But those eyes, God, those eyes did something to my heart. I suddenly felt like I could do it all again.

"Christmas dinner will be at the shop, is that okay?" I vaguely heard Tabitha ask.

"Jack?"

"Yeah, yeah that's fine," I said, distracted by Cora.

I would agree to anything at this moment in time. Our group dispersed. Eli moved away from Ayden to speak with Tabitha. Clio said her goodbyes and headed towards the cottage. I hadn't seen Ember since we'd split. That left me and Cora.

"So..." I prompted.

"Interesting day," she finished and smiled.

I fought the urge to lean towards her, to run my hand through her hair, to have my lips meet those luscious rose-tinted ones.

Christ, I was losing control.

She moved into my body, her head coming to a rest underneath my chin as she put her arms around me.

"Thank you for today," she spoke softly.

"Sure, no problem," I sighed and put my arms around her, enjoying the way she felt against me.

Cora

I woke to the sound of my mother's laughter. Excitement fizzed like champagne in my chest as I jumped out of bed, grabbed my dressing gown and ran down the stairs.

"Merry Christmas, darling!" My mother leapt up off the sofa and hugged me.

"Merry Christmas, Mum."

Ayden was sat on the sofa. "Merry Christmas, Ayden."

"Merry Christmas, High Priestess." He stood and placed his hand across his chest as he bowed.

I giggled and pulled him in for a hug.

"Do you want something to eat?" Ayden asked.

"No, I don't want to spoil the food Tabitha's prepared."

Silver, pink and purple shimmered as lights danced along the foil wrapping paper. I walked to the little cupboard under the stairs, my not so secret hiding place, and grabbed the presents. I walked back into the living room and ripped the bag, letting the many oddly wrapped presents spew all over my feet and the carpet.

I grabbed my first presents and ripped the wrapping paper. I laughed as I looked down at the book, '*How to be a witch for Dummies*'.

"I love it," I smiled. "Open one of yours."

She timidly peeled back the wrapping paper. She didn't allow one piece to be ripped. Her eyes flashed with excitement as she saw what it was. "This is wonderful, perfect. Thank you." She held up the witch shaped feet warmers.

"Laura, they are perfect for your cold feet."

"Ayden, you open one."

Ayden leant forward and picked up the first box he saw with his name scrawled on it. Ayden attacked the wrapping paper like a dog would a chew toy.

"It's a knife holder but in the shape of a witch. When you put the knives in, it looks like it is stabbing it. What do you think?"

"It's great!" Ayden exclaimed and then started ripping the box open to look at it properly.

After a blissful thirty minutes, my presents were piled up next to me. Socks, a dressing gown with witches all over it, people would definitely start to think things if they saw the entire stack of witch related items, slippers, books, DVDs and chocolates were from my mother. Ayden had bought me a beautiful satin ribbon watch. The thick ribbon was a luscious deep emerald green. The small face was surrounded by crystals that winked at me.

My first Christmas of many that I would remember now. This year it felt more important to me. Having Jack here made it special too.

I ran upstairs to get ready and stopped when I noticed the box sat on my bed with a white ribbon and bow sealing it. When had this arrived here? I picked up the label.

Wear this
Tab x

I eagerly ripped it open revealing an emerald green robe. Oh my God! It was stunning, not only did it look like liquid, it felt like it too. I contemplated what to wear underneath it. Surely you didn't go commando under it? I really hoped Tabitha didn't. Pulling a face, I searched among the pile of clothes finding a pair of white cotton trousers with a green top, I dressed quickly. The weight of the material surprised me, but it fit my body like a glove.

I'd never felt more like myself than this moment. Stood here, in witch robes representing my coven. I breathed through a surprising push of tears. I wouldn't cry today. Today was a good day.

I walked down the stairs, gliding my hands along the liquid material. My mother's hazel eyes widened when she saw me. "Cora, you look beautiful." She engulfed me in an embrace so tight I struggled to breathe.

"What time are we going?" I asked when I was free, and Mum moved to the kitchen.

"Now if you like?" Ayden suggested.

"Yeah."

"Cora, is that you?" My mother called from the kitchen.

"What?" I hadn't done anything.

"Have you looked outside?"

I moved to the window and saw big soft white flakes

falling thick and fast out of the dull slate sky. The flakes were already creating a beautiful layer of crystal white on the ground.

"Nope, that's not me, but it's gorgeous."

My phone bleeped. I rummaged in the pocket of the robe and looked at the message.

If that is you affecting the weather, I'm going to bloody kill you x

I laughed out loud. Heat moved into my cheeks. He'd put a kiss on the end of the message. Things happened to me when I was with him, my mouth always went dry, my heart bounced around happily. I felt safe wrapped up in his arms. I had to address it at some point…probably. Did I tell him? I'd never had the dilemma of telling someone I liked them before, and we'd had a bumpy start.

"Ready?" Ayden asked.

"Yep."

As the shop came into view I could see that the main window was concealed with dark green covers, so I couldn't see inside. Ayden stepped aside, allowing me to go first.

"Why do I have to go first?" I hissed.

"Because you are the High Priestess," he said and winked.

I took each step slowly and with a tremor in my hands I opened the shop door. My eyes widened in shock as a gasp escaped my mouth. The window area was the first thing that I saw. Thick garland weaved around the banister, thousands of tiny stars twinkled within it. The warm turquoise lights from the trees flashed across the green backdrop, creating the perfect winter wonderland.

Lining the floor to guide our path in to the shop were small glass lanterns that held a single candle. Along the floor, near the bookcase, cotton candy, sky blue, luscious purple and deep green presents were piled high in groups around the shop. As I approached Tabitha, I got a better view of the small table. But it was no longer the small table.

There were nine high back chairs placed around the new solid oak table. Each place was set with silverware that gleamed in the soft candle light. Four tall pillar candles stood in the centre of the table, two were emerald green and two were deep red. Tabitha had combined the two covens. The crackers were green and the foil stars sprinkled on the cotton white tablecloth were red. Above the table, floating in the air, were many more lanterns.

"You wore it," Tabitha whispered as tears filled her eyes.

"Of course," I hugged Tabitha. "You're wearing the same coloured robe as me."

"Yes, your mother and I used to wear the same robes on Christmas day, I thought we could continue the tradition."

That small piece of information pushed my emotions over the edge and the tears escaped their feathery prison, rolling down my cheeks.

"The place looks amazing, Tab!" Ayden exclaimed.

"Thank you." Tabitha wiped away my tears. "We must open the presents before the others arrive, Ember?" Tabitha called behind her.

Ember walked up the staircase whilst holding presents stacked against her chest. Ember was wearing the same robe as us. I received a present that was the colour of a cloudless sky in summer. Ayden had already ripped his open, revealing a ruby red jumper. I ripped mine open and found myself staring at a picture.

I stopped breathing. I'd told myself I wouldn't cry and yet, here I was, crying.

"This is you and your mother. You were only two, I believe. She used to hold you high in the air and swing you around like that for hours. I've been working for quite some time on this picture, the spell was very difficult, but I think it has turned out rather beautifully. Not your traditional photo, but it works." Tabitha moved aside to allow my mother to see.

The photo wasn't traditional. It wasn't a picture on glossy paper. The image had been burnt on to the paper. The details were so intricate that I could see every line, it was as though the picture had been drawn on with fire. My mother was smiling as she swung me high in the air. We were both wearing robes, mine the tiny version of hers.

"This... this..."

"I know." Tabitha hugged me.

"Thank you," I whispered.

Ember placed the presents in the stock room just as the bell above the door sounded.

Eli walked in first and whistled. "Bloody hell, Tabitha, this place looks amazing."

"Thank you, Eli," Tabitha smiled.

Eli was followed by Clio who looked pretty, wearing a pair of dark jeans and a red jumper. Clay followed. He was brooding, I knew the look. The door shut and then jingled as Jack bounded up the stairs with a huge smile on his face. He lifted his hand to sweep his hair to one side. Then his eyes widened as he surveyed what I was wearing. My heart galloped. I wanted him to like what I was wearing. His lips curved into a smile which made my stomach somersault.

"Merry Christmas, Cora, you look beautiful."

He pulled me into a hug, I breathed deeply letting the smell of him wash over me.

"Merry Christmas," I murmured into his chest. "I know how difficult today must be for you. I want you to know I'm here if you need to talk."

His sister had been taken on this day. He took a deep breath; I felt the rise and fall of his chest. He moved his mouth closer to my ear. His lips brushed my ear ever so gently, his words a deep rumble in his chest that made me shiver.

"Thank you."

"Right, it's time for food." Tabitha clapped her hands together.

Ayden, Eli and Clay stood and followed Tabitha up to her flat. I reluctantly pulled away from Jack and sat down next to my mum. Jack sat down next to me.

"I've got you something," he whispered.

"But I didn't get you anything," I whispered, feeling guilty.

He shook his head, dismissing my comment. He handed me the gift. Inside, I found a box, I opened it and felt the walls around my heart crumble.

I realised in that moment that I was falling for him, and fast.

Inside the box was a silver necklace. Delicate swirls looped into a tear drop; inside the tear drop was an emerald green crystal which glittered in the candle light.

"I saw this and it was your coven colour, so I thought you would like it..." he said, looking embarrassed.

"Jack, it's beautiful, thank you," I whispered.

He picked up the necklace and opened the clasp. Leaning closer to me, he moved my hair aside. My breath stalled as his fingers brushed against the back of my neck. Once he'd fastened it, his hand cupped my cheek and I saw something flash in his eyes. Chocolate swirled as his eyes studied my face. I felt the urge to kiss him and the smirk that played on his lips told me that he knew what I wanted. His breath brushed against my lips.

"Grub's up," Ayden's voice boomed from the staircase.

We jumped apart.

Trying to ignore the growing tension between us, I focused on the food. The golden turkey rested in the centre of the table and Ayden had taken the liberty of carving it. Everyone tucked into the food and pulled their green crackers. I moved closer to Jack as his hand brushed my hand under the table.

"I have one last present," Ayden announced, clearing his throat and bringing my attention to him. "Well, I should say *we* have one last present."

Ayden looked at my mother and lovingly kissed her hand. Putting his napkin to one side, he stood up. He looked around the table until his eyes rested on me.

"Cora, everyone, Laura and I will be having a baby."

My mouth dropped open. Tabitha squealed and launched herself at Ayden. Jack had stood and was hugging my mother.

"I'm going to be a sister?" My voice was high pitched and squeaky.

"Yes."

I choked on a sob and launched myself at my mother.

"How far are you?" I stepped back, looking at her belly like it was going to grow.

"It's early days yet. I'm only 5 weeks."

Ayden leant over the table and took my hand. "Do I have your blessing, High Priestess?"

How could I deny this man anything? "Yes, Ayden."

"I'm really happy for you, Mum." I squeezed her hand.

"I'm happy too, darling."

"I would like to propose a toast," Jack said as we sat around the table. He raised his glass. "Here's to those that couldn't be with us today but who are here in spirit. And to Laura and Ayden who begin their journey today. We wish you all health and happiness."

"Health and happiness." We clinked our glasses together.

Cora

It was a cold, slate grey New Year's day and Tabitha had been true to her word, we were training. According to Tabitha this was the New Year. I couldn't complain. Train or die, those were my choices.

I'd left my mother in the capable hands of Ayden who was currently holding her hair out of her face as she threw up. Even as they sat on the bathroom floor surrounded by a cloud that smelt of vomit, they still smiled.

As I approached the training area, Tabitha was stood conspiring with Ember. Clay and Clio were training in a little circle of their own. I couldn't see Jack or Eli. As I made my way to Tabitha I could sense Clay watching me. He was making things worse, dragging things out, unable to forget and leave what was never meant to be.

"Ember," I said, smiling as I hugged her. "How are you?"

"I'm well, thank you. How have you been? How is Laura?"

"I'm good, and she's currently throwing up."

Ember pulled a face which made me laugh. "So, who am I training with?"

"Me."

His voice drifted from above, the sound making my insides fizz excitedly. I looked up to see him floating slowly down towards me, his lopsided grin was firmly in place. I resisted the urge to run and hug him the minute he landed.

His eyes latched onto mine and that was all it took for my heart beat to accelerate and literally smash out of my chest. I felt the explosion of pink flood my cheeks.

"I know its New Year's day, so I've decided to let you work on what you think are your weaker points. Have fun."

Tabitha turned and walked away rather abruptly with Ember. Frowning, I studied their body language. They were huddled close together with serious expressions on their faces. What was happening between them? Whatever it was, they weren't telling me. I sensed Jack edge closer to me.

"Does Tabitha seem off today?" I asked him, trying to ignore the heat between us.

"Not any more than usual, but I suppose you know her better."

Clay and Clio walked across to us. There was an awkward pause before Clio spoke. "We are heading out in the woods so you can have the circle if you want it."

"Thanks."

Clay glanced at me. Shaking my head, I turned to Jack and found him watching me.

"What happened between you two?" he asked.

I squinted up at him. "It's nothing."

"Doesn't look like nothing. Are you two... still...?" His voice trailed off.

"Nothing happened between us then, and nothing is happening now."

"I was such a muppet that day on the lawn outside your house," he chuckled.

"What else is new? So, what do you want to do today?"

"I wouldn't mind just levitating, just to make sure I've got it."

"Sure." I shrugged.

We split within the area, giving the other plenty of room just in case unexpected things went flying. Jack began by levitating several large pieces of wood in the air. One plummeted to the floor, smashing on impact. I heard him curse and then he picked up another to join the five already in the air.

I turned and concentrated on my element. It scurried happily around me. I pushed it and watched as it picked up various twigs, branches and stones along the way. I looked across at Jack, saw the way his back muscles rippled and stretched. His blue jumper stuck to his body as the effort to lift the wood made him sweat.

I hit the floor and yelped as something sharp hit my head. The ground thudded beneath me as Jack bent down beside me. My fingers came away sticky and warm.

"What happened?"

His fingers gently moved my chin to one side so he could get a better look at the wound. His lips teased me as he moved closer to my face.

"I guess I smacked myself with a rock."

"I'm sorry if this hurts."

He moved aside strands of my hair, the tickle of it made me sigh. And that sigh escaped my mouth. Damn. He stopped and leaned back to look at me. My skin tingled as his thumb grazed my cheekbone and continued caressing my skin until it came to a rest in the dip of my chin. I felt the overpowering urge to just grab him, so I bit the bullet.

My hands slid through his hair and I found it softer than I'd expected. I kissed him.

The spark.

The fire.

It consumed me.

I felt his need spike and he took charge as he pulled my bobble free and pushed his fingers through my hair. He deepened the kiss and I lost the ability to breathe.

He broke the kiss, breathing heavily. "I've wanted to do that for a while," he admitted.

"Me too."

I closed my eyes as he kissed me again, and that right there felt like home to me.

"So, I guess training's over?"

The voice made us jump. The burning in my cheeks intensified when I looked at Clay. We stood up, I felt a little awkward, but I couldn't find my voice.

"Cora hurt her head, but why is it any of your business?" His warm hand filled mine.

Clay's eyes moved from my head down to our joined hands. "Just a bit of advice, what with you being so *young* and everything, but that wound needs an antiseptic wipe not your tongue." Clay cocked his head.

I held Jack's hand tighter. "Listen, let's not be stupid," I pleaded.

"That's easy for you to say, you lead me on."

"I did no such thing. You believed something would happen when it never would."

"You want to give us marks out of ten, *High Priestess*?"

I felt the painful slap of hurt. "How dare you speak to me like that?"

"Well, you haven't earned my respect. I was someone to keep you from growing bored, is that it, Cora? Well, you've run out of men. Is Eli going to be next? I doubt he would, his dead wife might come and haunt you. Perhaps your mother won't take it so kindly if you seduced Ayden!"

I gasped, shocked by his words and barely registered Jack's hand leaving mine. Jack launched himself at Clay and I heard the dull thud as Jack's fist connected heavily, saw the bright red blood spill out of Clay's mouth as they went down to the floor and wrestled angrily.

I charged towards them, hoping to pull them apart. "Stop it, Jack! Clay, stop it!"

Jack stood and kicked Clay in the stomach. Clay doubled over coughing and spitting out blood as Jack wiped his hand onto his jeans and took mine.

"Don't you ever disrespect her again! Do you hear me?! Because next time you'll get more than a bloody nose, you worthless piece of shit."

We walked away. The Corenthio Coven were coming and we were fighting amongst ourselves. The coven wouldn't have anything to do when they got here, we were doing such a great job of hurting each other already.

Cora

As we entered the house, I stopped in the hallway when I heard voices coming from the kitchen and looked back at Jack to see if he wanted to play this a different way. He nodded, giving me my answer.

Opening the kitchen door, I found Tabitha and Ember leaning over the kitchen table looking at papers. Ayden and my mother were stood with their backs to us. "Hey."

"Hello, love," my mother half turned to me.

"What's going on?" Jack asked.

"We need your coven here, Jack. Contact Eli, where's Clay and Clio?"

I walked over to the freezer and grabbed the nearest bag of peas. Handing it to Jack, he placed it on his hand. Ayden looked at Jack's hand and I saw something register.

"What's happened?" Tabitha asked.

"Well..." Jack began.

"What have you done to your head?" Ayden interrupted as he looked at me.

Now that Ayden mentioned my head, it throbbed with a new lease of life. Jack stepped to me, his lips curved and I knew what was going to happen. He kissed me.

Ayden looked disgusted. Tabitha appeared unsure; the main give away was the nibbling of her lip. Ember smiled.

"Okay." Tabitha broke the silence.

I didn't relax, that wasn't an okay, everything is fine. It was an acknowledgement of what Jack had just done.

"But that doesn't answer why you are bleeding from your head."

"I hit myself with some rocks whilst I was training. It happened before..."

"The two of you together, this could have major repercussions if it went wrong, are you sure about this?" Ember asked.

"I've fallen for her," he said, pulling me closer to him. "I wouldn't do anything to hurt her, you have my word."

My heart literally sighed. That had to be the most romantic thing I'd ever heard.

"So, what happened to Clay? I'm guessing something happened?" Ayden asked, suddenly interested when there may be talk of fighting.

"He caught us kissing after Cora hit her head-"

"I've heard of kissing it better, but you take the phrase to a whole new level," my mother teased.

"Thank you," Jack laughed. "Anyway, the whole situation escalated, so I punched him."

"What did he say? He must have said something for you to punch him," Tabitha reasoned.

"He said that Cora was a..." He stopped and looked at me. "Okay, he called Cora a tart. He said that she had been through all the men. He mentioned my sister and Eli and...then he said that her mother should watch out because she would take Ayden next."

My face felt like it was on fire. Ayden's face looked like it was on fire.

"He said bloody what?!" Ayden rammed past us, storming towards the front door.

"Wait! Ayden!"

"Cora, let him go," Tabitha said.

"I can't believe he said that. How very silly of him," Ember sighed.

"How good was the punch?" my mother asked.

I looked at her in shock. That wasn't the right question to ask.

"I split his lip and his nose was bleeding by the end of it," Jack grinned.

"Good."

"Maybe someone should go get Ayden?" I felt like I should be the adult.

"There's no point, he probably duplicated himself," Tabitha replied. "Jack, ring Eli and tell him to come here."

Jack left the room with his phone to his ear. Tabitha instantly invaded my personal space.

"Cora, are you sure?"

"Tab, I really like him. I've liked him for a while now but I just didn't want to admit it to myself. I just feel so right when I'm with him. I get goose bumps when he touches me. I feel butterflies when I see him," I confessed. "I'm falling for him pretty fast."

"Very well, if you're sure, then I'm happy for you. You know the two of you were a couple before."

"What?" My whole body stilled.

"You both were together before the trials, but I never thought it would happen now."

Well, that was something to think about…maybe Fate was playing a hand in things? No wonder I felt so right in his company. It would appear that I'd always been in love with this boy, and now that I knew who I was again, my heart was waking up and remembering the love I had for a boy a long time ago. Time hadn't killed that. We were lucky we were able to get a second chance.

"Eli's on his way over," Jack confirmed as he entered the room. Jack kissed my cheek. That simple act nearly made me sigh. "Jack did you know we were a couple before?"

"What? In 1612?"

I nodded.

"No. I didn't know. But it makes sense, with how I feel so strongly about you."

"Yeah, I agree. I'd never believed that things like this could happen and I feel overwhelmed by the rush of feelings I have for you, so soon. But we've always felt this way."

He smiled as his index finger caressed my cheek. "It all feels right."

Eli arrived and sat with a shocked expression on his face as he listened. Once Jack had finished I could see that the shock had turn to heated anger. He very nearly went out looking for Clay, but Jack managed to restrain him. Clio arrived moments after Eli and, having missed some of the story, she quickly caught up on the events. Her face had remained impassive. She was very much like Ember.

We waited another twenty minutes until Ayden returned,

by which time my mother had worn a patch in the carpet from her constant pacing. He didn't look battered or bruised.

"Right, we've nearly mastered our skills and we will continue to work on them before the time comes, but for now, we need to focus on our enemy."

Ember bent down and picked up a large piece of card and stuck it to the wall. My heart dropped to my gut as I focused on the faces.

Jesus. Was this really happening?

"This is the Corenthio Coven."

Ember pointed to a picture of a woman of Asian descent. Her cheekbones stuck out rather fiercely, the angles making her green eyes appear smaller. Her lips were set in a severe pout, but the thing that caught my attention was the orange, spiky hair.

"This is Akina. Her element is sublimation which means she can make you blind in battle. To do this she uses her ability to manipulate elements of the weather, more often than not, mist." Ember looked at me. I felt fear snake along my neck.

"She surrounds the enemy with fog. That is why we have our communication devices. Be very careful when near her."

Ember paused, allowing this information to sink in. I already struggled to breathe and that had been after the first one. My mother looked distressed.

"Mum, I don't think you should be in here, what with your condition and everything..."

"Yes, love, she's right," Ayden agreed.

"No, I want to see what my baby is up against." She stroked my face and looked at Ember. "You can continue."

Ember nodded. "Melitta is next." She pointed to the woman next to Akina on the board.

Melitta's vibrant blonde hair hung long and wavy down to her waist. Her beautiful face looked directly into the camera like she knew someone was watching her. Her cheekbones were carved high, her baby blues were wide and seductive.

"Her power is acedia," Ember continued, "*do not* let her touch you. One touch from her and your element is taken. However, over the past few centuries she has tried to find a peaceful resolution, she is rather averse to fighting. I guess she doesn't like damaging that pretty little face of hers," Ember sneered, "but if she doesn't find peace, if we persist in our defence, she will weaken us by taking our power."

I'd only just got my power back, there was no way she was taking it from me.

Ember moved across to the other side of the board. "Evander," she smiled but it was tight and unnatural. "You may think he looks like a male version of yours truly, what with all that white hair. But he has one of the meanest streaks-"

"So do you," Tabitha smiled.

"Yes, well," Ember smiled and focused her attention back to the group. "He will try and persuade you to agree to his way of thinking; that their decision is for the best. If you don't listen, and we won't, he will use his element which is kinetic energy.

"Now, I've seen him use this in the past few months and believe me when I tell you that he is very clever, very strong, and he finds great joy in crushing his victims."

Evander's eyes, a merciless, cold steel seemed to search me

out and glare at me. How could you stop someone from using that power on you? He could do everything he wanted from a distance. Jack's fingers stroked my hand, trying to give comfort.

"Last but not least, Varick."

The shape of his face was that of a tear drop, the sharp point ending with his chin. His eyes sat too close together, but what made my blood run cold was the colour of them.

They were pure black.

His hair was perfectly cut, just touching his shoulders, and was also black in colour. His nose was too long for his face and his lips were too big. In my mind, he was the epitome of evil.

"He is the unofficial leader of the Corenthio Coven. There has never been an official leader but Varick controls the group in his own way. He makes the decisions and the others seem to follow. It was his final decision to come here and *visit* you both."

"Nice little visit to come here and kill us," Jack sneered.

"Yes," Ember answered. "But you are prepared to fight him. You are prepared to fight them all."

"How can we win when they are so strong, so powerful? There are four of them and eight of us and I still feel outnumbered," I whispered.

"We need to do everything possible to live. We will die saving you two if it comes to that," Ayden said, determination in his voice.

I didn't want people to die. I didn't want this. I'd just found them. I'd just found my life and here they were, trying to take it away from me.

I would make sure they wouldn't.

"This is my fault, I caused this. It all began back at the shop." Jack shook his head.

"No, Jack. I did this too. We attacked each other." I wouldn't allow him to take the sole blame for this.

"Varick controls electricity." Ember turned back to the board, making us focus once again. "This is a powerful gift; I believe you could be as strong as him in years to come, Cora. He kills people by using a single strike."

The room was silent. Ember definitely hadn't held back with her information. Her choice of words were straight to the point. I liked that. I looked at the board, memorising each face and the details below their pictures until it was burnt to memory.

"Wait, Tabitha, it said in my book that you were apprehended by the Corenthio Coven when they came to see my mother, is that true?"

"Yes. It is true. Gosh, I nearly forgot-"

"How can you forget something like that?" I cut in, astonished.

"Time affects us all, details and events become distant memories. Your mother was questioned about the scandal involving Thomas. I ran to her aide. You were also there."

"I was there?" I hated not having my memories.

"Yes, you didn't fight, you were hidden. For her to deal with the four of them on her own was unthinkable. When I arrived, I was more uncooperative than they would have liked, so Varick struck me. He hadn't used enough force to kill me; he simply wanted to shock me. I was placed in the corner of the room surrounded by an electrical shield. Once they had completed their questioning, they left. I would say thirty minutes passed before the shield evaporated."

"Is there anything we can do to prepare against such powerful elements? How can we fight against electricity and kinetic energy?" Jack asked.

"We have to do everything we can. The only thing I can suggest is to constantly move, never remain in the same position longer than necessary. I did, and that was my mistake."

"Is this where you've been all this time?" The hushed conversations now made sense to me.

"Yes. It was easier for me to travel and get back here without interfering in the workings of our group. We needed more information on them. Tabitha thought it best that I went. If that has offended you, I'm very sorry."

"I'm not offended but I don't like being left out of the loop. In future I need to know all of this. I just hope we don't have another situation like this."

"Of course."

"I want you to leave the board here. I need to see them, it will help me prepare."

"I'm going to head back home," Eli announced. "I still need to speak with Clay if he's there. Do we need to hold a disciplinary meeting?" Eli looked at Tabitha.

"I'm not the one to make that decision."

"Well, I think he might have learnt his lesson, or at least I hope he has. We still need him when we face the Corenthio Coven, I'm not that stupid. If he does it again or speaks out of turn again, he is gone, is that understood?"

Jack sounded so authoritative, and even that was sexy.

"Yes, I think that is more than acceptable. Cora?"

"I agree. What with everything that is happening, we need everyone we can get."

"Right, that's fine. I will discuss his options with him. See you all soon."

Eli walked to the door and was followed by Clio who had remained quiet during the meeting. Others moved in the room, signalling their goodbyes. I stood up and hugged Tabitha.

Jack stood up next to me. "How's your hand?" I asked.

"The swelling makes it look worse than it is. How is your head?"

"It hurts a little, but the numbing cream Tabitha gave me has worked wonders." His lips feathered lightly against my head.

"He needs to apologise to you." His eyes latched on to mine, refusing to let them go.

"It doesn't matter, not in the great scheme of things. We have bigger things to deal with right now."

"I understand that, but he still needs to apologise. If it wasn't for the Corenthio Coven I would have let him go."

I agreed. How could you trust someone who said those things? I automatically tucked my head underneath his chin and breathed deep, he smelt like mud and it strangely calmed me. Like he'd always smelt of the earth to me.

"Everything's going to be all right," he whispered.

I didn't know if it was going to be fine. His lips touched mine and ever so gently lingered there.

"Want to watch a DVD?" I asked.

He nodded his head.

Images on the screen blurred with colour and motion. The film did nothing to take my mind off our situation. I couldn't forget the faces. I couldn't help but wonder which one of them would end my life. Which face would be my last. That thought made my blood run cold.

Cora

"Mum, I'm going to the training ground. If anyone needs me, you know where I am."

"Okay, love."

Since waking up that morning the wind had been my constant companion, it was still howling and bashing against the house. Sleet had been added to the mix during the last hour but that had now slowed. The ground was icy underfoot as I walked towards the little path at the side of the house that led to the training ground. I put my head down and walked a little bit faster.

I stopped at the end of the path and admired my view. Jack was stood facing a line of large pieces of bark, huge broken bits that had fallen when Clio had destroyed the area. He looked at the ground where they lay, silent soldiers waiting for their command. I held my breath. As they approached the height of his head, he lifted himself.

He moved around the large trunks and started casting his energy to other objects that lay on the floor. Several large branches joined him. Boulders rose, flying into the air with him. My feet instantly lifted off the floor as his energy wrapped itself around my body.

"I knew you were there," he grinned at me.

I floated across to him, having no other option.

"Hi, beautiful."

His energy vibrated around me. His arms wrapped themselves around my waist, providing a warmth that took away the chill of the morning. He kissed me, his lips teasing, making heat spread from my chest to my toes.

"Show off," I muttered when I got my breath back.

"So, what shall we do today?" He gave me a suggestive wink which made my insides turn to mush.

"We need to train, we have to be ready for them."

"You're ready. I need a little more practise."

My power had really come together over the last week. It was evident with the changing weather; I'd produced sleet. I bobbed up and down in the air, watching him. He walked into the woods, I could no longer see him but a huge tree complete with crinkled dead leaves floated across to me, I stiffened.

"Don't worry, it won't hit you," Jack shouted.

"Nice to know," I responded.

He levitated up towards me and pulled me back into his body, the cut of his abs pushed through his clothing making my stomach muscles quiver with pure lust.

"We need everyone here. I'm ready to pull everyone up."

I pulled my mobile out, my fingers making quick work of a text. "She's on her way. Eli knows and he will bring the others."

He played with my fingers, twining his own around them as he placed kisses along my jaw.

"Have you spoken to Clay since you know...?"

"Not the kind of conversation I want to start when I'm busy kissing my girlfriend," Jack commented, speaking in between kisses.

Girlfriend. The word made the butterflies in my chest go crazy. I laughed, the sound cut off when his mouth devoured mine.

"Nope, I haven't spoken with Clay," he murmured when he finally allowed me to breathe. "He'd gone by the time I had got home. Eli just said it was sorted. He hasn't been home in two weeks and wasn't there this morning when I left. It's not sorted yet." His eyes darkened, the chocolate becoming solid.

"Jack, just leave it, it doesn't matter anymore," I urged.

"It does matter."

We were interrupted by the sound of voices. I looked down to see Tabitha come through the path with Ayden right behind her. They both looked up and smiled.

"Wow, you've got plenty up there!" Tabitha shouted.

"Sure you can handle any more?" Ayden laughed.

"You just wait and see."

Eli came through the other side of the circle closely followed by Clio. A few steps behind, Clay came trudging through the trees.

"Right," Jack snarled.

I'd barely landed on my feet when Jack stomped towards Clay. "If this gets out of hand, will you stop it?" I asked.

Tabitha nodded.

"I'm just wondering whether I will get more enjoyment if I smack you in the face again or if I let Ayden do it," Jack snapped as he grabbed Clay's jumper in his fist.

Clay's nose was puffy and a little red and there was a nasty gash over his cheek. Ayden stood by the side of Jack, his fists clenched. The only time Ayden stands by Jack is when he wants to get in a fight, typical.

"Now, you, you foul mouthed piece of shit, you can apologise to my High Priestess. When you disrespect her, you disrespect me. Those cuts on your face, that bruising, that is nothing compared to what I was going to do to you if I found you. You're bloody lucky I didn't!" Ayden growled, angrily jabbing Clay in the chest.

Jack let go of Clay, a smile played on those perfect lips.

"You made the mistake of bringing my future wife into the mix and for that you will pay-"

"Ayden," Tabitha interjected.

My heart was beating so fast I thought it was going to explode.

"Tabitha!" Ayden snarled at her.

"No. We do not do this now. We have too much to deal with. I'm not saying Clay doesn't deserve it, I'm not saying he does. I'm just trying to keep these two covens together."

Ayden had grabbed Clay's jumper, his fist pulled back ready to make the connection. I held my breath and exhaled when he dropped it.

"Again, you're very lucky," Ayden sneered and stepped away.

"I'm sorry to all of you," Clay whispered. "My emotions got the better of me and they shouldn't have. I'm truly sorry."

I walked to Jack and pulled him back. "Clay, what you did was stupid and uncalled for. I made mistakes; my main mistake was not stating clearly that we were never an item. You said things that hurt me, but I know things can be spoken in angry moments and you have apologised so we need to drop this subject. We can't be fighting amongst ourselves anymore."

"I'm sorry, Cora. I'm disgusted by how I treated you. If you allow it and, of course, High Priest, I would like to remain within this group. I will leave when we are finished with the Corenthio Coven."

Going up against the Corenthio Coven meant death.

We all knew it.

There was no escaping it.

Tabitha sighed, making her feelings known about this.

"I accept your apology, Clay. I also accept your request to leave the coven," Jack spoke.

"I second that," Eli agreed.

Clay nodded and turned to look at Clio who wasn't giving her answer. She lifted her head and simply nodded. Her face held every emotion but the clearest one was hurt. It hurt her to be stuck between her High Priest and Clay, her friend.

I pulled Jack away from Clay not wanting to risk any more fighting. "Right, Jack wants to test his element."

"Yeah, I just need to make sure that I can get you all up there."

"Where do you want us?" Tabitha asked.

"Anywhere really, you could spread out to make it harder."

Jack stood in the middle of the group with his head bowed. He looked up and smiled as Clio was the first to start levitating. I was stood next to one of the trees quite a distance away from Jack.

"I'm testing to see how high I can get everyone but I'm going to do it one at a time to make sure everyone is safe. I think the higher, the better." Jack nodded.

Ayden was next, joining Clio in the air. Jack wasn't

showing strain yet. Clay was the third to go. I felt the vibrations snake around me.

"Hold on, beautiful," he grinned.

I smiled as I slowly joined the others and the debris floating in mid-air. Tabitha was the last to come up in the group.

"How are you feeling?" Tabitha asked, looking down.

"I'm fine. I'm handling it better than I thought I would. I can feel the tug deep in my gut but it's not painful. I think I can handle Ember when she's involved too."

Jack levitated and came to a stop next to me; he was smiling like an idiot. He moved us higher and I refused to look down. The unnatural force against gravity was showing on Jack's face. We stopped. I dared to look down then instantly regretted it when my heart fell out of my feet.

"I would say that is high enough, Jack," Ayden commented.

"Excellent!" Tabitha clapped her hands.

"Can you get us down without any broken bones though?" Eli teased.

Eli fell around five feet from the group, the drop forced a short squeal from his mouth. "You mock me brother and you will be the first to fall," he laughed.

He let us glide gently to the floor. As soon as my feet touched ground, Jack bounded up to me and lifted me off my feet. I laughed and then he noisily kissed me.

"They're coming!"

Everyone spun around to look at Ember who had popped up out of nowhere.

Cora

"What?" Tabitha demanded.

The laughter stopped.

"They're coming, Tabitha."

For the first time I could see the panic in Ember's eyes.

"When?" Tabitha asked as she took charge of the group.

"They are on their way now. It should take about three hours, at a push it could be four hours, they are coming from London."

"Cora's house, now."

Bulbous clouds formed, darkening the sky as thunder protested overhead, it reflected my mood perfectly. The group walked in a line, apart from me and Jack. Jack was jumping over old trunks and bushes so he could walk by my side as he held my hand.

We walked into the house and joined Mum who was sat in the living room, oblivious to what was about to happen. She didn't ask questions as Ayden started placing the table chairs within the room so the others could sit down. Clio took a seat next to Clay near the window. Ember remained stood and Tabitha stomped continuously behind us, creating a walkway in the carpet. Ayden sat next to my mother, one hand on her belly, his other hand held hers.

"Just to begin, I want to tell everyone that Ember and I have been working on a strategy," Tabitha began, "but we felt it would hinder you. You would be thinking of what comes next rather than what to do at that time... so we scrapped it."

"We have no strategy?" Clio's voice squeaked in shock.

"I think the best strategy is to do what comes naturally," Ember offered.

"But that means we have nothing!" Clay fumed.

"We have worked on our elements individually and we have come together as a group, a strong group at that. Jack and Cora have come a long way during the past few months. Just a few months ago they didn't even know they were witches, now look at them."

Everyone in the room looked at us. My cheeks flushed. "Okay, we aren't actually doing things *right now. Y*ou don't need to stare," I snapped and caught the tiny twitch of a smile on Jack's lips.

"So, what do we do?" Ayden asked.

"We need to direct them to the training area. We cannot let it go to the village. I don't think they would take it that far, it would alert the Commoners and the whole point of this little *visit* is to stop the Commoners from figuring out we are witches. Cora will have to lead them there."

"What? Me? Why me?" It was clearly my turn to squeak in shock.

"They will look for you first. Your mother, or so they believe, was the one who caused the most problems during the witch trials. They will no doubt think you are like your mother, the trouble maker," Tabitha commented, her voice dripping with hate. "Then they will focus their attention on Jack and then the rest of us if we stand in their way, and we will stand in their way."

"Why can't I be with her?" Jack added, squeezing my hand.

"You need to be with us. If we want to surprise them we can't be in plain sight for them to see, we need to be high. This means that Cora will have to get to the circle by herself."

"I can keep you in the air from a distance. I won't leave, Cora," he snapped.

"You haven't shown me that. How do we know you can do it? It's not worth the risk."

"And it's worth risking Cora who will be out there on her own?" Jack stormed.

"She will be safe. We will be there for her."

"I don't like it, not one bit."

"Jack, I know you want to protect her. What do you think we're doing?"

Jack's jaw popped with anger, but he didn't know what to say. I wasn't exactly thrilled about the whole thing either.

"So, Cora, you will bring them to us through the woods."

I did the maths in my head. By the time they got here the sun would have set. "I have to do it in the dark?"

"Yes. They need to follow you. I would suggest starting at Andrew Bruton's field and then making your way to the circle. Can you find your way there okay?'

"I think so. How do I know which direction to head in? If it's dark then I'll lose my sense of direction."

"We will give you a signal, something that will light your way."

"Great," I huffed, slumping back into the sofa. I could possibly be facing death within the next few hours and I was worried about the dark? "So, I run to the circle and then what?" I asked.

"Then we do what comes naturally. For now, we need to make some weapons, the extra bark in the woods can be made into sharp weapons. Gather bags of stones, maybe they won't expect such medieval methods of fighting, just gather anything that will help us."

"So, all we have to help us is a bag of rocks and some sharp pieces of tree?" Clay scoffed.

"Do you have a better idea, Clay?" Eli asked.

Clay shrugged.

"Eli, Ayden and Clay go and look at what we can use for weapons. Clio, you can come with me as we need some things from the shop. Cora and Jack, you wait here, we'll be back."

Everyone stood up and left to do their tasks. I envied those who had something to do to occupy their minds. I let go of Jack's hand and walked into the kitchen to look at the board of faces that threatened to change everything that I loved. The ache at the back of my throat flared as the tears blurred my vision. Jack's strong arms wound around me as his chin rested on my shoulder as we both assessed the board.

"I'm scared."

He sighed. "I know."

"We won't win."

"Don't be so pessimistic. You can't go into something believing you can't do it, we have to believe we can, what's the point otherwise?"

"Since when do people go up against a government type thing and live to see another day?" I questioned. "It's like attacking MI6 for crying out loud. People who walk out of their homes with a gun in their hand are going to be riddled with bullets. No questions asked. We're metaphorically waving guns at the Corenthio Coven. I'm scared for my mum. What if she loses me and Ayden? God, what would she do? The baby." I nearly sobbed but I held it together.

"Listen, I need to see the Cora that smacked my arse into the ground and smirked about it. I need to see the fiery spark that flashes in your eyes when you're pissed off. You need to be the bad arse out there, *my* bad arse," he smirked. "Plus, you're so sexy when you're angry."

I smiled as he wiped away the tears that slid down my face. Our kiss was slow, tender. Every unspoken word between us had been poured into that moment. Into that kiss.

"I need to go sit with Mum."

He took my hand. I couldn't think about the goodbyes. Not yet. I had to believe there wouldn't be a goodbye.

Cora

I sat on Andrew Bruton's fence waiting for Tabitha and Eli. Jack was with me, our hands linked. He hadn't left my side at all which I appreciated more than he knew. At this moment, he was my rock.

The night had become cold and our breath mingled together, rising into the night sky. Tabitha came to a stop in front of us. Eli put his arm around Jack's shoulders. Tabitha's leaf green eyes were focused on the task ahead, portraying nothing but strength.

"Everything is in place. Everyone is in the training area waiting."

"My mum, what-"

"Ayden has made sure she is safe," Tabitha reassured me.

The knot loosened a little.

"Ember has been in touch, they are close. The car is a silver Audi to be precise." Tabitha must have sensed my confusion. A car was just a car to me.

"Just look for the silver car. Ember will speak with you to

let you know the right one. Is that okay?" Tabitha passed out the ear pieces.

My hand shook so badly that I couldn't put the ear piece in. Tabitha took the piece from my hand and placed it in.

"Can you hear me?" Ember's voice was loud and clear through the ear piece.

"Yeah."

"They are just approaching the hill, ETA seven minutes."

"Right, Eli, Jack, we need to go."

I looked desperately at them, silently pleading with them not to go as my heart thumped erractically against the cage that contained it.

"Cora, the signal will fire, so follow it. Get to the training area and bring them with you. Do not stop running, do you hear me?" Tabitha urged. "You keep running until you are with us. I can only assume that they are travelling towards the shop as that is the only place they know where to find you, with me." Tabitha tucked some of my hair behind my ear.

"Tab?"

"Yes?"

"Has anyone ever..." Why had I even asked? Tabitha looked at Eli, who nodded.

"No, love. No," Eli answered.

I would die tonight and I accepted that, but I would die making sure I saved the others.

"Right, Eli." Tabitha motioned for him to move.

Eli hugged me. He stepped aside and hugged Jack. They did a lot of male slapping on the back and coughing.

"I love you," Tabitha whispered. "You've made me so proud. You're Alizon's daughter and don't forget that," Tabitha smiled, tears twinkling in the corners of her leaf green eyes. "I will be there with you until the end."

I nodded, not trusting my voice. Tabitha and Eli walked towards the woods and left me alone with Jack.

His eyes traced the features of my face. He slowly leant into me, his lips moving over mine, lovingly. He'd become so important to me, he was so much a part of my life, I refused to say goodbye to him. I couldn't do it.

"See you there," he murmured.

"Jack... I just want to say..."

"I know, beautiful. I know."

His lopsided grin calmed me. He took a deep breath and then turned and walked towards Tabitha and Eli. I knew how hard that had been for him because it would have been hard for me to do it too. I watched them leave and then the darkness crept in. Every little sound was magnified, the snap of a twig, the whoosh of wings as birds flew above. Everything set my heart racing.

"Cora, they are nearly here."

I hoisted myself off the fence and tried to stand on wobbly legs. Headlights lit the road ahead, casting distorted shapes around me. I walked towards the middle of the road as the light pushed the shadows back and illuminated me. The car stopped. The engine purred for a moment and then cut dead. I blinked when a door opened. The blonde hair was the first thing I saw.

Melitta.

The door slammed and another opened. Four dark shapes were stood around the car. The air above them became misty with their breath. This was it. I took a big breath and willed my legs to move. I sprinted towards the woods, hearing a male voice shout.

I sprinted into the darkness, digging deep, trying to push faster. The cold night air burned my throat, making my lungs scream in agony. Twigs snapped loudly behind me. The pursuer was gaining ground, and fast. The black trees towered dominantly over me.

The signal was all I had to wait for. I searched the dark sky. A thud of feet struck the hard ground behind me as the sharp crack of frozen branches echoed in the vast wooded area. I ran as each snap sent my heart into overdrive, that sound meant they were gaining ground, but I couldn't run any quicker. I couldn't pull the much-needed oxygen into my whimpering lungs.

My heart jackhammered, fighting its way out of its cage, trying to escape the overwhelming fear that coursed its way through my body. I feared the many things that could happen tonight. I feared that my lungs would give out, I would stop running and they would catch me…I feared who I would meet when my legs, which were as strong as jelly, finally crumbled beneath me.

My biggest fear ripped the remaining breath from my body.

That fear…

Would it hurt when I died?

The night was silent other than the pounding of our feet and my harsh, panicked breath. The person chasing me was silent, why? I could only guess from the louder punch of feet in the hard ground that it would be seconds before this stranger reached me. If a hand touched me, I would scream.

The signal fired.

A bright firework exploded in the night sky. Birds flocked from the trees, fluttering to escape the vibrations and sound. The boom rang deep in the woods, temporarily drowning the sound of the blood pumping around my head. The white gleam from the firework worked as it should, showing me the path I should take.

I found the training area and sprinted with every bit of energy I had left. I skidded to a stop as candles instantly lit the area. Closing my eyes, I searched within myself for the strength and the power to finish it. The united sound of crunching, twigs snapping, feet marching together reverberated within the dark woods.

The crunching sound abruptly stopped, followed by absolute silence.

I held my breath, it *was* rather distracting when I was panting like a dog. An eerie stillness consumed me. The icy fear that played along my spine remained, as did the frantic flapping of my heart. But I was ready.

Varick was the first to emerge out of the prison of trees. His black hair mixed with the cover of the night made it look like his head was floating. His black eyes popped out against the stark white of his face. A small smile travelled on his lips before they pulled straight.

"Cora Hunt, it is so lovely that we should meet *again*."

Certain words dripped with exaggerated power, it made my skin crawl.

"I don't recall ever meeting you before, I wouldn't want something so useless cluttering important space in my head."

Varick growled.

"That's my girl," Jack whispered in my ear.

Heat and confidence rushed through me. "By the way, you've got my name wrong."

"Oh?"

"My name is Cora Device."

"I see. Like mother, like daughter." He nodded his head.

"You also appear to be a trouble maker-"

"I'm no such thing," I snapped.

The air around us stilled. Varick stepped a little closer. The candle light flickered across his face, emphasising his features.

"You prove my point exactly."

A flicker of lightning struck the ground near my feet. If the next bolt struck me dead, then so be it.

"Bloody hell, let me down there!" Jack growled.

"No, Jack," Ayden hissed.

Varick looked like a smiling corpse. "I see," he said happily.

Another lightning bolt flew across the distance between us, branching out and narrowly missing me. He wanted me to run. The wind whipped around me, waiting for an instruction. Screw it, he'd snapped a few times. It was my turn. I threw it out, he stumbled, unprepared, but remained stood on his feet.

"Where are the others?" Jack asked someone above.

"They are here," Ember replied.

I tensed. Before Varick could respond to my attack, Melitta appeared.

"Hello, Cora." Her thick Scottish accent surprised me.

"Hello, Melitta."

The wind snaked around me as I watched Melitta and Varick exchange a glance.

"Hi," Ayden announced as he came bounding up with a huge smile on his face.

295

He was waving at them like they were friends, because I knew him so well, I could see that his body was alert, but his eyes conveyed nothing but warmth, a false kind of warmth.

"Welcome, Ayden, it's been too long," Melitta responded.

"Well, I did actually think it was time to meet you again," he smiled pleasantly.

What? Ayden had spoken with her before, why hadn't he mentioned anything?

"When was it last, 1724?"

"Yes, around then. I recall you setting fire to some crops and dancing naked there. Isn't that right?" Melitta picked up her hand and looked at her nails with a bored expression on her face.

"Yes," he chuckled. "Those were the days. I would say you look well, but... you don't."

Melitta dropped her hand and hissed in anger. A flicker of lightning struck my left leg. The pain shocked the breath out of me.

"That's it!" Jack shouted.

Ember's voice sounded in my ear. "Do not let her touch you!"

I looked at her and flung my energy. Melitta flew to the side, landing on the floor. I'd pissed off the white flag, there was no going back now. I'd felt pain before, I could handle this. As I moved, mini waves of white rolled in. My feet disappeared underneath the low clouds. Akina popped out from behind a tree and moved slowly towards us. The mist rose and as it did, Akina rose with it. She was walking on top of the mist.

"Now!" Tabitha cried.

Cora

Jack landed softly on the ground next to me; an instant later a bolt of lightning struck the ground inches from his head.

"Are you okay?" he asked.

I nodded, trying not to think about the pain as it throbbed in time with the rapid beat of my heart. I heard a pop and looked over Jack's shoulder as Ayden became four. The mist continued to rise, slithering up my body as it tried to consume me. I'd never been a claustrophobic person, but this was beginning to panic me.

Jack disappeared for a second. And then his head came back up, his eyes latched onto mine, calming me.

"Get under the mist," he instructed.

We ducked, crawling on our knees. I cried out as the pain in my leg intensified. We huddled together behind a tree.

"Tab, where are you?"

"I'm just coming up around the north side of the circle. How is your leg?"

"It could be worse."

"I'm going to freeze the mist. Everyone, stop moving and duck down," I whispered into the ear piece.

The mist slowed to a crawl until it eventually stopped, creaking under the pressure of the cold air. Akina growled and locked eyes with me as she slipped on the ice rink. Melitta was held in the ice, one move and the jagged edges would penetrate her. I had only minutes to enjoy this control.

The ground shook as Varick built an electrical current to the point where it cackled, almost laughing at my attempt to stop them. The static sound was deafening, the colour of the sparks a bright blue. Varick's body pulsed, visibly vibrating. It only took seconds and the ice completely shattered, falling to the floor. Akina started sprinting towards me.

"Clay!" I shouted.

The water bounded in. I watched Akina struggle against the current. Varick remained stood, his blue thread dug deep into the ground. If my science was correct , he should be toast around about now?

"The water!" Tabitha called.

I felt the pull and we were in the air. From above I could see the blue vessels running through the water. I gathered a mini tornado and pushed it from me, watching as it sucked up the water and splattered it in every direction.

A barrage of trunks, thick branches and rocks flew through the air. I added a little more power behind the bags, and saw one connect with Melitta's head. I had the satisfaction of watching her tumble to the floor.

As our feet touched the ground, I could see the ripple from Clio's power. The trees swayed, roots groaned. I turned in time to see Varick running towards Tabitha, an angry snarl fixed on his death white face. Tabitha was ready as she blew fire at Varick, who in return struck her foot with a quick flash of electricity.

Tabitha could blow fire?

Clay caught Tabitha as she stumbled on her injured foot. The wind scurried around me, I pushed it and watched as it picked Varick up. I growled and then threw him as hard as I could. In that moment I saw Clio who was unaware that Melitta ran directly towards her. I sucked in a breath to warn her but there wasn't enough time. If I screamed then that would distract her. Either way she was going to be touched. I held my breath.

Clio screamed at the contact.

I ran as Clio dropped heavily to the ground. Melitta gave a tiny wave with the tips of her fingers before she smiled and disappeared. Ember popped up beside Clio and quickly picked her up.

"Tabitha, Melitta has disarmed."

"Copy that," Tabitha responded.

I heard a screech and turned to see Melitta jump at me, almost catlike. I held the tornado, telling it to pick up speed, to protect me. It roared as it followed my command. I felt the burst against my element as Melitta hit me. I closed my eyes, half expecting Melitta to get through, but the wind continued to whirl around me. I pushed and watched as Melitta was sucked into the tornado and carried away. I rushed over to Ember.

"Her power has gone," Ember whispered sadly.

I felt sick with grief. This had happened because of me.

"I will put her somewhere safe, she isn't conscious right now."

I nodded just as I heard a growl come from behind me. I spun around as Ayden appeared out of nowhere and popped into four. He, all of them, grabbed Akina. Her wild orange hair was moving at a rapid speed as she struggled against his strong hold. Snakes of white slithered around his feet, making their way up his legs, tangling him. The lower part of his body was starting to look like a mummy. As the tendrils crawled around his chest, they tightened and I heard his intake of breath and knew that he was struggling to breathe.

I lurched towards him. As I ran, Tabitha rushed from the woods with her hands outstretched as fire burst from them. The white strands shrivelled, hissing as the warmth touched them. I grinned as the pressure built within me.

"Jack," I whispered.

He began lifting the others but he left me until last. Akina looked at me, her blue eyes unfocused with rage. Jack lifted me just as a tornado burst out of me.

Akina's mist swirled, creating a cloud which blocked their view. Lighting flashed across the bed of the woods. I took this moment to look down at my leg. My jeans were ripped where the lightning bolt had seared through it, the blood around the area had dried, clinging to my jeans. The skin looked disfigured as areas of it clumped. My stomach rolled.

Jack squeezed my hand as we landed, and then I saw a bobbing head. "Clio."

Ember ran to me. A second later, Ember's head fell down to her chest. Before I could even blink, Ember lifted her head again. "She's not where I left her."

Varick appeared from behind a tree. He grinned in that sleepy way of his.

"Oh my God." I pointed to where Clio was wondering aimlessly.

Ember's head dropped to her chest in the same instant that Varick lifted his hands. I watched, unable to do anything, as the lightning bolt, so quick, so clean, sliced straight through Clio. Clio fell to the floor. Ember had reached her but she was too late. Ember projected back into her body.

"Shit," Jack whispered.

I couldn't hold back the rush of bile. The smell of burning flesh hit me. Eli, screaming with rage, had begun his attack on Varick who had taken cover once again. Large pieces of wood flew above my head. Eli was seriously pissed. Water smashed against trunks in the hope that Varick was behind one of them.

Melitta was heading towards Tabitha, and Tabitha hadn't seen her. I pulled my power just as Ayden, one of them intercepted, cutting Melitta off. He struggled to stay out her grasp. I held my breath as I saw Melitta's fingers brush against his clothes. Pulling the wind, I threw it towards Melitta, praying that it would knock her off balance long enough for Ayden to regain the upper hand. Melitta stumbled. I used this weakness and attacked her again. Jack must have influenced the lift as Melitta seemed to really fly. Melitta screeched before she hit the tree with a thud.

In the next second, Ember popped up behind Melitta and grabbed her neck. I gasped, expecting Ember's powers to vanish. Ember forced her to stand even though the woman was unconscious. Melitta stood with her hair hanging in front of her face. Her power must not work when she's unconscious.

Lightning flew across the air, striking the ground angrily, Varick wasn't happy. With a flick of her hands, I heard the bones snap in Melitta's neck and then a heavy thud as her body hit the floor.

Varick charged at us. Jack's element latched onto Varick, flipping him in the air. He spun around several times before crashing into the floor. Electricity buzzed in the air, bright blue lines of death narrowly missing Jack. Before I could rush to him, tendrils of snow white mist wrapped themselves tightly around my legs. My legs were pulled from underneath me.

My body slammed to the floor, knocking the breath out of my lungs. The cold mist moved around my body, grinding my bones, creating a cold so deep I feared I would never feel the warmth again. Pins and needles popped up and down my arms. I could feel the strain against my bone, could almost hear it groan under the pressure. I held my breath as a loud snap exploded in my right arm. I screamed as black dots flitted across my vision.

Jack's cry rang in my ears. The mist had travelled the full length of my body. I was cocooned. I couldn't do anything. Akina's face was going to be the last I saw. I heard a battle cry and Akina's body weight was thrown off me. Tabitha's hand shot to the middle of my chest and the explosion of heat made me sigh. The deathly wisps thawed, melting into a pool of water. My arm hung limp and detached from my body.

Akina quickly jumped on Tabitha's back. Tabitha spun around and lifted her hands to Akina's face. Akina's scream made me cringe as the smell of burning flesh drifted across to me. I saw something glint in her hand as Akina held a knife up against Tabitha's neck.

"Jack!!"

I lifted my good hand and flicked it, the wind did nothing. It was paralysed, my fear rendering it useless. I watched helplessly as the knife dug into Tabitha's neck and moved across it in one final sweep. Red liquid seeped out, spilling along the cream of her neck. I hurled the wind, trying to make Akina fly. Akina had her knife positioned ready to go at Tabitha again. I pushed at my element. Her knife hand was pushed aside.

"Jack!"

Jack's power mingled with mine and I watched as Akina flew in the air, away from Tabitha. Tabitha stumbled towards me as the neat red line continued gushing blood. My arm screamed as I caught her. Tabitha's hands fluttered around her neck. The cut hadn't been too deep.

"You're okay," I assured her. My hands and voice shook.

Tabitha's body stiffened. Akina was charging towards us. She was waving the knife in her hand. I could see the white wisps swirling at her feet. They pulsed ready to attack.

"Enough!"

I jumped at the sound of the voice. A smile spread across Akina's charred face. Varick sauntered away from Jack and Clay. Jack moved towards me. Tabitha slowly stood up as Ayden ripped some of his shirt and tied it around her neck.

I looked towards the trees, waiting for him to appear. I didn't have to wait long. Evander emerged from the darkness, his white hair flapped in the wind I'd conjured. I heard a yelp and watched as Ayden, all eight of him, suddenly stuck together in a tight bind. Ayden struggled against the invisible hold but the more he struggled, the more they crushed each other. Ayden bellowed in pain.

"Stop!" I yelled at Evander.

The wind picked up as my anger spiked. Jack flew back and slammed heavily into a tree. "Jack!"

Jack cursed and pushed against the tree. He moved his chest which instantly hit the rough bark, making him wince in pain. Before I could do anything, Clay flew back and slammed against a tree. This was Evander's game. I turned to face Evander, waiting for the force.

"Can you only fight when you have the men wrapped up against the trees?" I spat.

"What a big strong man you are!" Jack sneered and then paid the price as his body was pushed further into the bark making him cry out.

Flames erupted around us, creating a semi-circle, a shield. Tabitha grabbed my good hand and we stood together.

"So be it," Evander spoke. His voice was barely a whisper, but we heard it.

A figure hurtled at considerable speed towards a tree not far from us; it hit the bark with a sickening thud. I heard a muffled scream of pain. I screamed, but my legs refused to move, refused to run.

How had he found her?

Evander glided towards my mother and moved her hair from her face. Her wide eyes found me, her muffled cries incoherent because of the cloth in her mouth. Ayden roared. My ears should have bled with the noise, but my whole world was muffled by shock. My mother lay hurt against a tree under the control of Evander.

"No!"

Jack and Ayden struggled like madmen against the hold on their bodies. Tabitha was trying to move but she was fighting against the hold. Ember appeared to be paralysed. Why was I the only one who could move? Did he find pleasure in this sick game?

"This could have been very different, Cora." He shook his head. "You could have done something-"

"We had no chance!" I screeched.

"We all have chances, Cora. Take this woman, your mother, for example. She had a chance to escape this predicament. She would have been safe if only you had turned around when you ran to this little training area. Do you usually run from your mother?"

"I wasn't..."

"You were running away from your mother. She was so close to reaching you, so close," he said. "But you continued running."

I was dizzy, sick with grief. The stranger behind me, the one that had nearly grabbed me when I'd run here, that had been my mother? If I'd stopped, turned, my mother wouldn't be here...

I charged at him, but my feet were knocked from under me. I hit the floor and quickly scrambled back up. Before I could run, a heavy weight dropped onto my body. I was pushed down to the ground. I screamed as I pushed harder, as I tried to get up.

Tabitha suddenly ran towards my mother with fire balls flying from her hands. Evander laughed as Tabitha flew at a great speed, hitting the ground behind me. She screamed in anger. Ayden was still struggling against the hold, his screams broke my heart, a heart that could take no more.

I pushed against the force he placed on me, adamant that he would not touch her. "Don't touch her, you arsehole!" I roared and pushed again, trying so hard to get up.

"*Tsk Tsk,* Cora. Please respect your elders. Didn't your mother teach you manners?" Evander advanced closer to her.

"Don't touch her!" I screamed and fought against his hold on me. "We've done nothing wrong!"

"We will not have a repeat of history. Your mother paid the price and you must too."

"My mother didn't do anything wrong. We have the proof," I cried.

"Everything you know is lies. We know the truth."

I pushed the wind from me as the crack of thunder boomed above us. The sudden gush of wind made him stumble but he remained on his feet. I'd made him stumble, I could do it again. I pushed, and this time Evander barely stood. My body ached and protested but I would not stop.

"Jack!"

I pushed again. His element combined with mine lifted Evander. The pressure on my body intensified. Jack screamed in pain. Evander regained his footing. I watched, helpless, as Evander stepped behind my mother and brushed her nutmeg curls behind her ears. Evander placed his death white hands on either side of her lovely face.

"Get off her!" I lurched forward again only to be forced back to the ground. "No!!"

Rage made me blind. The pressure on my body lifted and I stood to run at him.

The snap echoed around the woods.

I slammed my eyes shut as the bile rose and erupted out of my mouth. Sobs wracked my body. My breath came hard and heavy as rain poured down on us. I opened my eyes and saw my mother's lifeless body, my legs buckled underneath me as my heart shattered into tiny pieces.

"Cora! Get up!" Jack bellowed.

I couldn't move. Evander stalked towards me. My vision

blurred, a mixture of tears and shock, making it difficult to see.

Before the darkness took me, Jack's voice was the last thing I heard.

THE END

Printed in Great Britain
by Amazon